50690010317791
Dickson,
Jewel of ☞ **W9-AQB-038**

SEP 1 9 2002

LACKAWANNA COUNTY
LIBRARY SYSTEM
520 VINE STREET
SCRANTON, PA
18509

'By what right do you appoint yourself my guardian?'

His eyes seized hers in an unrelenting gaze. 'I don't. Miss Powell has placed you under my mother's care and my own.'

'Then I sincerely hope it is a habit you do not feel obliged to continue.'

'Until such time as your aunt returns, you will abide by my rules and accept the hospitality of this house. Is that clear?'

Judith grew pale. Her pride had been pricked, and she was hardly in the mood to forgive Jordan his high-handed manner, but his words were an order. 'Yes—I understand.'

Jordan had caught the flare of anger, but he also saw something in the depths of her eyes. Their warm colour was brightly exposed to the sunlight slanting in through the window. She really was quite lovely and he couldn't believe he had once thought her plain...

Helen Dickson was born and still lives in South Yorkshire, with her husband on a busy arable farm where she combines writing with keeping a chaotic farmhouse. An incurable romantic, she writes for pleasure, owing much of her inspiration to the beauty of the surrounding countryside. She enjoys being outdoors, reading, films, music and travel. History has always captivated her, it is what drove her to writing, and she spends hours in reference libraries researching her subject. Her ambition is to continue writing, but whatever the future holds she hopes it will be exciting and challenging—with many surprises.

Recent titles by the same author:

LORD FOX'S PLEASURE
CARNIVAL OF LOVE
CONSPIRACY OF HEARTS

JEWEL OF
THE NIGHT

Helen Dickson

MILLS & BOON®

 Interboro Public Library
802 Main St.
Peckville, PA 18452

All the characters in this book have no existence outside the imagination of the author, and have no relation whatsoever to anyone bearing the same name or names. They are not even distantly inspired by any individual known or unknown to the author, and all the incidents are pure invention.

All Rights Reserved including the right of reproduction in whole or in part in any form. This edition is published by arrangement with Harlequin Enterprises II B.V. The text of this publication or any part thereof may not be reproduced or transmitted in any form or by any means, electronic or mechanical, including photocopying, recording, storage in an information retrieval system, or otherwise, without the written permission of the publisher.

MILLS & BOON and MILLS & BOON with the Rose Device are registered trademarks of the publisher.

First published in Great Britain 2002
Large Print edition 2002
Harlequin Mills & Boon Limited,
Eton House, 18-24 Paradise Road, Richmond, Surrey TW9 1SR

© Helen Dickson 2002

ISBN 0 263 17327 5

Set in Times Roman 14¼ on 15¼ pt.
42-0802-87996

Printed and bound in Great Britain
by Antony Rowe Ltd, Chippenham, Wiltshire

JEWEL OF THE NIGHT

Helen Dickson

Chapter One

1822

Long of limb, six foot three of lean hard muscle, his handsome face with its imperious profile and strong features as fine drawn and almost as tanned as those of the native Indians, Captain Jordan Grant—a cavalry officer tailor-made—stepped out of the boat that had rowed him from the *Eastern Lady*, and climbed the ladder onto the bustling wharf at the East India dock yard at Blackwall. His thick dark hair gleamed beneath the morning sun, and his wide-set silver-grey eyes, beneath winged black brows, were hard and intent.

A man who inspired awe in all those he met, he was completely unreadable and single-minded—and at that particular moment he had an uneasy feeling. He looked back at the ship that had brought him from India, a muscle ticking in his clenched jaw. He searched the faces of those around him, wanting to discover the identity of whoever had invaded his cabin and searched his personal property when he'd been breakfasting with the captain. Nothing was missing, so he assumed they had been unable to find what they were looking for. Instinctively his hand went to his breast pocket, and he was reassured when his fingers closed over a hard object.

His gaze sharpened when he recalled the man with pale features and a drooping moustache he had seen on deck earlier, a man who hadn't been on the ship from India, so he must have come aboard after the vessel docked some time during the night. Something nagged at his memory. His face had been vaguely familiar—seen in very different circumstances. He followed the recollection down the alleyways of his memory. It had to be in India. But where, precisely?

Jordan was still frowning when further along the wharf a carriage pulled up. When the door was flung open and the familiar face of his younger brother Edmund appeared, he immediately put the disturbing incident to the back of his mind, but it was not forgotten. A smile broadened his mouth, revealing a lightening glimpse of very white teeth, and with ground-devouring strides he moved towards him. It was two years since he had last been home on leave, and he was impatient to see his family. The two men shook hands and embraced affectionately, speaking rapidly for several moments.

There was a similarity between them. Like Jordan, Edmund was dark-haired, but he was not as tall, nor was he was so ruggedly virile, and he lacked the aura of authority, of forcefulness and power, that surrounded Jordan. Edmund was friendlier and more approachable, but he did not possess the full measure of the legendary Grant charm that had been bestowed on his older brother.

'Welcome home, Jordan. Good Lord, it's good to see you! You're still in uniform, I see,' he said, passing a quizzical eye over his brother's red jacket. 'Does that mean you will be returning to your regiment?'

'I've worn this uniform for so long that it's become a part of me,' Jordan replied, his voice richly textured and deep. 'But—no, I won't be going back.'

Edmund looked at him steadily. 'Do I detect a note of regret?'

Jordan shook his head as they walked slowly towards the carriage. 'No—although after ten years of military life, it won't be easy adjusting to being a civilian again.'

'I needn't tell you how relieved Mother will be. We'll all be happy to have you back at Landsdowne. Mother has invited Emily and me to spend the summer with you, by the way.'

'It will be good for us all to be together again.' A pensive frown creased Jordan's brow. 'It was rotten news about Father, Edmund. I was stationed in Calcutta when I heard about his ship going down off Madagascar. Tropical storm, I believe. How's Mother taken it?'

'It was a terrible tragedy. Mother was stunned by her grief. As you know, her constitution is delicate and we were all deeply concerned. It might have been easier to bear had there been a body,' he said quietly. 'Still, she's over the worst, thank God, and coping rather well. She's looking forward to seeing you.'

'And Charlotte?' Jordan asked, enquiring about his sister.

'I broke the news to her at the academy. She was devoted to Father and quite devastated. But the tragedy was three months ago, and our sister is young and healthy and strong. She'll be all right now.'

'Is she still at the academy?'

'Yes. She came to Landsdowne for a few days to be with Mother and although Mother suggested that she remain at home, Charlotte was restive. It was her wish to return to her friends. Her education is almost complete. Anyway, she'll be home in three weeks.'

Jordan looked at his brother in astonishment. 'Good Lord! Is she eighteen already?' he asked, as a picture of a golden girl, all ruffles and lace with ribbons in her bouncing hair and a laughing face, danced across his mind.

Edmund laughed. 'She is. Our sister is a woman grown—and a lovely one at that. Mother is going to have her work cut out fending off Charlotte's admirers when she takes her bow. I'm afraid you've been away too long, brother.'

They climbed inside the coach, and Jordan lounged in the corner with his usual careless elegance. Edmund subjected him to close scrutiny. There was an aggressive confidence and strength of purpose in his features, and he had the air of a clever man who succeeds in all he sets out to achieve. From the arrogant lift of his dark head and casual stance, he was a man with many shades to his nature, a man with a sense of his own infallibility.

Whenever Jordan had been home on leave, he'd been much sought after by every hostess and unattached female in town. Dazzling women always surrounded him. They found him irresistible. Edmund had watched with amusement as they had flirted shamelessly with him, using all their feminine wiles to hold his attention. Jordan was not immune, and his name had been linked to some of the most beautiful women in town. But with all his attention pinned on his career, marriage was not on offer. Now he was home for good and still a bachelor, he presented a challenge few would be able to resist. In no time at all half the mamas in London would bring their daughters into his line of vision.

'So, Jordan, you are no longer a military man,' Edmund stated.

'No. I put in my discharge before Father's ship went down. His death has brought my retirement sooner rather than later.'

'I dare say you'll miss India.'

He nodded. 'Very much—but it's good to be home.'

It had been a long voyage—almost five months. When at last the fifteen vessels of the East India fleet—protected by watchful frigates of the Royal Navy—had sailed heavily laden up the Channel and he had seen the English coastline with its crying gulls, it seemed that he had been a lifetime in that swaying, creaking wooden world.

'Still,' he went on, 'involvement with the Company will take me back from time to time. Now, tell me everything that has been going on in my absence—

and about Emily. I'm glad the two of you finally tied the knot—and I'm sorry I couldn't be with you.'

Edmund had married Emily Paxton, a young lady of good breeding and enormous wealth, twelve months ago. Being the eldest of two girls, she was her father's heir. Her mother was dead, and when they had married her father had insisted that they live at the family seat in Kent. The old man liked Edmund, and stressed that as his son-in-law and—God willing—father of his future grandchildren, it was important that he learned all about the running of his estate.

Of an indolent nature and without his brother's drive, Edmund had been only too happy to oblige. Jordan was Lord Grant now, and Edmund was content to stand back and let all the responsibilities of running the family's many business concerns—which included being a director in the East India Company—rest on his capable shoulders.

As Judith walked across the street to Miss Powell's house opposite the academy clutching a letter in her hand, it was not the first time that she had entertained uncharitable feelings towards her Aunt Cynthia. Her shame at her own thoughts in the face of her aunt's generosity swamped her. When her parents had been killed in India four years ago, her aunt, being her only living relative, had sacrificed a great deal to pay for her education. That her aunt held no affection for her—indeed, her manner often bordered on antipathy—had saddened and hurt Judith deeply in those early days.

She felt friendless and totally dependent on her aunt, who saw her as a financial burden and endured her presence at her home in Brighton with resentment. Never had she felt so alone—abandoned, almost—and when her aunt had enrolled her at Miss Powell's academy for young ladies in a quiet part of Chelsea, telling her that she should be grateful, for she was under no obligation to pay for her education, and that if it were not for her she would have been sent to the poorhouse, Judith's misery had been complete.

Miss Powell was seated at a table in her drawing-room reading some correspondence when the maid showed Judith inside. It was a lovely room, homely and full of light, and a fire spluttered cheerfully in the hearth. Miss Powell, the proprietress of the academy, who preferred to live not on the premises but close enough to keep her finger on the pulse, was a tall, stately woman. Her neatly arranged fading dark hair crowned a lined, intelligent face and shrewd blue eyes. Her graceful movements, calm features and soft voice disguised a formidable efficiency and energy. She smiled a warm welcome at her favourite pupil.

The light from the window fell onto Judith's face, illuminating her fine skin to a soft shade of golden honey, and lighting her serene hazel eyes with a luminous quality. Her dark brown hair, with highlights of red and gold, was gathered into a knot at the back of her head, a style Miss Powell considered far too severe for one so young, although today the effect was softened by several escaping stray curls brushing her cheeks. She was of medium height and as slender as a wand. Her gown was dark green, the bodice tight-fitting, which drew the eye to her narrow waist and small breasts.

The young woman had a natural poise and unaffected warmth, but there was always an air of seriousness about her, a primness, which manifested itself in the square set of her chin and the firmness of her lips. Some people thought she was aloof and cold, while others thought she was quiet and refined. She had a way of looking at a person, silent and unblinking, like the dark-eyed Indian women in the land of her birth, with their unfathomable stares. Having lived among them until she was fourteen, it was something she had unconsciously acquired.

'What have you there, Judith?' Miss Powell asked, seeing the letter in her hand. 'Is it for me?'

'It's from Aunt Cynthia, Miss Powell,' Judith said, moving close and handing it to her. 'I think you should read it.'

Quickly Miss Powell's eyes scanned what was written. When she had finished, she sighed low and was pensive for a moment, then, rousing herself, she looked at the young woman with some concern. 'So, your aunt is to leave for Europe with friends for an indefinite period, and suggests that you remain at the academy for the summer vacation. How do you feel about that, Judith?'

A small shadow passed over Judith's face. 'I am disappointed, of course,' she said slowly. 'I do so love Brighton and the sea. But Aunt Cynthia is entitled to do as she pleases. Despite existing on a small income, she has placed an excellent education within my reach. I will not repay her generosity by complaining and showing ingratitude. It's no good fretting over something that cannot be changed, so if you would allow me to remain at the academy, Miss Powell, I would be most grateful.'

'Of course you may. Your loyalty to your aunt does you credit, but you've too generous a spirit, my dear. As your father's sister and your only living relative, your aunt had a duty to take care of you when your parents died so tragically—and from what you have told me they were an admirable couple and you are a credit to them.'

Judith felt her heart warm. 'Thank you for that, Miss Powell. No one understands the way you do.'

'You have taken advantage of all the academy has to offer and excelled admirably in all your studies. They would be extremely proud of you. You will make an excellent teacher, Judith, and a valuable addition to the academy—of that I am convinced.'

'At least I will be able to support myself, which is a relief. Apart from visiting Aunt Cynthia in the future, I cannot accept anything now that comes from her.'

Miss Powell had always been extremely sympathetic to the trials and tribulations of Judith's situation. She was eighteen and in three weeks time her education would be complete. Despite the friction that existed between Judith and her Aunt Cynthia, Miss Powell knew how much the young woman had looked forward to going to Brighton for the summer, before returning to the academy in the autumn when she would take up her employment as a teacher. No doubt her aunt thought she had done quite enough, and now Judith was eighteen and old enough to earn a living, she desired to rid herself of her tiresome niece as soon as possible.

The fact was that Judith's parents had died penniless. Her father had held a minor post in the Indian Civil Service, and both he and his wife had been killed. Judith had never recovered from the shock of losing both her mother and father so tragically, and it was something she never spoke of.

Apart from a small allowance her parents' deaths entitled her to from the Company, she had no money of her own and couldn't live off her aunt for ever. She had to find some means of earning a living, and teaching was a respectable occupation for a young woman.

Miss Powell put great emphasis on learning and devoted all her time to crusading for the education of women. She ran her academy efficiently and employed only the best teachers. Judith was her star pupil and well qualified to teach English, French, the arts and the classics, and so she'd had no qualms about offering her employment. She would be paid accordingly, and would occupy a room at the academy. However, when the young woman had accepted her proposal, Miss Powell was saddened, because she knew it wasn't from choice or inclination, but because it was the only thing she could do.

* * *

Resigning herself to spending the entire summer in London—although she had to concede that it was a splendid city and had plenty of attractions to keep her occupied—Judith returned to the room at the imposing red-brick establishment in Chelsea that she shared with her friend Charlotte Grant. Not in the least interested in art, Charlotte had gone reluctantly to an exhibition of paintings with one of her tutors and a group of other girls.

Feeling dejected, with a sigh Judith lay on her bed and stared up at the ceiling, her mind going back over the four years she had been in England, with fragmented images of her life in India intruding. She'd been born there, and had been so happy that she hadn't wanted to leave, but she'd been given no choice.

Oppressed by a terrible feeling of isolation, when she had first come to England she'd felt out of place. With her exotic upbringing and the freedom and vibrant colour of India coursing through her veins, it had been difficult that first year, try as she did, for her to conform to an English young lady's way of life. Eventually she had settled down, but there were times when she still felt like a stranger in a strange land.

She would never forget the day she had come to the academy. She had stood in front of the other girls, stiff and awkward. Self-consciously she had looked down at her boots, twisting her handkerchief in her fingers, feeling the eyes of every girl in the school looking at her. Tortured by shyness and painfully aware of the sorry spectacle she made in her plain grey dress, tears had been very near to the surface.

Brought up in India, she had imagined that she would be at a disadvantage among the other girls, but thankfully she had inherited her parents' gift for learning and had applied herself to her studies with diligence and determination that had surprised herself and brought praise from her tutors.

Charlotte Grant had been her salvation. She had burst into her life like a shining light and, unlike Judith, there was nothing prim about her. When she was not under the watchful eye of Miss Powell, her manners were quite outrageous, her conduct reprehensible. She was wilful, obstinate and made everyone laugh, but she also had a kind heart and a caring nature, for which Judith loved her. All pink and white, with a pair of languishing cornflower blue eyes that twinkled mischievously and a profusion of golden curls, she charmed all her companions and could not be found wanting in those accomplishments that characterise a young lady. She could play the pianoforte well, dance like a fairy and sing like a lark—attributes unequalled by Judith.

She envied Charlotte her home in Greenwich, her family, and their closeness. The enormous wealth of the Grants brought Charlotte many luxuries. Her elder brother and father showered gifts on her when they returned from India—glorious silks, cashmere shawls, and pretty trinkets.

On the whole life at the academy was pleasant. Judith was reconciled, and the background that made her different from the other girls didn't worry her quite so much any more.

Charlotte returned from her visit to the exhibition in subdued spirits. After removing her cloak she plopped onto the bed, sighing deeply. 'When I leave the academy I swear I will never look at another painting again.'

Judith sat up, her lips curving into a smile at Charlotte's frowning vexation. 'Oh dear! Was the exhibition that bad?'

'Worse,' she grumbled, producing a small novelette from her pocket and beginning to thumb through the pages.

'What is that?' Judith asked, eyeing her friend's reading material suspiciously. 'Is it a romantic novel, by any chance?' Charlotte was certainly not of a literary bent, but she did try.

'Yes, but I didn't buy it,' she was quick to inform Judith. 'One of the other girls has let me borrow it.'

'Then for heaven's sake don't let Miss Powell see you reading it. You know she considers that kind of literature as frivolous and uninstructive—"it could fill the reader with delusive ideas and even lead to degeneracy,"' Judith said, quoting the proprietress, and yet not unkindly.

'I know.' Charlotte sighed, not in the least concerned. 'But I love reading romances, and if it produces a moral degeneracy and makes me unable to control my passions, then so be it. At least I won't die of boredom from reading the curriculum we are made to absorb day in and day out to improve our minds.' She glanced across at Judith. 'Is something the matter,

Judith? You look quite miserable. Has anything happened?'

'I've had a letter from Aunt Cynthia. She's going away for the summer and closing the house. Miss Powell has agreed to let me stay at the academy.'

Charlotte sat bolt upright. 'What? All summer?'

'Yes. Oh, it won't be too bad. London isn't Brighton, I know—but there will be lots to do. There will be one or two other girls staying on, so I won't be here alone.'

'But that's positively ghastly. I can't let you stay here all alone. You must come to Landsdowne and spend the vacation with me,' Charlotte pronounced with her usual enthusiasm. 'Besides, when we leave here neither of us know when we will see each other again. It would be fun to spend the whole summer together—before Mother begins planning my future and finding me an eminently suitable young man to marry.'

'It's generous of you to offer, Charlotte,' Judith smiled, 'but I couldn't possibly.'

'Yes, you can. I shall write to Mother immediately and ask her. I know she would love to have you stay. She likes having people around her—especially since father died. Edmund and Emily—that's Edmund's wife—will be there, and Jordan will be home from India.'

'All the more reason why I must stay here. You will all be together as a family for the first time in two years, Charlotte. I couldn't possibly intrude.'

'Don't be silly, Judith. You wouldn't be intruding. Mother is always urging me to bring you to Landsdowne, and Edmund has expressed his eagerness to meet you. You will like Emily, and Edmund is nice—unlike Jordan, who can be a dreadful ogre at times. Oh, you must come.'

'Very well, Charlotte—but only if your mother agrees. I shall look forward to meeting your brother and his wife, and forget all about your ogre of an older brother,' she teased.

'Good. I'll write to Mother at once.'

The letter from Charlotte's mother arrived the day before the end of term. It was raining hard that evening and Charlotte had just come in from the street. She was standing by the door shaking the wet off her plum-coloured cloak and trying to stifle a sneeze when Judith handed it to her. Tearing it open, she scanned it quickly.

'There you are,' she cried happily. 'I told you Mother would be delighted to have you stay with us. You must go and tell Miss Powell immediately, and then we'll go to our room and pack our trunks.'

Judith was apprehensive about going to Landsdowne and at the same time excited. She knew she would cut a sorry figure staying in such a grand house without the right clothes. Nearly all her dresses were serviceable and hardly the kind young ladies wore to soirées and such, but since she wouldn't be invited to any, it didn't really matter. 'Yes, I'll go right this minute.'

'Wait,' Charlotte said, as she was about to go outside. 'It's raining quite hard. Here.' She handed Judith her cloak. 'Put this on, otherwise you'll be soaked before you cross the street. It's damp, I know, but it will cover you.'

Judith slipped outside into the rain, drawing the large cowled hood over her head. It was almost dark and the street was quiet. She fixed her eyes on the light shining from Miss Powell's windows, knowing she would find her in her drawing-room at this hour. As she was about to step off the pavement she drew back when a coach and matching pair of horses drew near. It halted, and she gasped as the door opened and a black garbed figure with a hat pulled well down over his face emerged.

There was something sinister and threatening about that figure. Becoming alarmed, she turned to go back inside the academy, casting an anguished glance at the closed door, but everything happened with such dreadful speed. The man was on her before she could take a step, his arms going round her. Even as she drew breath to scream, he dealt her a ringing blow on her chin and she went spiralling down into a black hole.

Judith stirred and moaned. As she gradually regained her senses she tried to move, but it was impossible. Her hands were bound tightly behind her back and a blindfold prevented her from seeing. An ache throbbed in her jaw and her head swam as the ache became a pounding pain. She was lying on a hard floor and it was extremely cold.

There wasn't a sound to be heard, but it was an unnatural silence—which was an enemy in itself, while the air was charged with an ugly tension. Menace bristled all around her, and she sensed she was not alone. She strained her ears, her heart pounding with a mixture of rage and fright. Only once before in her life had she experienced the kind of terror that gripped her at that moment. A presence surrounded her like a sickening wall of hatred. She struggled to stay calm, to stop her limbs from trembling. She had no idea what was happening to her, who would want to abduct her—or for what reason.

Finding her voice, she whispered through parched lips into the dark. 'Please—I know someone is there. Why have you done this? What is it you want from me?' There was a rustle as someone moved close and she could hear his breathing.

'So,' a voice hissed quietly, 'our little captive is conscious at last.'

Judith let out her breath on a long sigh of relief. 'Why are you doing this? Why am I a prisoner? At least tell me that.'

'It is not for you to concern yourself with that.'

'My disappearance from the academy will have been noticed. Someone will find me,' she said on a note of desperation, trying to conceal the raging anxiety in her heart.

'No one will find you here—and screaming will do no good. There is no one to hear you. And do not try to struggle,' her captor said, his voice having become flat and deadly. 'If you are to remain here indefinitely, it could save you much pain in time to come.'

The fact that she had been trussed could only mean that her captors were afraid she might escape, and the blindfold was to prevent her from seeing their faces. If there were anyone to hear her screams they would have gagged her. 'But what is it you want from me?'

'From you, nothing. You are merely a pawn, that is all. When your brother has complied with our demands you will be released unharmed.'

Judith puzzled on this. 'My brother?' she asked at last. 'But—I don't have a brother.'

There was silence.

'I said I don't have a brother,' she repeated forcefully, her voice raised.

'I heard you the first time,' the strained voice hissed, as though purposely keeping his voice low so as to disguise it.

Suddenly, realisation of what must have happened hit Judith with the stark clarity of a blinding flash. It was Charlotte they had meant to kidnap, not her. She was wearing Charlotte's cloak and must have been mistaken for her. If she hadn't taken it this would not have happened. Hope stirred in her heart. 'Clearly you have made a mistake. I am not who you think I am— whoever that may be. My name is Judith Wyatt. Don't you see? You have kidnapped the wrong person.'

The terrible silent stillness around her told her that her captor must believe her—that he had irretrievably blundered into an appalling error, for after a long moment of deliberation, he uttered a string of savage curses and moved away. She heard a door open and close and voices raised in anger. Then all was quiet. And so, huddled in her dark retreat, despite her numbness and pain, she waited, vulnerable and afraid, praying that now they knew they had the wrong person they would release her. But then again, in another minute she could be dead, pointlessly murdered by someone she had never seen.

Chapter Two

Jordan was not in the best of moods when he arrived at the academy to escort his sister and Miss Wyatt to Landsdowne.

Being a powerful proprietor of the East India Company and a member of a group representing the banking, commercial and shipping interests of the Company—a position held by his father until his tragic and untimely death—he had yesterday come to town to India House in Leadenhall Street for a shareholders' meeting.

Alighting from his carriage, the sight of three men leaving the building had suddenly caught his attention. His heart gave a sudden jolt of recognition and his face hardened. Quickly he stepped back, not wishing to be seen. One of the men was Lord Jeremy Minton, who had been employed as a district officer in the northern region of India, and whose career in the Company's service spanned fifteen years.

The Company provided useful career opportunities for sons of impoverished landowners, and Minton's family had become almost destitute. Jeremy had been a youth when his father died, and seeking ways to boost the dwindling income derived from his estate, he joined the East India Company.

Opinionated and susceptible to demonstrations of arrogance that he could not disguise, pride was evident in all Minton's dealings. He was also a man who couldn't hold his temper, and as a result had few friends. He had joined the Company for personal gain, and he had very soon developed a hunger for gold and jewels that amounted to a personal sickness. If ever there was a man whose judgement could be tempted by greed, it was Minton. It was rumoured that he had grown immensely rich in the Company's service.

Slightly over average height, he was certainly a fine figure of a man, with a bull-like strength, the muscular swell of his shoulders straining against the seams of his coat. His pale blue eyes were set too close together beneath a heavy brow for his features to be described as handsome.

Jordan's dislike of the man was intense—the dislike being mutual—but it was not Minton's looks he disliked as much as the stench of corruption that surrounded him, and the suppressed violence within. He was like a dangerous animal trained to behave, while retaining the menacing, wild ways of his birth. But while Jordan kept him at a distance, he could also keep at bay the memories and feelings he stirred.

Jordan's eyes shifted to one of Minton's companions. Suddenly his mouth went dry and clammy sweat sprang out on the palms of his hands, for he recognised the pallid features and the thin, drooping moustache of the man he had seen on board the *Eastern Lady*. At the time he had been unable to remember where he had seen him before. Now he knew. The man was Minton's servant, and Jordan was a hundred per cent certain that under his master's instructions, he was the one who had searched his personal property in his cabin.

He gave his attention to the third man—a splendidly dressed turbaned Indian with an effeminate face, flat black eyes and a cruel mouth. His name was Jehan Khan, once a humble retainer of the Rajah of Ranjipur. During his time in India as a soldier of the Crown, Jordan had become closely acquainted with the Rajah, whose small state bordered on Nepal. He had been a man of honour and had earned Jordan's respect and admiration. The same accolade could not be applied to his cousin, Prince Chandu, who had wheedled Jehan Khan into his own service.

What perturbed Jordan was seeing Jehan Khan here in London with Jeremy Minton, whose district had included Prince Chandu's domain. And what deepened his concern was the fact that there was little love lost between them and their distrust of each other ran deep. When Minton made common cause with Khan, Jordan had reason to think something serious and of a sinister nature was afoot. But then, both men were corrupt and ambitious, and corruption and ambition could make strange bedfellows.

Jordan had a multitude of reasons for wanting to avoid contact with either of them. A thunderous frown drew his black eyebrows into a single line as he watched the three men climb into a waiting coach and drive off. Cursing softly, a dull rage ate into him like acid, filling him so completely that for a moment everything went dark around him. He strode into India House, determined to discover the purpose of their visit.

After all those years serving as a soldier in India, wasn't it time for pleasure and peace at his home without the intrusion of Jeremy Minton and the corrupt machinations of Prince Chandu?

Amidst a great deal of girlish laughter and tears of departing pupils—happy to be going home but sad to be leaving their friends—trunks and bonnet-boxes and a paraphernalia of other articles were being arranged onto carriages by frustrated coachmen in the street outside the academy. When Jordan enquired after his sister he was directed to Miss Powell's house by a sombre-faced teacher. Looking forward to seeing Charlotte, he was quite unprepared for the reception he received when he was shown into the drawing-room.

Charlotte was seated on the lemon and green cushions of the window seat in an extreme state of distress, with Miss Powell doing her best to comfort her. On seeing her brother she rose and flung herself into his arms.

'Oh, Jordan—I'm so happy to see you—relieved, too. Thank goodness you're here.'

She didn't look at all well and her tearful greeting alarmed Jordan. 'Charlotte, what is it? Has something happened to you?'

'No,' she wailed, 'not to me. It's Judith.'

'Judith?'

'Judith Wyatt,' Miss Powell explained. 'As you will know, Lady Grant has very kindly invited her to spend the summer at Landsdowne with Charlotte, and has agreed to assume complete responsibility for her. Unfortunately she has disappeared. We are all so worried as to what can have happened to her.'

Jordan's stare was probing. He had the distinct feeling that he was about to be inconvenienced by a girl he had never met. 'Disappeared? How? How can a pupil go missing?'

'I wish I knew,' Miss Powell replied. 'Yesterday evening she left the academy to come here to see me but never arrived. A thorough search has been made, but there is no sign of her. It is all very distressing.'

Jordan was incredulous. 'You mean she disappeared crossing the street?'

'Yes, so it would seem. No one has seen her since.'

Jordan frowned impatiently. He had no idea what to expect of Charlotte's friend, but in view of her impoverished state, which left her with no alternative but to earn a living to support herself, he didn't expect much. 'You have informed the constables?'

'Of course. Everything possible is being done to find her, but as yet their enquiries have come to nothing.'

'Is it possible that she could have run away?' he asked shortly.

'Judith had no reason to run away, Captain Grant.'

'Does she have any friends she could have gone to visit—a young man, perhaps?'

Charlotte was clearly shocked at what he implied. 'Jordan, really!' she gasped. 'Of course she hasn't. Judith isn't like that.'

'I apologise, but every possibility has to be considered.'

'You are right, Captain Grant, but Judith's parents are dead,' Miss Powell explained. 'She has no friends outside the academy and her only living relative is an aunt in Brighton.'

'If anything untoward has happened to her I shall blame myself,' Charlotte wailed, crumpling down onto a sofa and giving vent to a fresh outburst of tears. 'I should have gone with her. It was almost dark and Miss Powell has always stressed that we must not leave the academy unaccompanied. I hate to think of her being kidnapped—or worse.'

'Stop it, Charlotte,' said her brother sharply. 'You are jumping to conclusions.'

'I can't help it,' she whispered, sneezing and wiping her nose, for she had contracted the most wretched cold after spending too long in the rain the previous day. 'I can't leave here until I know what has happened to her. I simply can't.'

'I am sure Miss Powell will send word to Landsdowne if she hears anything,' Jordan said, gentling his tone, a sympathetic smile softening his grim features.

'Please, Jordan. Let me stay,' she begged, almost choking on her emotion.

Relenting, Jordan sat beside her and placed a calming arm about her shoulders as she began to cough. 'You look as though you should be in bed, Charlotte. Very well. We will both stay—if that is all right with Miss Powell.'

'Of course. You must remain here. With all the activity going on at the academy, you will be more comfortable. If you will excuse me, I have some parents waiting to see me before they whisk their daughters away for the summer. As you can see, Captain Grant, Charlotte has caught a chill. I'll instruct matron to make up a powder for her and have refreshment sent in to you while you wait.'

An hour after Jordan's arrival, Judith was unceremoniously deposited at the end of the street. Dazed and shaken, and struggling to find some sort of mental equilibrium as she adjusted her eyes to the bright light when she removed the blindfold, she walked unsteadily past a line of carriages towards the academy. Parents and pupils swarmed all over the place. Seeing her, a concerned-looking tutor disengaged herself and came to her. Reassured that she was unharmed, the tutor immediately took her to Miss Powell's house.

When she entered the drawing-room Charlotte threw herself at her friend, enfolding her in the protective warmth of her arms and love. 'Judith! Thank goodness you're all right. I have been so worried. Where on earth have you been?'

Judith swallowed down the lump in her throat, and the tears she'd fought all night finally slid down her pale cheeks. In all the years she had known Charlotte, she'd never seen her so upset, and she felt sick with remorse that her disappearance was the cause of her distress. The heat of the cheek pressed against her own also alarmed her, telling her that her friend was most unwell, which was confirmed when she looked into her fever-bright eyes.

Miss Powell interrupted the reunion, saying in a calm voice, 'I can't tell you how relieved I am to see you back, Judith. Everyone has been most anxious. First of all I must ask if you have been harmed in any way?'

Judith shook her head, brushing the tears from her cheeks. To surrender to the full intensity of Miss Powell's solicitude was a luxury she would have to forgo until she had explained all that had happened.

'No, Miss Powell. I am tired and my head aches, that's all.'

'Nevertheless, you must go to bed and I'll send for Dr Gardner to take a look at you. But first there are a few questions that must be answered.'

Miss Powell placed an arm about Judith's shoulders and turned her round. From across the room a man of uncommon height with his hands clasped behind his back was studying her closely, his lean frame clad in an impeccably tailored black suit, a white shirt and neckcloth at his throat. Dark hair was swept back from

 Interboro Public Library
802 Main St.
Peckville, PA 18452

his wide brow and curled on his collar. 'This is Captain Grant, Judith.'

Miss Powell left the three of them alone to ask her maid to arrange for Dr Gardner to call.

As Captain Grant crossed the room with long, vigorous strides, Judith stifled an unexpected attack of nervousness. She admitted to herself that Charlotte's brother was a splendid figure of a man, whose movements bespoke a life of action and adventure. His face was darkly handsome, almost saturnine, his nose well-formed above unsmiling lips, and those eyes—silver-grey and almost transparent—which gleamed like bright gems against his skin, bronzed by the Indian sun, seemed capable of piercing her innermost secrets, causing a frisson of unease bordering on fear to course through her.

There was something unbending and self-contained about him, an air of the professional soldier displayed in his dignity and bearing and crisp manner. He moved with the confident ease of his own masculinity, and he had a powerful presence, an undeniable magnetism— a ladies' man, Charlotte would say, the kind of man who filled the pages of those romantic novels she so ardently devoured.

He had done nine years of military service in India—her own beloved country, where she had spent a greater part of her life—and her senses swirled as something as mystical and primeval as India and the ancient rivers that journeyed through that land entered her soul. In that moment all her senses were intensified almost beyond endurance.

She recalled the tales of destiny her Ayah had immersed her in as a child, of how all their lives were dictated by the stars and the heavens, and she wondered if some master plan had been at work and marked her path to cross that of Jordan Grant's. Mentally she shook herself out of her trance. She didn't believe in the influence of fate, nor that she was destined to meet a man who wouldn't give her a second look.

Towering over her and having no knowledge of her thoughts, Jordan saw a young woman of medium height, extremely pale and tense. Her eyes were lowered. She was dressed in a high-necked, unrelieved charcoal grey dress, unbecoming on a girl so young. Her hair was also drawn back severely. He was just deciding that she was the plainest young woman he had ever encountered, when she raised her startling hazel eyes and fixed him with an unfathomable, unblinking gaze.

His breath caught in his throat, for in their depths was the look of another world. He was surprised to find there was nothing actually objectionable about her. Her skin was golden and absolutely without blemish. Her face didn't change as she held out her hand, small, slim, though still slightly swollen from the tight bonds that had secured her wrists during her captivity.

'I'm pleased to meet you, Captain Grant,' she said, with all the confidence she could raise. Regardless of all that had happened to her since she had left the academy, she was determined not to portray herself as some weak-kneed schoolgirl. She sensed that he found her something of an encumbrance and that he was vexed that her disappearance had inconvenienced him. He concealed his impatience well, but it was there, in the tightening of his jaw and the narrowing of his eyes. Captain Grant was an aloof, icy stranger who was inspecting her closely. She was certain that if she were one of his soldiers he would lose no time in telling her that she did not pass muster. 'I am sorry to have caused you so much trouble, but I assure you it was not of my making.'

Jordan was somewhat taken aback by her calm approach, but he would have been surprised to know how exceedingly nervous she was about meeting him. He took her hand lightly in his strong fingers. 'I'm pleased to meet you, too, Miss Wyatt,' he said, with flawless formality and no warmth, which, to Judith, seemed like an unpromising beginning. 'I assure you that you have been no trouble. I am relieved you are returned to the academy unharmed—although,' he said sharply, his gaze shifting to the bruise on her cheek, 'not entirely, it would appear. Who did this?'

'I—do not know.'

His granite features softened. 'Does the bruise cause you pain?'

Judith had recovered both her equanimity and her air of command. 'I'm perfectly all right. It is nothing,' she replied, touched that he should ask. 'I—I was accosted last evening—when I was coming to see Miss Powell—and bundled into a carriage. It was raining and everything happened so fast. I tried to get away, but my assailants were strong. There was nothing I could do.'

Charlotte was outwardly shocked. 'You mean you were kidnapped?' she gasped, staring at her friend in terror, the inadequacy of the question in the face of that monstrous bruise angering her to bitter tears. It was unthinkable that anyone would want to hurt Judith. 'How frightened you must have been.'

'I confess that I was,' Judith admitted, laying a calming hand on Charlotte's arm, 'but please don't distress yourself, Charlotte. I am recovered now.'

'Have you any idea why anyone would want to accost you?' Jordan asked.

'No—or what I mean to say is that they didn't. They had no reason to—although they didn't realise this at the time. Please understand that I lost my senses for a while, and when I recovered I was terribly confused and had no idea what was happening to me. One of my assailants—although I must tell you that I was wearing a blindfold and didn't see his face—told me I was merely a pawn, and that when my brother had complied with their demands I would be released. That was when it occurred to me that they had made a mistake.'

'Mistake?' Jordan frowned, puzzled.

She met his gaze calmly. 'Yes. I don't have a brother, you see. I—I believe it was Charlotte they meant to kidnap.' On hearing a fearful cry, she turned to Charlotte, who was frozen in shock, her eyes staring in consternation.

'Me?' she uttered, a slight tremor detectable in her voice. 'But why would anyone want to kidnap me? For what reason?'

Knowing how fearful Charlotte must be feeling, Judith's heart swelled with pain for her friend. 'Oh, Charlotte,' she whispered, reaching out and taking her hand. 'I'm sorry to have to worry you, but that I cannot tell you.'

'But—am I in danger?'

'I cannot tell you that, either.'

Jordan was giving Judith a strange look, staring at her hard, his eyes boring holes into hers. 'What are you saying? How can you possibly know it was Charlotte they wanted? Did they say as much?'

'No, they didn't. However, I have no doubt in my mind whatsoever that Charlotte was their intended victim. She has two brothers and I was wearing her cloak at the time.'

'And this is significant?' Jordan snapped the question.

'I believe so. I am quite certain that whoever it was that abducted me mistook me for your sister.'

Jordan raised his brows in a scornful gesture. 'Forgive me, Miss Wyatt, but I find that difficult to believe. You and my sister are not remotely alike,' he remarked pointedly.

His reply was startlingly abrupt—almost rude, and Judith flinched. She heard the insult in his smoothly worded statement, and a wave of anger brought a sudden flush to her cheeks. She knew she wasn't as pretty as Charlotte—who was the very picture of perfect sweetness in comparison with what Judith felt to be her plainness, but she didn't care to be reminded of it. Her eyes did not flinch from the piercing silver gaze and she faced him with a flicker of hauteur she could not quite conceal. Pushed to retaliate by his arrogant calm, and the recollection of her own ill-use at her assailants' hands, when she spoke her voice was cold and threaded with sarcasm.

'You are absolutely right, Captain Grant, and it is an affliction I have learned to live with.'

'I apologise if my clumsy words offended you. It was not intended. I am sure you have many admirable qualities.'

'If I have then I doubt very much that they are of the kind you would admire, Captain Grant,' she replied tartly. 'However, I don't know what it was the men who abducted me want from you—or your brother, but it has occurred to me that they could decide to pursue whatever it is and that Charlotte's life might be in danger. Being extremely fond of her, this concerns me greatly, as it should you.'

'No,' Charlotte cried, choking on her emotion. 'Surely not.'

Judith turned and saw naked fear in her friend's eyes. 'I'm sorry, Charlotte, but it could happen.'

Affronted and furious that this chit of a girl had the temerity to remind him of his duty, Jordan's voice turned positively glacial and his eyes gleamed like shards of ice. 'Be assured, Miss Wyatt, if, as you say, my sister was their intended victim—and I have to say that I am inclined to believe you—then every precaution to safeguard her well-being will be taken by me.'

'For heaven's sake, Jordan,' Charlotte intervened, distressed by the thought that some unknown assailant might be planning to abduct her and carry her off to heaven knows where. 'Do you have to be so unkind? Why, anyone would think Judith asked to be kidnapped. You must realise that if she hadn't borrowed my cloak none of this would have happened—although I shudder whcn I think that if they had been successful and abducted me, then I would still be their captive waiting for you or Edmund to concede to their demands. Goodness! What can it be they want? Have you any idea, Jordan?'

Guilt tore at him as he abruptly replied, 'None.'

There was an edge to his voice which made Judith glance at him sharply. She looked at the tight line of his mouth and the disturbing light in his eyes, and the truth hit her then. Captain Grant did know, and knowing this cast a haunting and uneasy cloud over her. She could not have put into words the feeling of discomfort, but it was as though some spirit had groped its way into her heart.

'Then when we arrive home we must ask Edmund,' Charlotte quipped. Taking Judith's hand she drew her down onto the sofa beside her. 'Please forgive my brother, Judith. He's not usually such a crosspatch—although I do recall that he has an evil temper when vexed.'

'I have a rather formidable temper myself when roused,' Judith admitted, meeting Captain Grant's gaze. It was true, although no one had tested it for some time.

Mild interest stirred in Jordan's eyes and warmed with a mixture of amusement and admiration. For one brief moment he glimpsed the proud, spirited young woman hidden behind that calm façade.

'Really?' he drawled. 'I am surprised, Miss Wyatt. To me, you have the appearance of placidity and patience personified.'

'Appearances can be deceiving, Captain Grant.'

'It would appear so,' he said, inclining his head slightly, the rigidity leaving his jaw and a smile lurking at his mouth.

After her gruelling night, all Judith's defences were down, her spirits low. As a result her deep sigh and the weary smile she gave him was unintentionally personal. 'Please forgive me. I feel quite worn out and truly do not want to argue with you.'

'I am glad to hear it. And I don't argue—I'm diplomatic,' he stated. 'How quickly you become angry and defensive, Miss Wyatt, which is something I shall have to guard against since you are to be our guest at Landsdowne.'

'I am only angry when I feel the need to be defensive, Captain Grant,' Judith countered.

A smile moved across his lean brown face. 'Truce?'

Judith told herself that her presence at Landsdowne would be of no real consequence at all to Captain Grant, but she smiled anyway, her first genuine smile of their meeting, her soft lips curving with winsome humour that made her eyes glow. 'Truce,' she agreed.

'Now—tell me what you remember of your ordeal.'

'It was all very confusing at the time. I was knocked senseless out in the street, and when I came round I had no idea where I was.'

'Miss Wyatt, I am extremely sorry that you have been drawn into a matter which is none of your concern. However, I don't think I need to stress how important it is that you remember something so these men can be apprehended. Nevertheless, if they do intend pursuing this matter with either me or my brother, then they will have to show their hand sooner or later. Do you remember anything? The smallest detail could be crucial. Did you see your assailant? Did you get an impression of his build?'

'I didn't see anything. My eyes were covered the whole time. The blindfold remained in place until I was released at the end of the street.'

'Do you remember anything about the location of the place they took you to?'

'No, nothing—except that it was extremely cold.'

'How long did the journey take from where you were being held to the academy?'

'About fifteen minutes.' She sighed, suddenly tired of his questions, which bordered on interrogation. 'I'm sorry I cannot be of more help. What I do know is that there was more than one person involved. I heard them arguing when they realised their mistake. Before that, one of them told me I would not be released until my brother had conceded to their demands. That was when I realised there had been a mistake. I don't have a brother, you see.'

Jordan nodded, becoming detached and cool once more. 'Yes, I do see,' he said, moving towards the door, intending to leave. 'I also see that you will not be travelling to Landsdowne with Charlotte and me this morning.'

Her heart leapt with disappointment. 'Oh—but after a change of clothes and—'

'Please don't interrupt,' he said with an insistence that brooked no argument, his face having set itself into the implacable mould which would have been instantly recognised by the men in his regiment. 'Clearly you need to rest after your ordeal, and Miss Powell is quite right to ask the doctor to examine you. Charlotte is feverish and I want to get her home as quickly as possible. My brother and his wife will be coming to town tomorrow, in which case I shall instruct them to collect you at three o'clock. Now, before we leave I must have a word with Miss Powell.' He glanced at his sister. 'Be ready in a few minutes, Charlotte. Goodbye, Miss Wyatt. It's a pleasure to have met you.'

His curt dismissal of her annoyed Judith, but she was too well schooled to show it. She rose, making a conscious effort to keep all emotion from her voice. 'Goodbye, Captain Grant,' she said with quiet dignity. 'And thank you.'

He gave her one last look as though he wanted to say something further, but then he changed his mind and left.

Chapter Three

The following afternoon, feeling rested and pronounced well enough to leave the academy by Dr Gardner—despite having slept fitfully and dreaming she was still tied up in that cold room—Judith was ready when Edmund Grant and his wife arrived to take her to Landsdowne. But her ordeal at the hands of her assailants was still at the forefront of her mind, and she wondered what was behind it and how deeply Captain Grant was involved. It was all very mysterious.

In spite of the fact that she had prepared herself for what she must expect at the Grant family home at Greenwich, she viewed the proposed visit with some trepidation. Her trunk, which had seen much service over the years, seemed even more battered as it was placed on the rack at the back of the splendid coach.

With her husband, Emily got out of the coach and greeted her warmly, referring with a great deal of concern and sympathy to her abduction. Emily was petite, fair-haired and extremely pretty. There was an air of kindness about her and Judith liked her immediately.

Edmund Grant was natural in his behaviour and charming. His looks were pleasant and friendly, and he put on his most engaging smile when he saw her.

'It's good to meet you at last, Miss Wyatt—or may I call you Judith?'

'Yes—I would like that. Thank you for collecting me, Mr Grant.'

'Edmund,' he corrected firmly. 'I have been urging Charlotte for a long time to bring you to Landsdowne. Unfortunately my poor sister was quite unwell when she arrived home yesterday.'

'I know. She did have a sore throat and a headache. She was out in the rain the day before and got quite wet, I'm afraid.'

'Mother took charge of her at once and in no time at all she was tucked up in bed with a hot water bottle. But please don't worry, Charlotte has such miraculous powers of recuperation that I'm sure she'll be on her feet in no time at all. Now,' he said as he handed her into the coach, 'come and meet Emily's sister, Alicia. She's been staying with friends in town and is coming to Landsdowne with us for an indefinite period.'

It was only then that Judith became aware that there was another occupant inside the coach. At the sincerity and warmth of Edmund's and Emily's greeting, Judith knew she would enjoy her visit to Landsdowne. This opinion lasted only a moment. One look at the beautiful young woman Edmund introduced her to—whose nose was long and straight and perfect for looking down, and with a mouth resembling Cupid's bow—made Judith's heart sink. It only took her a moment to realise that Alicia, who was twenty years old, was unlike Emily in every aspect.

As Judith settled herself opposite this aloof young woman, Alicia gave her a faint inclination of her elegantly coifed auburn head and a frosty smile, before settling her austere gaze on her in a cool and exacting way. Impersonally her eyes raked her with a single withering glance, noting her plain attire with a look of distaste. Judith knew she had decided there and then that she was as poor as a church mouse and had no social credentials to recommend her. Immediately a wall of antipathy seemed to spring up between them, and Alicia seemed bent on putting her at a disadvantage from the start.

'So you are Charlotte's friend,' she commented wryly and with a practised smile when Edmund had introduced them, giving Judith a flash of sharp white teeth from between her parted lips.

There were hidden connotations behind the smile and Judith was not quite sure how to read them, but whether meant as insult or compliment, the two of them were both to be guests in the Grant household and it would not do to get off on a bad footing. There was nothing like a smile to confuse a foe or charm a friend and Judith's lips curved graciously. 'Yes, I am,' she replied pleasantly, self-consciously tucking a stray curl beneath her bonnet. She might resemble a pauper, but she had no wish to look as dishevelled as one into the bargain. 'We have been friends ever since I began attending the academy four years ago.'

'And have you finished your education at the academy, too?'

'Yes—although I am to return in the autumn to take up a teaching post there.'

Alicia gave her an arch look. 'You are to be a teacher? Goodness! How awful for you. I cannot imagine anything worse than having to teach hordes of children how to read and write.'

If Alicia hoped to see a flicker of emotion pass across the girl's face she was disappointed, for Judith continued to smile. 'Your conjecture is quite wrong, I assure you. I'm looking forward to it.'

With a slight nod and a look of boredom, Alicia turned to look out of the window at the passing scenery. She made no further attempt at conversation, clearly considering Judith of no consequence.

There was a strange air of unreality about the journey as the coach travelled through London and across the river to Greenwich. She chatted amiably with Emily and Edmund and, having decided to ignore Alicia, Judith found that the couple had succeeded in putting her at ease.

Almost at their journey's end, they travelled down a lane which brought them to a set of tall iron gates. A wide avenue of stately limes led to the most beautiful house Judith had ever seen. Built in warm red brick, its lines were pure and simple, with tall windows of shimmering glass. As the coach passed through the gates, which swung open on well-oiled hinges, she gazed at the exquisitely landscaped gardens, which consisted of acres of rolling green lawns and clipped box hedges, of sculpted pools reflecting flowering shrubs and trees with variegated leaves.

After climbing out of the coach she entered the house in dazed disbelief. Standing in the spacious marble hallway with a graceful, curving staircase sweeping upwards in the centre and forming a gallery, it surpassed anything she had ever seen.

'Mother is resting just now, Judith. You probably know she hasn't been too well of late. I dare say she'll be down later,' Edmund informed her, explaining his mother's absence. 'Jordan is in town and hopes to be home for dinner. Emily will show you to your room.'

'I'd be happy to,' Emily said obligingly. 'Come this way, Judith.'

Judith's room was pale blue and cream, charming and restful, with a splendid view of Greenwich and the Thames in the distance. Immediately concerned about Charlotte, she asked Emily if she might see her. Emily could see no reason why not and took her to Charlotte's room, which was just next door.

Propped against her pillows, her eyes red, cheeks flushed and sneezing into a handkerchief, poor Charlotte really did look quite poorly, but she was delighted to see her friend.

'I'm so glad you're here, Judith,' she said, patting the bed for her to sit down when Emily had left, 'but how I wish I didn't have this wretched cold.'

'You'll soon be feeling better, Charlotte.'

'I do hope so. If I have to stay in bed another day I'll go mad.' Rearranging her pillows with Judith's help to enable her to sit up, she settled back. 'Tell me about your journey and what you think of Edmund and Emily.'

'They are everything you said of them. They were both charming and very kind.'

'And Alicia? What do you think of her?'

In Judith's uneasy mind the memory of those cool green eyes resting on her was far too vivid. 'I—have to say that her manners are not equal to those of her sister's,' she replied cautiously, without implying that she had found offence in Alicia's behaviour towards her, 'but she is extremely attractive,' she conceded.

Charlotte glanced at her sharply. 'Alicia can be quite stuck up sometimes. I do hope she wasn't rude to you, Judith.'

Judith smiled, having already decided to avoid Alicia's company as often as possible. 'I think Alicia sees me as something of a ''blue-stocking''—one of that frightful band of women who openly parade their intelligence. I always find it strange that those who are prejudiced against educating women to the same level as men are those that one might expect to appreciate them. I suppose Alicia finds somebody as plain as I am, who has been taught to a degree that enables me to teach others, thoroughly unfeminine and therefore unattractive.'

'That's because she doesn't have an imaginative brain. Alicia puts great emphasis on fashion, status, social advancement and being seen in all the right places. She is a dullard and has no literary leanings, you see, that's why she resents it in others.'

'Then perhaps she is to be pitied and better understood and I have been too harsh on her, Charlotte.'

'No, you weren't. It's very rare that you see fault in anybody, Judith, but I'm afraid that where Alicia is concerned you are too generous by far—which, in my opinion, is more than she deserves. Every time she opens her mouth I expect to hear her rattle,' Charlotte said unkindly. 'She is a natural flirt, proud, vain and conceited, and thinks far too highly of herself, if you ask me.'

'I suppose with her looks and being the daughter of a very rich man, she has everything in her favour and is entitled to think highly of herself.'

'That may be, and I would be ready to forgive her, if she had not been rude to you. You are a guest at Landsdowne as much as she is, and I won't have her upsetting you.'

'She won't,' Judith smiled. 'I won't let her—but you didn't tell me she was to be here.'

'I didn't know myself until I arrived home and mother told me—although my dear brother is her true reason for coming to Landsdowne, not, as she would have it, to be with Emily. When Jordan came home two years ago, Alicia had visions of being his wife, but however much she hoped he would ask her, he went back to India without saying a word. Yet when he returned and she saw him in town recently, I suspect her aspirations have been revived. She's quite besotted by him—and I know Emily would be delighted if anything were to come of it. Although I'm not so sure about Mother.'

'And your brother? How does he respond?'

'He's not immune to the overtures she's making towards him,' Charlotte told her, stifling a yawn. 'When it comes to wheedling her way around people Alicia is a genius—and when it comes to affairs of the heart, in my opinion all men are weak and foolish. From what I have seen when the two of them are together, Jordan is no exception.'

Judith disagreed with this. There was nothing weak or foolish about Jordan Grant. 'Then I wish her success.'

'Perhaps she was rude to you because she sees you as some kind of threat for my brother's affections.'

'Me?' Judith responded incredulously. 'Don't be ridiculous, Charlotte. As plain and ordinary as I am, what man would give me a second look? Especially when the competition is someone as beautiful as Alicia.'

'Plenty would, if you'd encourage them more. If only you would accept some of my dresses and do something with your hair—which is lovely when you brush it out—you would confound them all.'

Judith was saved having to reply, for at that moment Charlotte was overcome by a fit of sneezing. Her refusal to accept any of her friend's dresses was an old argument, one she preferred not to enter into just then. She sat with Charlotte a while, but as her eyelids began to droop it was clear she was not up to any more conversation. 'Do you think anyone will mind if I take a walk in the gardens before it gets dark, Charlotte? They look so lovely.'

'No, of course not. I just wish I could come with you,' she grumbled miserably, closing her eyes and settling down to sleep.

Realising she had strayed further that she had intended, Judith was about to turn back when she saw Captain Grant walking with long strides towards her. She was totally unprepared for the way her heartbeat suddenly started to quicken and the warmth that flooded her whole being. He had returned to Landsdowne from his business meetings in town, and when he had enquired of the butler if Miss Wyatt had arrived, he had been told that she had gone into the gardens. Immediately he had come to look for her. He was frowning and his jaw was tightly clenched.

Frozen into stillness, Judith waited for him to reach her. With his tall, lithe figure, she thought how handsome he was, how confident and assured of himself, and she wondered what it would be like to be close to such a man. But Judith knew, and her heart lurched with pain, that she was a million miles away from being his equal, that she was not of his world and never would be. The realisation shook her out of her trance, and she was shocked that she should venture to think this way.

'Miss Wyatt! I wish you wouldn't walk too far away from the house alone,' he said curtly.

Judith bristled at his tone. His coolness damped the warmth she had felt on seeing him walk towards her, and when she looked into his eyes, unable to find any gentleness or kindness, and seeing that they were as cold and unwelcoming as glaciers, she withdrew inside herself. 'I—I am sorry. I didn't think anyone would mind if I took a stroll before it gets dark.'

'Usually it would be perfectly in order for you to do so, but in the light of what happened to you the other day, as a precaution I would prefer it if you didn't,' he said. His tanned features were set in lines of implacable authority, and he spoke in a voice of strained patience, reminding Judith of the brutality of her abduction and the terror of her incarceration.

She gasped with alarm. 'Captain Grant! Are you saying I might be abducted again? You seem to forget I was released—that it was not me those men wanted to kidnap but Charlotte.'

'I do not forget, and I can see you are still upset by what happened.'

'Of course I'm upset,' she said heatedly. 'I'm not used to being set upon in the street by a total stranger, viciously attacked and bundled into a carriage, where whoever it was bound my hands and tied something over my eyes and carted me off to heaven knows where. Are you going to tell me what it was all about? You know who was responsible, don't you?' she challenged.

There was a hard gleam in his eyes when he looked at her, giving no inkling of his thoughts. He nodded slightly. 'All I can say is that I have my suspicions and no proof. However, if the people who abducted you are still intent on kidnap—for whatever reason— then now that you are our guest they may realise they were too hasty in releasing you and abduct you again.

The truth of it is I don't know what they intend, but I am sufficiently worried not to take any chances until there is an outcome to my enquiries. I tell you this for your own safety. Come—I'll walk with you back to the house.'

Jordan's quality of detachment as they walked side by side was peculiar to himself. It wasn't until the house was within their sights that his mood softened. Slowing his pace, he looked at the young woman properly for the first time, his silver-grey gaze considering her closely. When he had first seen her he had looked at her with a critical eye, but on closer inspection he found her features uncommonly intelligent. She was a strange young woman, and with her looks and plain attire did not belong to the fashionable world. But with her fine, slender form and handspan waist, which reminded him of the frail white moonflowers that grew in abundance in India, she was deserving of a second look.

She moved with a natural grace and poise that evaded most of the European women he knew, in fact her movements were more reminiscent of Indian women. There was an aura of prim innocence about her that he found appealing, but behind her calm façade he sensed an adventurous spirit tinged with obstinacy.

She really was the opposite of Charlotte in every way. Charlotte could be described as adorably pretty, whereas Judith Wyatt's face was arresting. Her hair was a rich dark brown, attractively highlighted with shades of red and gold. Her face was heart-shaped, with a small determined chin and soft, pink mouth. Her hazel eyes, outlined with thick sooty lashes, were large and slanted slightly.

They were lowered as she walked beside him, so he was unable to read their expression—which was just as well, for Judith was irresistibly drawn to her companion from that moment, and the realisation of it shone deep in their depths. Her profile was pure and serene, and Jordan was suddenly curious to know her better.

'I trust you are suffering no ill-effects from your ordeal?'

'No—none.'

'Tell me about yourself,' he said without preamble, watching her steadily and fixing her with a lazy smile.

Turning her head she looked up and met his gaze, her incredible eyes candid and expressive. 'There's nothing to tell. Usually I never talk about myself.'

'Never? Might I ask why not?'

'Because there are so many other things to discuss that are far more interesting.'

Raising his brows he looked at her expectantly. 'Come now,' he prompted softly. 'You are eighteen years old, Miss Wyatt. There must be something.'

Clearly he had no knowledge that she had been born and raised in India. If he did she was certain he would have asked her about it. But she was glad he didn't know, since there were some memories that ran deep and were too painful to recall. 'There isn't. I'm quite ordinary, really. My parents are dead, and when I'm not at the academy I live with my aunt in Brighton.'

'I understand that your aunt is abroad just now.'

'Yes—which is why Charlotte kindly invited me to Landsdowne. I did thank her for her consideration for me. I would not have you or Lady Grant believe me ungrateful. I confess it sounded more agreeable than spending the summer at the academy.'

'I suspect you will miss not going to Brighton. Is that correct?'

'Yes, I will. I love the sea.'

'And your aunt? Do you love your aunt, Miss Wyatt?'

Judith opened and closed her mouth without uttering a word before turning her eyes away from his penetrating gaze, wishing he hadn't asked such a personal question.

Her face was a mirror of such confusion that Jordan took pity on her. 'I apologise. It was rude of me to ask that. You don't have to answer.'

'No—it—it doesn't matter,' she said, looking at him once more. 'I—I respect her—and I will always be grateful to her.'

He frowned, eyeing her quizzically. 'But you are not close. Why?'

Perhaps it was the low timbre of his voice or the intensity of his gaze, for as Judith looked at him, the truth seemed to be squeezed from her. 'Because she dislikes me. I am also burdensome and an expense she can ill afford,' she answered, wondering what a man with all his privileges would make of that.

Jordan nodded, digesting her words. 'Why do you want to teach?' he asked pointedly.

His question took her wholly by surprise and she felt herself flushing. She was in a situation for which she was ill-trained, but she answered with admirable calm. 'Why does anyone want to do anything? I want to teach because I can—and because I need to. I find it necessary to support myself. Besides, I like being independent and self-sufficient. I prefer it that way.' When he gave her an enquiring look she said, 'I have my pride and my reasons, Captain Grant.'

'You have just given me three answers to my question, Miss Wyatt, but you have not given me the most important one. You have not said that you enjoy teaching.'

'Oh, but I do,' she said on a rush. 'And teaching is a respectable profession for a woman.'

'And being respectable is important to you?'

'Of course. Miss Powell already allows me to teach French to the children in the lower school, and I shall be happy to take up my position in full at the academy in the autumn.'

'Does being a governess not appeal to you instead?'

'Not really. I enjoy teaching more than one person.'

'And no doubt you are well-drilled in all subjects necessary to make a good teacher.'

'I hope so, Captain Grant.'

Having come to a small gate in a beech hedge, he paused in opening it, looking down at her upturned face. 'And what are your pleasures?' he inquired softly, waiting for her reaction and her reply with enigmatic eyes, knowing perfectly well that her idea of pleasures would not conform to his own—which were

the kind she would not approve of and certainly not
admire. He was ten years her senior, wiser and centuries older than she in experience. There was an innocent vulnerability in the purity of her features, and
when she replied and he noted the enthusiasm that
crept into her voice and the glow that lit her wide
hazel eyes, he suddenly felt ancient and worn out beside her youthful idealism.

'I have lots. I take pleasure from listening to music,
reading and painting and visiting various exhibitions
when I can. I also enjoy discussions on current affairs—but I do have opinions of my own which do
not always agree with those of my associates and that
often leads to arguments,' she told him, her light
laughter bursting from her like sunshine. 'I like walking and sight-seeing in town—and I do so look forward to going to my first opera or a play.'

Jordan's reaction was sharp, his voice holding a
trace of irony. 'Whatever happened to such things as
needlework and housewifery and etiquette? I was under the impression that the curriculum was heavily
weighted in favour of those accomplishments as might
make an appealing wife.'

'And so it is, but unfortunately—and much to my
tutors' dismay, I am not much good at any of those
things,' she confessed without embarrassment.

'I expect you play the pianoforte and sing, too, Miss
Wyatt?'

'Unfortunately I do not excel at playing any instrument—no matter how hard I practise,' she answered,
undaunted by his tone and with laughter still shim-

mering in her eyes. 'I don't play the piano half as well as Charlotte—who puts me to shame, and my voice is less than tuneful so I always avoid inflicting it on sensitive ears.'

A faint smile tugged at the corner of Jordan's mouth. 'And will you go on teaching at the academy until you are of an age to retire?'

'Maybe.'

'That is certainly proof of your attachment to the place,' he remarked. 'And marriage? Does that not enter into your scheme of things? Doesn't every young woman want to marry and have children?'

'Marry? Why is it that men seem to think the goal in every woman's life is to marry and have children?'

'So, you plan to remain a teacher all your life?'

Judith flushed. 'Well—no—I mean—I do not know at this time,' she replied with some confusion. 'If it happens then maybe I will consider it.'

Jordan simply smiled crookedly and opened the gate, standing back to let her pass through.

They walked on in thoughtful silence for a few moments. Having studied Captain Grant's profile from beneath lowered lashes, Judith recognised authority when she saw it, and everything about this man bespoke power, control and command. The hard set of his face did not suggest much tolerance or forgiveness, and she felt quite small and vulnerable when she was in his presence.

'What about you, Captain Grant?' she asked courageously, capturing his gaze with her mesmeric eyes.

'I imagine you must be missing India. Are you enjoying being a civilian again?'

'My mother is happy to have me back in one piece—and my brother is relieved to have someone take over my family's many business affairs. Since Father died he's had his work cut out keeping the wheels turning and travelling between here and his home in Kent.'

'I was sorry to hear about your father. I met him several times when he came to collect Charlotte from the academy. I liked him. Poor Charlotte was inconsolable for a time. But—that is not the question I asked,' she said quietly.

His face took on a masklike look, deliberately expressionless, like his voice, and his eyes narrowed on her face. 'True—and please feel free to ask any question you like. I am tied to India by affection, not by blood, and for now, Miss Wyatt, I must give my heart and soul to the task of the moment.'

'I suppose you must find life here very different.'

'I do, but no doubt I'll adjust given time.'

'And can you turn your back on your military life in India with no regrets?'

'No. That is not possible. No one can have no regrets. Whatever military duty I carried out, I did so with a clear mind and never sought to justify myself— even though I am convinced of the fallibility of all human judgement. Most of the officers of my acquaintance and subordinates accepted the ideal of working hard and playing hard. I believe it was playing hard that kept everyone sane.'

'You sound hard, too, Captain Grant,' Judith stated, in a tone that was not meant to give offence.

He looked directly ahead, his face set in harsh lines. 'I was in India for nine years, Miss Wyatt, and it would be hard for you with your English upbringing to understand the nature of the people there.'

Judith stiffened and was about to inform him that she knew all too well the nature of those people he spoke of, but he gave her no time.

'India is a country where a man has to rely on his own wit and his own power of command to survive. It is a country accustomed to stern measures and respectful of power—be it Indian or British—and it is careless of human life. The things a soldier does and sees tend to harden him.'

'But not beyond recall.'

'No,' he said, smiling, his gaze warm and gentle as he captured her own once more and looked deep into her eyes. 'I hope not.'

Judith returned his smile, and in that second she saw something in his gaze that spoke of his interest, and she knew that for the first time he was aware of her.

They had reached the house and before either of them could say anything else Alicia hastened to claim him. Her appearance had a sobering effect on Judith. Alicia's cold green eyes met the hazel ones of the young woman by Jordan's side. For the merest instant a current of tension passed between them, and then, with a little smile, Judith turned away, breaking the contact.

Alicia looked extremely elegant in a lime-green shot silk dress, making Judith feel positively shabby beside her. 'You look very nice this evening, Alicia,' she said generously. 'Please excuse me. I will go and change for dinner.' She knew as she said this that she had nothing better than what she was wearing to change in to.

Not waiting for either of them to reply, she slipped into the house, but not before she had seen Alicia bestow on Captain Grant her most dazzling smile. Charlotte was right: it was plain that Emily's younger sister was very taken by him. The fact that he had first sought out Judith on his return to Landsdowne—who was not even a member of the family—was quite clearly indefensible to Alicia.

When she had changed into a lavender muslin dress she looked at her solitary figure in the long mirror, finding no comfort in what she saw. The dress, with its high neckline and long sleeves, was far from flattering. How she wished she'd something pretty to wear and someone to arrange her hair in a grand style like Alicia's.

Feeling oddly alone, and wishing Charlotte was not indisposed, she went to the open window and looked out. The sound of Alicia's tinkling laughter drifting up to her from below and echoing around the walls of her room with merciless mockery made her feel worse. Looking down into the garden, she saw that the auburn-haired beauty was still in conversation with Captain Grant, who was perusing her in the ageless way in which a man looks at a beautiful woman.

Judith watched Alicia laugh and lean towards him, placing her hand in a familiar gesture on his arm, and what she said was soft and muted. Her companion said something in reply and laughed with her, gazing down into her upturned face, and whatever it was he said to her, she lapped it up like a kitten with its face in the cream.

It amazed Judith that Alicia could remain so calm when she was so close to him, when she herself—just an observer—was as much a-tremble as a blade of grass in strong wind. Charlotte was right, Alicia was very taken by him, she could see that. She was not sure of Captain Grant, but there wouldn't be a man alive who didn't find Alicia attractive, and Captain Grant was certainly speaking to her and looking at her in a way that bespoke interest.

Quickly she pulled back from the window, feeling ill at ease and very much the intruder, yet at the same time a warmth began to course through her body. Suddenly the thought of being as near to him as Alicia was, of having him lean close and speak tender endearments, made her heart knock frantically and a strange excitement pulsate through her veins, and she felt a yearning that was completely alien to her. Catching sight of her reflection in the mirror once more she sighed, wishing she weren't so plain and uninteresting. Compared to Alicia she was as naïve and unsophisticated as a babe in arms.

As Jordan prepared himself for dinner with the aid of his valet, he was quiet and detached—lost in his secret self. He tried to concentrate on the meeting he'd had at India House earlier that day, and the information he'd been given regarding Jehan Khan's reasons for coming to London, but in his relaxed state he was more inclined to dwell on the quirk of fate that had caused Miss Judith Wyatt to be a guest in his home.

As he'd begun to escort her back to the house he'd tried to ignore her, to pretend she wasn't there, and after their few minutes of conversation he had been sorely tempted to do so once more. She had made him reflect on his life in India, on all the things he was missing, and on what his life in the future would lack.

There had been many pleasurable diversions for him in India, but none of them had been of a serious nature. This had been mainly down to him. Because of his military duties, which were often fraught with danger and took him away for many months at a time, he had purposely steered clear of becoming closely involved with any woman.

Until he began his military career he'd been surrounded by family and servants, whose presence and the things they did for him reminded him of his social superiority. He couldn't remember a woman ever talking to him with such unaffected candour as Miss Wyatt had done. He had never met anyone like her—but then, he hadn't been anywhere to meet anyone like her.

Young ladies of Miss Wyatt's station in life had never entered his sphere, and if she had he would have overlooked her because she wasn't spectacularly beautiful like all the other women who floated around in his social world—women of unbridled self-indulgence, whose lives revolved around the latest fashions and expensive jewels, women who had a raging ambition to marry a high-ranking officer or a nabob—women like Alicia Paxton.

It had been brought to his attention by one of the gentlemen at his club in town that Alicia had been more than generous with her favours with one of her father's employees last summer. Alicia was one of those women so basically beautiful that even artificiality heightened her, with all the confidence of a young lady born of a well-to-do family. She had a way of smiling teasingly into his eyes, and from witnessing her body language her interest seemed genuine enough.

Her sole priority was marriage. Unfortunately Jordan found her shallow, somewhat lacking in intelligence, with her head stuffed with nonsense. Nor had she any perception of what love between a man and woman could mean. She might have hopes in his direction, but he had no intention of becoming romantically involved with her. Her slightly slanting green eyes gave her a feline look, and he'd wager she could produce claws if necessary! But whatever shine she possessed had become somewhat tarnished by the presence of Judith Wyatt.

Chapter Four

Judith was the last to come down to dinner. The butler showed her into the drawing-room where everyone was gathered, all partaking of a glass of wine. It was the first time she had been inside this luxurious room, and the sumptuous decoration, the paintings, the furniture and silk upholstery, the porcelain and the Aubusson carpet, were far removed from her little room at the academy and her Aunt Cynthia's modest house in Brighton.

Unable to stave off looking at Captain Grant, her eyes immediately sought him out. She was surprised to find he was watching her entrance like a large, predatory hawk, his wineglass arrested halfway to his lips.

He had changed his clothes and looked extremely handsome and dignified in a rather splendid ivory silk embroidered waistcoat beneath his black suit, which stretched without a crease over the breadth of his shoulders. His shiny black hair had been brushed in merciless neatness, but an errant lock threatened to dip over his forehead at any moment. There was a restlessness about him which reminded her of a caged animal, and she sensed he would feel more at ease outdoors than confined to the house.

He was standing with Edmund by a huge, heavily carved mahogany sideboard, pouring wine. Alicia, her face aglow and clinging to his side like a limpet, was more haughtily, breathtakingly beautiful in the candles' glow than Judith had realised earlier.

Judith went directly to Lady Grant. She was always struck by the elderly lady's dignity. Like her friendly, charming manner, it was so much a part of her and demanded immediate respect. She was seated on a sofa beside the fire, discussing a variety of topics with Emily, who sat opposite.

Lady Grant was slight in stature, softly spoken and her movements graceful. Her brown hair was sprinkled with grey, her skin smooth, and the appealing beauty of her youth lingered on into middle age. Having met her on those occasions when she had come to the academy to collect Charlotte, Judith thought her a lovely lady, and was saddened that her husband's death seemed to have affected her health. They had been very close. Today she looked pale and drawn and had been lying on the sofa in her room for most of the day, but she had come down to dinner to welcome Alicia and Judith to Landsdowne.

'Judith! I'm so happy you're here,' Lady Grant said, her face wreathed in a smile. Taking her hand, she drew the young woman down beside her. 'When Charlotte wrote and asked if you could come I was delighted. You are so sensible and level-headed and

such a great influence on my daughter. I do so hope
you enjoy your stay with us.'

'I know I will. I just hope Charlotte is soon better
enough to get out of bed. I'm so sorry you're not
feeling well, Lady Grant. If there's anything I can do
to help, please don't hesitate to ask.'

'Thank you, Judith. That's extremely kind of you.'
She glanced to where Jordan stood. 'Be so kind as to
bring Judith a glass of wine, will you, Jordan? I'm
sure she could do with one.'

It was quite unnecessary for her to remind her son
of his duties, since he was already halfway across the
room with a glass in his hand. Alicia, evidently resentful of Jordan's brief desertion, scowled her displeasure, her black brows drawn together like wings.

Lady Grant looked at Judith once more, her eyes
filled with concern. 'But how are you feeling, my
dear? Jordan told me all about your abduction. I'm so
relieved you were unharmed. I was very concerned
about you. It was a dreadful business—truly dreadful.
Whatever it was those men wanted, we must all be
very careful until Jordan's enquiries can throw some
light on the matter.'

Handing Judith the glass of wine, Jordan bowed his
head with a studied degree of politeness. 'Is your room
to your satisfaction, Miss Wyatt?'

'It's charming, thank you. I'm sure I shall be comfortable,' she replied, trying to ignore the warmth tin-
gling up her arm as her fingers accidentally touched
his when she took the glass.

'I thought you might like to have the one next to Charlotte,' Lady Grant said. 'It also offers a splendid view of the park and the river.'

'That was very thoughtful of you. When I go down to Brighton my room overlooks the sea. I hear it every morning when I wake.'

'Which you will miss, I'm sure,' Lady Grant sympathised. 'Do you swim, Judith?'

'Yes—when I can.'

'Don't you find the sea cold?'

'At first. But you soon get used to it.'

'What else do you do when you are in Brighton—when you're not swimming?' Jordan asked.

Shifting her gaze from Lady Grant's, she gave him a hesitant smile. 'I love the beach—collecting shells and things. I suppose it's the child in me,' she laughed. 'I also walk a great deal, and Aunt Cynthia has friends calling all the time. I often accompany her on her visits to them.'

'Well, we can't promise you any swimming but there are some lovely walks in Greenwich,' Lady Grant said, 'providing you don't wander off unaccompanied, that is. If it rains—knowing how much you enjoy reading, there are plenty of books in the library. I'm sure you'll find something to your taste.'

'Do you ride, Miss Wyatt?' Jordan asked.

'Not since I was fourteen.'

'Then it's time you were back in the saddle. We have some excellent horses. I'll select one that is suitable.'

Her face brightened, her expressive features glowing with such genuine delight that Jordan was completely captivated. 'Thank you. I would like that,' she replied, although having heard nothing but praise from Charlotte for Captain Grant's horsemanship, she prayed she wouldn't make a fool of herself if she rode in his company.

At that moment the butler entered with great dignity to tell them that dinner was ready.

The Grants lived in a style of elegance Judith was not accustomed to and she felt completely out of her depth, despite Lady Grant's efforts to put her at ease. She hardly noticed what she ate or drank, but the food was delicious. The conversation was interesting and animated, although Alicia, who was seated across from her, tended to raise matters completely alien to her. Judith felt it was intentional, to make her feel excluded. Alicia also had a subtle way of disparaging her through compliments, telling everyone how clever Judith was, that her intellectual powers were no different from those of the opposite sex—a blue-stocking personified, in fact. Judith was irritated by it and tried to laugh it off, but she knew Alicia was placing great stress on what some considered to be unfeminine traits in order to emphasise her own femininity.

'Judith was telling me on the journey down that she is to return to the academy to teach in the autumn,' Alicia said over dessert.

'That is what I intend,' Judith responded calmly.

'Do forgive me,' she smiled, 'but I can't help thinking how very odd that seems.'

At first Judith believed Alicia jested in light repartee, but the malevolent gleam in her eyes destroyed all such thought. She felt her cheeks go hot. 'Odd?' she queried.

'Yes. I find it quite extraordinary. Apart from my governess, I've never met a female teacher before. It's hardly a profession one would embrace from choice,' Alicia remarked with a tight smile.

'It was not forced on me. I enjoy learning for its own sake. It is necessary that I provide for myself,' Judith explained unashamedly, in a controlled voice, determined not to let this rude woman score a hit. 'So it is indeed fortunate that I do enjoy teaching.' Out of the corner of her eye, from where he sat at the end of the table, she could see there was a mixed expression on Captain Grant's face. It was one of disbelief and amusement. She shot him a look and he arched his brows and grinned lazily in the face of it, before settling down to watch and listen in speculative silence.

Alicia saw the exchange and seethed to think that Judith shared some secret with Jordan. 'What is the use of science and commerce and such like to a woman who will spend all her time making her husband happy and raising children?' she went on clumsily.

Judith listened patiently to Alicia's antiquated ideas. Much as she would like to give her the setdown she richly deserved, four years of strict adherence to rules and good manners, and not wishing to give offence to her hosts, could not be disregarded. Clearly Alicia hadn't excelled at her studies, and resented those who did.

'Father doesn't hold with boarding schools for girls,' Alicia went on. 'A governess taught Emily and me everything it is necessary for young women to know at home—is that not so, Emily?'

Emily responded with amused indulgence, but she was determined to have a quiet word with Alicia later, to remind her of her manners. 'So we were, Alicia, but I do envy both Charlotte and Judith the freedom of being taught at a boarding-school with other girls. Miss Powell is respected and very much admired by those both inside and outside her profession. I hear she is to found a charity school for both boys and girls in Chelsea. Edmund has already offered to subscribe to the school—you too, I believe, Jordan.'

Jordan's reply was a barely discerned nod and a sardonic lift to his brow, and Edmund heartily aired his opinion in support of education for women.

Miffed that she didn't have the support of either Edmund or her sister, and beginning to feel her cheeks grow hot with the sting of defeat, Alicia raised her chin haughtily. 'Nevertheless, one cannot escape the fact that the stain of being a ''blue-stocking'' is enough to scare away certain gentlemen, and as a result the accused woman may remain a spinster until the day she dies.'

Judith suppressed a smile, pitying Alicia her ignorance. 'Oh, my,' she said in a moment of sheer mischief. 'Now that is a daunting prospect for any woman. You make securing a husband sound like a holy crusade for all women, Alicia. Still, I have no intention of breaking one of my cardinal rules.'

'What rule is that?' Alicia enquired reluctantly.

'Never to accept a proposal of marriage from a man unless he is of the same intellectual calibre as myself. We must be equal in all things. I refuse to dance attendance like a witless fool on any man who will expect me to submit to his authority, and not to say anything other than yes and no, and insist on my calling him my lord and master, a man who will list me among his possessions, like his dogs and his horses. I consider ideas such as these unacceptable and more than a little insulting.'

'You are rather harsh on the male sex, Miss Wyatt,' Captain Grant remarked coolly.

She turned her head and met his gaze directly. 'It was not my intention to give offence.'

'None taken,' he smiled, 'but you have just damaged my ego beyond recall. How about yours, Edmund? Still intact?'

'After that? Hardly,' Edmund laughed in mock horror.

'I think what you were trying to say,' Jordan went on, returning his sparkling, penetrating gaze to Judith, 'is that you have no intention of being owned by any man.'

'Yes, that's exactly what I meant,' she replied, her eyes holding his. 'Although I must make it quite plain that I believe it is a wife's duty to be an asset to her husband in every way, and that there must be respect and consideration on both sides.'

'It sounds quite mad to me,' Alicia quipped.

'Sane, I think,' Judith countered.

'Oh, I don't doubt your sanity, Judith. It is simply that with ideas such as these, a woman is in danger of becoming eccentric and developing undesirable characteristics.'

Judith arched her brows at Alicia. 'If you mean she is capable of taking care of herself, then I admire her for it. In my opinion men are superior to women in one thing only.'

'And what is that, pray?'

'Brute strength.'

Judith's reply brought laughter from all present, which increased Alicia's irritation further. 'Really? Then I wish you success in your hunting,' she remarked frostily. 'Among the gentlemen of my acquaintance, most of them are opposed to the idea of having an intellectual wife.'

'In which case I shall have to remain a spinster and bear it as best I can,' Judith said, sighing with mock resignation and folding her hands quietly in her lap. 'Although some women might consider it a privilege to enjoy such independence without the shackles of matrimony.' Was she mistaken or did she see a smile of frank admiration gleam in Captain Grant's eye? As if to confirm it he cocked an eyebrow and raised his glass in a subtle salute, before drinking his wine.

After dinner, while Judith exchanged pleasantries with Emily and Lady Grant over coffee, Alicia was noticeably silent as she watched Edmund and Jordan across the room. When she'd finished her coffee Judith rose.

'Please excuse me. I'm very tired and would like to retire,' she said in a quiet voice.

'Of course, my dear,' Lady Grant said. 'I shall be going up myself presently. Is there anything you need?'

'No, thank you. I'll look in on Charlotte before I go to bed. Goodnight.'

With a thoughtful frown Lady Grant watched her go. She had carefully noted the warmth of Jordan's smile and the absorbed way he had watched their young guest as she had valiantly responded to Alicia's barbed questions during the meal, and was both pleased and encouraged by it.

Jordan was in quiet conversation with his brother. He had not so much as glanced in Judith's direction since they'd left the table and she'd assumed he'd forgotten her presence, but when she moved towards the door he lifted his head and looked straight at her. When she was about to climb the stairs she was surprised when he came out of the drawing-room to say goodnight, closing the door behind him. Clasping her hands together, she waited for him to speak to her.

'Congratulations,' he said, striding towards her. 'You did well.' Admiration had swelled in Jordan at how valiantly this young woman had faced up to Alicia's barbs at the dinner table. He was beginning to see that she was a mass of contrasts, most of them vastly appealing.

'Did I?'

'When you imparted your pearls of wisdom earlier I confess to being a little alarmed at the content—but I admired the sense of what you said. There does seem to be a great disparity between the sexes, which I have not given much consideration to before tonight. However, there's nothing that pleases a woman more than victory over another.'

'Oh? Please explain to me what you mean.'

'That when one woman strikes at the heart of another, she usually hits the target.'

Her mouth twitched. 'You mean it's fatal?'

His silver eyes danced as though he had found her altercation with Alicia vastly entertaining. 'Nearly always—but in your case it was an exception. Alicia was too outspoken about your profession. You were too tolerant.'

'One thing I was taught at an early age, Captain Grant, was how to employ tact when it is most needed. As a guest in this house I would not be so rude or so ill-mannered as to argue with her. Besides, it was nothing really. I refuse to let Alicia upset me.' Inexplicably, the laughter was rekindled in her eyes and Jordan saw her bite back a smile. 'I'll do better next time.'

One dark brow arched and his eyes danced with devilish humour. 'How? Would you like to ask her outside onto the lawn, so you have the requisite twenty paces?' he asked, gently teasing.

Judith's lips answered the laughter in his eyes in a smile that revealed shining teeth. 'If I do, will you be my second, Captain Grant?'

Jordan shook his head with mock gravity. 'I'm afraid that would not be appropriate. You are both guests in my home, so it is only right that I remain neutral. Besides, I think you are more than capable of taking care of yourself.'

His expression became serious as he continued to hold her gaze. The depth of this young woman's composure amazed him, as did the delicate softness he saw in the expressionless young face that was looking up at his. He had seen enough of her to realise she had many pleasing attributes, and he was surprised to find that she stirred his baser instincts. 'You should laugh more often,' he murmured. 'It suits you. Tell me. Are you always so outspoken?'

'It's an attitude I seem to be growing into. No doubt you must have found some of my remarks quite outrageous and think that I'm dreadfully ill-bred.'

'Nothing is further from my thoughts. I thought you were quite magnificent,' he said softly. 'You, my dear Miss Wyatt, are a refreshing alternative to all the other ladies of my acquaintance. Something tells me there's more about you than being a blue-stocking. Did you mind Alicia accusing you of that?'

There was laughter in her voice when she answered. 'I could be called worse, I suppose, but—perhaps you share Alicia's opinion and cannot imagine what could be worse than for a young woman to be accused of blue-stockingism.'

'I hope,' he said softly, 'that I'm not so antiquated in my ideas as to think that. I'm not prejudiced against brains in the opposite sex—indeed, it should be considered a premium amongst both sexes. You are a remarkable lady, Miss Wyatt. All my life I've harboured the delusion that all young ladies yearn to snare a husband—and the wealthier the better. You have just taught me something new. I'm beginning to think there is no substitute for a clear-sighted, intelligent woman.'

Judith warmed to the compliment. 'Then I am pleased my outspokenness has achieved something. I'm not like other young ladies, Captain Grant.'

'I sensed that the moment I met you.'

His remark was by no means insulting, in fact the warmth in his voice indicated quite the opposite. Aware of the searching intensity of his gaze, embarrassed colour stained Judith's smooth cheeks. Perplexed, she lowered her eyes and moved away, convinced that he could see the pink flush which heated her body. Making a conscious effort to keep her voice from shaking, she said with calm dignity, 'Thank you. I must go. Goodnight, Captain Grant.'

'Goodnight—and—Judith?'

She lifted her head. 'Yes?'

'I may call you that?'

'Yes. I would like that.'

'My name is Jordan. I'm not a soldier any more.'

It was the first time in five days that Judith had left the confines of the house and grounds when she at-

tended the morning service at the parish church of St
Alfege, which was situated on Greenwich High Road
beyond the woods. She was glad that Charlotte was
sufficiently recovered to accompany her. Lady Grant
preferred to ride in the carriage with Alicia—whose
manner towards Judith was more amiable since that
first day, which gave her reason to think that Emily
must have had a quiet word with her.

Charlotte and Judith declined the use of the carriage, for they both sought the exercise provided by
walking. Besides, the sun was shining and the air was
fresh. Judith's abduction and the dangers that still
threatened were uppermost in all their minds, but with
Edmund and Emily accompanying them they felt quite
safe. With pressing matters of business to attend to in
town, Jordan had left Landsdowne the day following
Judith's arrival and was due back some time that day.

When the service was over and they were walking
back to the house, Emily and Edmund paused to speak
to some people they knew. That was when Judith discovered she had left her prayer-book in the church.
Her parents had given it to her on her tenth birthday
and it was one of the most precious things she possessed. She couldn't bear to think of losing it. Telling
Charlotte she wouldn't be long, she hurried back to
retrieve it, finding it on the pew she had occupied.

Leaving the church she hurried to catch up with the
others, slightly concerned when she found they had
gone on ahead without waiting for her. Entering the
woods, she followed the path that snaked between the
trees, welcoming the chill that fell on this twilight

world after the heat of the sun. As she walked she sensed that she was being watched. She paused and turned to look to her left, seeing a man standing among the cover of the trees staring at her strangely. But what she found stranger still was that the man was Indian. His turbaned figure was dressed in a glistening silk mulberry tunic, his heavily ornamented belt shining with jewels. A feeling of unreality crept over Judith and she shuddered, feeling extremely vulnerable and afraid. It seemed that someone had stepped onto her grave.

Through a veil of confusion and fear, what she now saw was a scene from her past. She glimpsed the dark, shadowy images creeping with stealth out of the locked doors of her mind, and she was sure they were catching up with her. All her deepest, darkest fears lay among the ghosts this Indian resurrected. Since coming to England her nightmares had lain dormant, but now those ghosts were beginning to raise their ugly, dangerous heads once more.

Overcoming her initial shock, she automatically found herself speaking in Hindustani, a language she was fluent in, even though she had not spoken it for four years. 'Who are you? What do you want?'

The man remained silent, but there was puzzlement in his eyes, which narrowed when he heard her speak his own tongue.

Judith forced herself to back away. With her heart thumping she turned and walked quickly towards the others, who had paused to wait for her, and when she glanced back the man had gone. Gradually her pulse steadied, but she wore an air of acute fear as she re-counted what had happened. Deeply concerned, Edmund told them to go to the house. He went back and searched the woods, but there was no sign of the man Judith had seen.

When Jordan arrived home Edmund lost no time in informing him of the incident. Jordan listened, and when his brother had finished speaking, for a split second there was total silence. But then Jordan's face hardened.

'In spite of all my warnings Judith was alone in the woods, you say?'

Edmund nodded. 'Emily and I had paused to speak to an acquaintance and had no idea she had run back to the church to retrieve her prayer-book. We began to walk on and it wasn't until we were halfway through the wood that we realised she wasn't with us. When she appeared her eyes were full of fear. She was clearly quite upset.'

'Where is she now?'

'In her room, I think.'

'Ask her to come to the study, will you, Edmund? I'll speak to her privately.'

Chapter Five

Ever since Judith had arrived back at the house she had puzzled over her encounter with the Indian. Who was he? Undoubtedly he was somehow linked to Jordan and had something to do with her abduction, but what did he want?

When she was summoned to Jordan's study she found him alone. He was sitting at his desk in his shirtsleeves, looking through a pile of correspondence. Uncertainly she moved across the carpet. His dark head was bent over his work and she felt a pang of longing and a need so strong she felt weakened by it. How she wished he might find her as pleasing to look at as she found him.

'You asked to see me,' she said quietly.

He raised his head and looked at her, throwing down his pen. 'Yes,' he answered sharply. Shoving back his chair, he stood up and walked round the desk. Perching his hip on the edge, he crossed his arms over his chest. His face was set hard, the lines around his mouth tight, and his silver eyes bored into hers. When he spoke his voice was like steel.

'Tell me, Judith. Do you make a habit of being disobedient—of doing the opposite to what you are told to do? What did you think you were doing?'

Judith started, her eyes snapping wide open at this surprise attack, her heart contracting at his tone, merciless and cutting. 'Why—I—I cannot think what you mean.'

'No? I thought I told you not to wander off on your own. No sooner do I return home than Edmund is telling me that you did precisely that. You, more than anyone, must be aware of the dangers. It was the height of folly. I advise you to heed my warnings in future.'

The unexpected rebuke stunned Judith into momentary inaction, but she regained her senses quickly and drew herself up with cool hauteur. 'If I wanted advice,' she retorted indignantly, her eyes sparking with ire, 'I would ask for it. I should tell you that I have a streak to my nature that fiercely rebels against being ordered what to do by anyone.'

'I have a formidable temper myself,' he informed her with icy calm, his eyes locking on hers with a deadly glitter.

'So I've been told. If you must know why I was alone, it was because I discovered I had left my prayer-book in the church. It happens to be extremely precious to me and I returned to retrieve it.'

Jordan's black brows snapped together and his eyes narrowed, but his voice was carefully controlled when he spoke. 'It doesn't matter why you disobeyed me— it makes no difference. From this day forward, while the threat of further abduction remains, while you remain in this house you will do as I say,' he continued, immune to the wrathful expression on her face.

Hot colour of indignation exploded on Judith's cheeks and his look warned her not to cross him, but this merciless analysis of her behaviour and the unfairness and harshness of his attack was too much. If he thought for one moment he could dictate where she went and what she should do then he didn't know her. She should have withered beneath his icy blast, but she was too angry to be intimidated by him. Undaunted, she lifted her chin with a small but obstinate toss of her head. It was a gesture of defiance.

'By what right do you appoint yourself my guardian?'

His eyes seized hers in an unrelenting gaze. 'I don't. While your aunt remains abroad Miss Powell has placed you under my mother's care and my own.'

'Then I sincerely hope it is a habit you do not feel obliged to continue.'

'Until such time as your aunt returns or you go back to the academy, you will abide by my rules and accept the hospitality of this house. Is that clear?'

These words were delivered in a cold, lethal voice, and Judith grew pale. She bristled inwardly. Her pride had been pricked, and she was hardly in the mood to forgive Jordan his high-handed manner, but his words were an order and, automatically, she managed to dominate her anger and obey. 'Yes—I understand.'

Jordan had caught the flare of anger his words brought to her face, but he also saw something that resembled pain and hurt in the depths of her lovely eyes. The complexity in them stunned him. Their warm colour was brightly exposed to the sunlight slanting in through the window. She really was quite lovely and he couldn't believe he had once thought her plain. Feeling his anger begin to fade, he relinquished his perch on the desk and walked slowly to the hearth to escape the fresh tender smell of innocent youth that stood before him.

'I apologise if I spoke harshly to you just now, Judith,' he said, still with his back to her, 'and you have every right to be angry. It was insensitive of me. I was alarmed when Edmund told me what occurred earlier. I am concerned for your well-being while you are here. You could so easily have been hurt. Clearly the incident has upset you.'

Perhaps it was the low timbre of his voice or the steadiness of his gaze when he swung round and came to her, but as Judith stared at his grave features she began to relax, finding herself believing him. 'A little,' she confessed. 'But coming upon the man in the wood like that reminded me of something else I would like to forget.'

He raised his brows. 'A secret?'

'No—not really. It—it's something I prefer not to talk about, that's all.'

Jordan was curious to know what it could be, but it was her own private affair so he asked no further questions. Shoving his hands into his pockets, his eyes held by the pale, graceful figure, he moved closer. He contemplated her for a moment and Judith stood, riveted by that sparkling gaze, like a sparrow mesmerised by a bird of prey.

'The man you saw,' Jordan asked at length. 'Tell me what he was like.'

'I am sure Edmund told you he was an Indian. Apart from that I cannot tell you anything else.'

'He didn't speak to you?'

'No.'

'What did he look like? Describe him to me.'

Judith quickly gave Jordan a description of the Indian, omitting nothing, not even the rather splendid huge black pearl she had seen fastened in the centre of his turban. 'Who is this man?' she asked when she had finished. 'You know him, don't you?'

Jordan nodded. 'His name is Jehan Khan.'

'And was he responsible for abducting me?'

'I suspect he might have been involved in some way.'

'The man who spoke to me when I was blindfolded was English. I'm certain of that. Who is Jehan Khan?'

'Apart from being the envoy to an Indian prince called Chandu, by all accounts he is enjoying himself and has become extremely popular. He's cutting quite a dash about town and is frequently seen in society with his entourage of servants and seemingly unlimited funds. What he is doing here in Greenwich, however, is a mystery.'

'Did you know him in India?'

'Yes, we met several times.'

'And Prince Chandu? Were you acquainted with him, also?'

He nodded.

'Why is Jehan Khan in London?'

'To negotiate with the directors of the Company for the return of his master's land, which was annexed by the British when the Prince's cousin—the Rajah of Ranjipur—died leaving no direct male heir.'

'And will he succeed?'

'No. The Company has no intention of doing anything that is against Company policy. Besides, being guilty of crimes against Company property and maladministration of his own domain and his people, Chandu has not adhered himself to the British.'

'So, Ranjipur has become just another bastion of British India,' Judith commented, not without bitterness, for she did not approve of the way the British gained control of disputed territory. But her opinions on this very sensitive and highly controversial issue she diplomatically kept to herself. 'Where is he staying—this Jehan Khan?'

'At the home of Lord Jeremy Minton in Highgate—which, I confess, confuses me. An open dislike and distrust existed between them in India. Khan deeply resented the closeness between Chandu and Minton, which is why I'm surprised they're here together, and that Khan is partaking of Minton's hospitality.'

'What kind of man is Lord Minton?'

'Ambitious. Like others before him, Minton saw India as a place for quick riches. He lived like a king in his district way up country—close to the border with Nepal. It was so remote he had no reason to fear interference from Delhi, so he was able to do very much as he liked—while portraying himself as a gentleman of business carrying out his work for the Company rather than himself.

'He is unscrupulous and avaricious, and has acquired a private fortune while in the Company's service. There is a restriction on receiving gifts and private trading by Company workers, and with a huge question mark over him he has been recalled to London, where he is to be investigated by the select committee. It is highly probable that he will have to face charges of native intrigue and the abuse of his office—which is no bad thing, for there are many more like Minton who need weeding out—pompous men with an inflated sense of their own importance, their brains addled by the sun, liquor and opium.

'The Jeremy Mintons who have grown fat on vice have to be curbed, or everything and everyone connected with it will become so mired in corruption that the rot it will generate will spread and destroy everything admirable about the Company. Whatever the outcome, with his name tainted by dishonesty and dissolution, his career with the East India Company is over.'

Judith was quite bewildered. 'But—what has all this got to do with you?'

'As to that I'm not certain.'

Judith eyed him quizzically. 'You have an idea, don't you?'

His expression became grim and his voice stern. 'You are very persistent, Judith, but that need not concern you.'

'I beg to differ. I have every right to know who abused me that night. I cannot forget it.'

'You have need to remember,' he said, glancing at her sharply, 'and to fear both Jehan Khan and Jeremy Minton. If I discover that either of these men were behind your abduction, then I promise you they shall pay.'

There was a quiet warning in what he said. 'If you're thinking of me, then please don't waste your time. One thing I have learnt is to rely on myself.'

'I know, but I do worry about you,' he said softly, his eyes fixed on her face. 'For all your courage, you are a fragile thing, Judith Wyatt. You put me in mind of a moonflower—a slender, beautiful white flower that grows in India. They are so transparent you can hear them pop when they open.'

She smiled, remembering them, too, but she made no comment. Tilting her head to one side, she looked at him with speculative hazel eyes. 'Do you suppose whoever abducted me intended abducting Charlotte and holding her until you paid them ransom money?' she asked, her agile mind having already reached this conclusion.

A hint of humour stole into his face as he met her gaze. 'There's maybe a bit more to it than that.'

'Is there? Well, I could be right. After all, it's no secret that you are immensely rich,' she reminded him with artless candour.

'Do you always speak your mind?' Jordan asked, astonished by her unguarded question.

'Always. I think it's best, don't you?'

He nodded. 'At least one knows where one stands—
although your question is difficult to answer just now.
It's possible that you are right and those men were
intent on procuring money from me. Greed is a powerful motivation for risk. However, I strongly believe
it was for something else.'

'If not for money, then could it be of a different
nature entirely?' Suddenly her eyes opened wide as a
fascinating yet outrageous thought occurred to her.
'Are you involved in some kind of conspiracy. Is that
it?'

He raised an eyebrow at this, and when he looked
at her, amusement struggled with amazement on his
face. For a moment he didn't say a word. His eyes
gleamed as he shook his head slightly, but he had a
peculiar trick of hiding all his thoughts behind an inscrutable mask. 'I can assure you that I am involved
in no such thing.' Suddenly his expression relaxed and
his eyes brightened as a smile moved across his lean
brown face. 'And now I think it's time we did something else.'

'What have you in mind?'

'Edmund, Alicia and myself are to take a ride in
the park before dinner. Perhaps you would care to join
us. As you know, Charlotte has a fear of horses and
doesn't like to ride, so she won't be accompanying
us.' The way her face lit up with a radiance like the
sun coming out from behind a cloud Jordan found utterly endearing. Captivated by the depths of the hazel
eyes looking into his and by the freshness of the lips
slightly parted to reveal small, perfect teeth, he felt an

unfamiliar ache in his heart and his mind became momentarily preoccupied with how adorable she looked, and another, less welcoming but undeniable awareness—desire.

His growing attraction to Judith Wyatt astounded him. It was insane! His tastes ran towards sophisticated, experienced women and he had diversions a-plenty—with Alicia hovering persistently by his side and the pick of every beautiful female in London society eager to trade themselves for an alliance with the Grants of Greenwich. The notion that a young woman fresh out of the schoolroom could arouse him was almost comical.

'Unless you wish to offend me, you won't refuse,' he said gently.

Judith lowered her eyes beneath the heat of his gaze in case they should give her away. Even as the blood raced through her veins and her heart was doing strange, unfamiliar things, there was a voice reminding her firmly of pride, self-discipline—and the foolishness of unrequited love. She could not believe the effect this man always had on her—but Jordan Grant, titled, wealthy, and devastatingly handsome, would never be interested in a penniless, plain young woman, whose only ambition in life was to teach.

'Come, what do you say?' he persisted. 'You're not thinking of an excuse, I hope?'

She smiled shyly. His gaze never wavered from hers, and she wondered if anything escaped those alert grey eyes. 'I wouldn't dare.'

'Good. Now that's settled I'll see you at the stables in fifteen minutes.'

Fifteen minutes later Judith watched a groom leading a white mare into the stable yard, her coat gleaming silver in the afternoon sun, her floating mane and tail brushed to perfection. Edmund was already mounted, and so was Alicia, who looked stunning in a blue velvet riding habit with gold frogging, and a matching hat, cocked at an impudent angle atop her hair.

But Judith only had eyes for the white mare and the man who came to take the reins from the groom. The horse stretched out its nose and shook its mane vigorously when Judith moved confidently towards her. The animal's soft brown eyes were alive and intelligent, and removing her glove Judith rubbed her velvety nose affectionately.

'She likes you,' Jordan said, pleased that Judith wasn't nervous about approaching the horse.

'The feeling is mutual. She's beautiful. What's her name?'

'Tilly.'

'And does she have any peculiarities that I should know about before I risk life and limb?'

'None that I know of. She's as docile as a lamb.'

'I only hope I haven't forgotten how to ride.'

'Four years is a long time, but don't worry. Once you're in the saddle it will come back.' He grinned when he saw her wrinkle her nose at the side-saddle. 'What is it? Do you have an aversion to the saddle?'

'I've only ever ridden astride. Seated on that, it is more than likely that I shall become unseated at the first hurdle and make a complete fool of myself—providing I don't break my neck. And if I do,' she said, smiling up at him, 'no doubt you'll blame my poor horsemanship and not the saddle.'

He grinned down at her. 'I'd offer to change it but should you be seen you will be ostracised from society for ever.'

She gave him a wry smile, probing the depths of those clear grey eyes. 'Since I cannot claim membership to that ancient and exclusive set, that does not concern me. Society can be vindictive, and I am glad I don't have to worry about social acceptability. Now,' she said, turning her attention to the instrument of torture she was expected to sit upon, 'about this saddle.'

'If you're afraid to ride side-saddle—if it's more than you can handle, simply say so,' Jordan generously suggested, a lazy, challenging, almost taunting smile tugging at his firm lips.

Judith glanced at him and laughed brightly. 'I'm not afraid, so don't you dare try putting me off.'

Jordan felt total admiration for her competitive spirit, and before Judith knew what he was about he'd placed his hands on her waist and lifted her effortlessly into the offending saddle, watching as she hooked one knee around the pommel and placed her small foot in the stirrup, letting his hand linger for a moment on her thigh.

'Does that feel comfortable?' he asked, his forehead suddenly furrowed in concern.

'Yes,' she replied, taking the reins with one hand and stroking the mare's neck with the other. 'We'll soon get used to each other—won't we, Tilly,' she murmured into the horse's ear.

'You don't feel faint?'

'Not a bit,' she smiled, controlling her mount easily when she moved restlessly and danced a couple of steps to one side.

Jordan swung himself up onto his own horse, a huge nut-brown stallion, and together they rode towards Edmund and Alicia. Alicia, coolly poised and elegant, her nose tipped disdainfully high and her green eyes hostile when they settled on Judith, had to struggle to hide her annoyance at the attention Jordan was showering on her. She walked her horse beside Judith's out of the stable yard as the two men went on ahead.

Although Alicia considered Judith far too slender to be described as womanly—presenting no competition to her own roundly proportioned form—she had to concede that dressed in the right clothes and with her hair arranged in a more fashionable style instead of that ridiculous bun at the back of her neck, with her wit and brightness, she could attract a covey of young men to her side. Alicia considered it high time she knew her place at Landsdowne.

'I've just been telling Jordan that I've never ridden side-saddle before,' Judith said in an attempt to relieve the tension between them, her nostrils invaded by a heavy scent of French perfume that wafted across to her from the other woman.

'You mean you have always ridden astride?' Alicia said, favouring her with a cool, level stare.

'Yes—always.'

Alicia's eyebrows raised as she stared across at her, her red lips twisting scornfully. 'Really! Another peculiarity of yours,' she quipped with silken malice. 'How very unladylike.'

Judith adopted a tolerant smile. 'Considering I was a child at the time, Alicia, your accusation is somewhat misplaced.'

They rode on in silence for a few moments until Alicia calmly said, 'I don't know what you have in mind where Jordan is concerned, Judith, but whatever it is, forget it.'

Judith stared at her with a coolness that astounded Alicia. 'Would you mind telling me what you mean, Alicia?'

Alicia returned her stare, her green eyes shining ruthlessly. 'That no matter how much you throw yourself at him, you'll never succeed in getting him to look at you the way he looks at me.'

'Do not suppose that I would encourage him to do so,' Judith laughed, delighting, as she always did, in the ridiculous. 'Dear me, Alicia. What on earth's got into you?'

'Righteous anger, if you must know,' Alicia flared, astonished and infuriated by Judith's calm, cool manner, 'which means that I have just cause. So don't deceive yourself into believing Jordan's interested every time he speaks to you. He's being polite to a guest in his house, and nothing more. Why,' she scoffed, wanting to humiliate and shatter this woman's most sensitive feelings and wipe the simpering smile from her lips, 'he'd laugh you right out of bed.'

'I doubt it, since such a thing is unlikely to happen,' Judith responded, meeting her gaze squarely, refusing to be intimidated by such cutting remarks. But Alicia was right. Any healthy, virile man would desire Alicia, with her voluptuous curves, her beauty and her sensuality. She was also ruthless, and any man she desired she would want to possess body and soul. Judith began to feel sorry for Jordan, and she also felt a small frisson of distaste when she thought of her own plainness. 'You're being quite absurd, Alicia. You let your imaginings run away with you to the point where you are in danger of becoming hysterical.'

'I don't think so. I've seen the way you look at him, how much you want him. But I'll get him in the end. I've been patient. I've waited for two years for him to come home, and now he has I won't see them wasted. I won't stand by and watch a mere schoolgirl jeopardise my plans.'

The anger and bitterness seeping out of Alicia was so palpable that Judith could almost feel it. 'You may be assured that I have no intention of doing any such thing.'

'Then we understand each other. You will stay away from him?' Alicia queried.

'I'm sorry to be a fly in the ointment, Alicia, but that's going to be difficult, since we inhabit the same house,' Judith answered flatly. 'But I'm sure if you want him so much then nothing will stand in your way.' She looked at Alicia and calmly pointed out, 'But the matter between the two of you is not absolutely settled, is it? First, you have to make him want to marry you.'

'And I will,' Alicia continued emphatically. 'I will do everything within my power to bring about a relationship that will be completely advantageous to myself.'

Judith gazed somewhat pityingly at her. 'If that's what makes you happy then I see nothing wrong with it. But don't overestimate your ability to manipulate him, Alicia. I would not equate Jordan Grant with the other gentlemen of society. I have known him just a short time, but I already know he is nothing like them.'

'How can you—a pupil at Miss Powell's academy, a person who is quite destitute—possibly know anything about gentlemen of breeding? Such things are way beyond your sphere,' Alicia said scathingly, her eyes travelling with abhorrence over Judith's plain garb. 'Why, you'll be lucky if a man ever looks at you.'

'How coarse you are, Alicia. If you're through with your insults,' Judith murmured, flinching inwardly at Alicia's words, half convinced that what she said was true, 'I'll ride on.'

Perceiving that her thrust had hit its mark, Alicia watched her go, her eyes shining with triumph.

Having nothing but contempt for Alicia's paltry attack, seeing nothing in it but ignorance and malice, refusing to be hurt by the cruel barbs, Judith shoved them to the back of her mind and rode on to join Jordan and Edmund.

They walked their horses towards the park, where they gave them their head and galloped over the grass. Judith breathed in deep, delighting in the feel of the horse moving beneath her and riding better than she'd imagined. She might not have a fashionable habit to wear and she might not sit her horse as elegantly as Alicia, but she didn't let it spoil her enjoyment or take away the pleasure of being on a horse again. How she wished Charlotte was there to share it with her, but Jordan was right. His sister had an aversion to horses and you couldn't get her near one.

She sneaked a glance across at Jordan admiringly. There was an aggressive virility about him and an uncompromising authority and arrogance that had been imbued into him during his years as a soldier. Alicia was right. Jordan Grant was beyond her sphere of things and she didn't know how to deal with him.

He made her uneasy and made her heart do strange things, but in a moment of dreaming of what might have been had she been born with a silver spoon in her mouth, she allowed herself a moment to dwell on how handsome he looked astride his powerful horse, with his shining dark hair ruffling in the light breeze, and his swarthy features enhanced by the gleaming whiteness of his neckcloth. He was resplendent in an impeccably tailored dark green riding-coat that stretched across his broad shoulders without a crease, and snug-fitting buckskin breeches disappearing into highly polished tan riding-boots.

They rode among the tall elms and chestnuts and up the hill to the Observatory, where a splendid view of the Queen's House and the busy river was to be had. Riding back they slowed their horses to a leisurely walk, Jordan and Edmund pausing now and then to acknowledge others they knew who were either strolling or riding in the park. Alicia, who was doing her utmost to engage Jordan in bubbling conversation, never left his side for a moment.

Happily chatting to Edmund, Judith failed to notice that Jordan was studying her. His sharp eyes told him that despite being out of the saddle for the past four years she could certainly ride, and her handling of Tilly was impressive. She adopted a no-nonsense attitude and dealt firmly with the skittish mare, commanding her movements superbly. His gaze rested with admiration on the confident poise of her head, her straight back and perfectly relaxed shoulders and arms.

His curiosity about her increased. She must have had an excellent teacher. Where had she learned to ride like that? He suddenly realised that apart from what she had told him, he knew absolutely nothing about her. It was a situation he was determined to rectify at the earliest opportunity.

Chapter Six

A gold-embossed invitation was delivered to Landsdowne inviting Lady Grant, her family and house guests to a ball to be given by Lord and Lady Penrose in town. The Penroses were close friends of the Grants, Lord Penrose being a director of the East India Company. The ball was in honour of their youngest daughter's betrothal.

Immediately Lady Grant started discussing the arrangements and Charlotte excitedly began deciding what dress and jewellery she would wear, speculating on the gentlemen who would be present. But she was not insensitive to the feelings of Judith on the matter, who had quietly and firmly proclaimed she would not be going.

'I can't possibly go, Charlotte,' she said when they were alone cutting flowers for the house in the rose garden.

'Of course you can,' Charlotte said, snipping a splendid red bloom and placing it neatly in her basket. 'You have been invited—and if you're worrying because you have nothing appropriate to wear, that's easily remedied. I have plenty of gowns you can choose from—although no matter which one you choose it will have to be altered to fit. You are much more slender than I am. Mother's maid can arrange your hair.'

'I like my hair the way it is,' Judith told her stubbornly.

'We are to travel up to town two days before,' Charlotte went on, ignoring Judith's comment about her hair. 'Edmund has promised to escort us to Vauxhall Gardens, and we are to go shopping with Emily. I dare say you would prefer a more cultural repertoire of exhibitions and museums, but you get enough of that at the academy. You are on holiday and should enjoy yourself.

'Jordan continues to rent the house in Piccadilly our father used whenever business commitments kept him in town. It's large enough to accommodate the whole family when the need arises. The Penroses live in a magnificent house in Mayfair, Judith, and there's not a society girl in London who wouldn't kill for an invitation to their ball. You really can't allow yourself to miss such an opportunity.'

'No, Charlotte.' Judith was adamant. 'I'm just a dowerless girl from Miss Powell's academy. I'm not a society girl.'

'You're going to be—even if it's just for the one night.' Charlotte glanced down the garden and her face broke into a joyous smile when she saw Jordan striding towards them, having just returned from spending three days in town on business. 'Hello,

Jordan! Come and help me persuade Judith to go to the Penroses' ball. I've tried my best but she refuses to consider it.'

'I am not going, Charlotte,' Judith said, happiness soaring through her on Jordan's arrival. Suddenly the garden, which had been up till then just another garden, became an enchanted place. The banks of roses became more splendid, the scent of flowers sweeter, the air warmer. It was absurd, she thought, for she seemed to be in danger of falling in love with this handsome captain.

Jordan looked at her for a long moment with those incredible silver eyes of his, one of his sleek black brows elevated, and then he smiled.

'We'll see about that,' he told her.

Judith's abduction and the mysterious threat of further danger hung uneasily over the household. No further light had been thrown on the incident, but Jordan reassured them all that it was still being thoroughly investigated. Apart from everyone being careful not to wander off unaccompanied, everything carried on as normal.

After dinner on the same day that Jordan arrived home, Emily became engaged in a game of piquet with Lady Grant, while Alicia observed with an expression of extreme boredom. With profound annoyance she kept glancing across the room to where Jordan and Edmund were in deep conversation.

Emily always looked faintly anxious when they were all gathered together, as though worried that the obvious antipathy her sister felt for Judith would break into open warfare. Whenever the two of them looked at each other it was with something less than pleasure. There was always a curious sense of constraint between them, and yet they felt obliged, because they were both guests at Landsdowne, to converse in the most formal and stilted manner. Emily was thankful that Judith was a sensible, level-headed young woman who knew better than to provoke Alicia, and was always careful to avoid sitting next to her.

Charlotte was entertaining them on the pianoforte, and Judith sat apart from the others, engrossed in a book. Unable to stand being ignored any longer, Alicia got up and sauntered over to Jordan and Edmund.

'Why are you neglecting us?' she complained, pouting sulkily. 'It must be a full fifteen minutes since either of you spoke to us—and you just back from town, Jordan. I have not set eyes on you for three days. I object to being excluded from your conversation and cannot imagine what you are discussing that is so interesting.'

'It may be of interest to us, Alicia,' Edmund said lightly, 'but I doubt you would find a discussion on industrial investments and the continuing famine in Ireland of any interest whatsoever.'

She wrinkled her nose with distaste. 'You're right, I wouldn't, and I don't see why you have to discuss such matters now.'

'I apologise, Alicia,' Jordan said, smiling in an attempt to dispel her sullen look. 'It's simply that now I've left the army and taken over my father's affairs,

I must familiarise myself with everything and fit myself to the role—which is the reason why I am frequently absent from Landsdowne for several days at a time.'

'Are you missing India and your regiment, Jordan?' Emily enquired politely, pausing in her game of cards to look across at him.

He seemed to contemplate her question before answering, and when he spoke his face had taken on a grave look. 'I shall always regard England as my home, but I became truly fond of India. I do miss it, yes.'

'I cannot for the life of me see why you should, and nor can I understand what the British are doing there,' Alicia said in some indignation, for she had resented the time Jordan had spent in India with his regiment, and her resentment was increasing daily now he was home, for he seemed in no hurry to press his suit as she had hoped. 'India is so far away.'

The mention of India interrupted Judith in her reading and she raised her head. A cold, tight feeling began to form in the pit of her stomach as she desperately tried to think of a way to avert a topic she feared would strike straight at her heart. Her palms were perspiring where they rested on the book in her lap.

'There are trading posts there, Alicia, and trade is necessary and important not only to the prosperity of Britain and India, but also to the entire world. It's called progress,' Jordan explained, patient as a teacher with a slow pupil. 'The British army is there to sustain order and to protect them and the people who are employed to run them from rebels, whose aim it is to disrupt the peaceful order of things—not without a heavy cost in human life, I might add.'

'Nevertheless the natives must feel oppressed beneath the might of the British.'

'They have suffered oppression for centuries at the hands of their own overlords,' Jordan commented dryly. 'It is our aim to bring peace to India.'

'Still—it seems to me that the Indians have exchanged one master for another and their oppression is no less,' Alicia continued with all the clumsy ignorance of a person unfamiliar with their subject, stubbornly refusing to let the matter drop. 'From what I hear and read in the newspapers of the British in India, they consider the natives to be culturally inferior and themselves a superior race.'

'From my own experience,' Jordan went on, 'much of their prejudice is rooted in fear and ignorance, and unfortunately some of the Company servants are not renowned for the sophistication of their manners.'

'I suppose that if the Indians do feel oppressed, they don't have to put up with it.'

'And in your opinion, Alicia, what should they do?' Edmund asked quietly.

'Why, there are millions of them to a handful of Company workers and the army. If they feel they are suffering hardship and injustice under British rule, then why don't they do something about it?'

'That's a very unpatriotic thing to say, Alicia!' Emily rebuked, scowling darkly at her, quietly wishing her sister would cease her mindless chatter and sit down. 'Besides, from what we read in the newspapers they do revolt—all the time, and the massacres and atrocities they carry out on British communities are quite dreadful. Is that not so, Jordan?'

'I regret that is so. But I must point out that there is often savagery on both sides.'

Alicia shrugged. 'I fail to understand why Company workers want to take their wives and children there anyway—to live among uncivilised heathens who worship heathen gods, killing each other and burning widows—where one is likely to be attacked and carried off by a tiger.'

Judith saw Jordan suppress an amused, tolerant smile, while she existed in a state of jarring tension as she sat perfectly still and listened to Alicia air her misinformed views.

'How they can take on a mode of life that strikes me as being the very epitome of stupidity never fails to surprise me. I cannot think of anything worse than exposing oneself to the fevers that are prevalent there, of adopting a nomadic existence, sleeping under canvas and travelling about in that intense heat, forgetful of the conventions that dictate our own lives.'

'And I, Alicia, cannot envisage you suffering such discomforts, either,' Emily said sharply. 'But you really should go to India and see for yourself, before you condemn what the British are trying to do there.'

'No, thank you. I have a fair skin,' her sister quipped, touching her cheek to indicate this well-known fact. 'The hot sun would not treat it kindly.'

'Nonetheless, I think you have said quite enough on the subject and it would be nice if you remembered your manners,' Emily rebuked.

In her vulnerable state Alicia's careless remarks had hit Judith like daggers, gouging holes into her emotional barricade. She put down her book and in a trice was on her feet, her eyes blazing at Alicia, unable to conceal her feelings.

'Nobody in their right mind would endorse your ignorant view, Alicia. You have no idea what you are talking about. Like most people outside India you are abysmally misinformed of the nature of the people and the country. However, being unacquainted with the East I suppose you can be excused what you have just said. But has it not occurred to you that husbands and wives should be together wherever that happens to be, that they may have no wish to be separated, often for years at a time? Many people who go to India find it enchanting and actually enjoy the nomadic existence, and rejoice in the absence of a social system that stifles freedom of any kind in the modern world.'

Alicia, somewhat shocked by Judith's outburst, looked at her directly. 'Nevertheless, one cannot help but wonder what would happen in a society where everyone could do very much as they please, where there were no rules to be broken. No doubt everyone would become tired of it and die of boredom. And in India where there is a lack of rules to dictate how people should live, one cannot escape the fact that there are tribesmen who can be described as nothing less than murdering savages.'

'Yes,' Judith replied angrily, feeling her legs begin to tremble. 'I know that, too.'

'Why, Judith,' Alicia mocked, 'anyone would think you speak from experience.'

The eyes of everyone in the room snapped wide open, and they looked at each other with an identical look of consternation.

As he was about to drink his brandy, Jordan's hand paused with the glass halfway to his mouth. Judith had caught all his attention. Her face was a mirror of anguish, and he watched it lose what little colour it had.

Judith swallowed, the faces around becoming blurred, but she was wretchedly aware that she had become the focal point of five pairs of eyes. Quietly and with a trembling voice she answered Alicia's question. 'I do. Please—excuse me.'

Her words scored through Jordan's brain as he stared at the closed door through which she had hurriedly disappeared. She had been close to tears, he had seen that.

'Good gracious!' Alicia exclaimed, seemingly amused by Judith's angry reaction to what she had said. 'Who on earth would have thought it?'

An uneasy silence had fallen on the room and Lady Grant was looking decidedly uncomfortable. Charlotte rose from the piano stool and strode towards Alicia, incensed.

'Alicia! How could you! That was the most insensitive, cruel thing you could have said to Judith. You have no idea what you've said, have you?'

Jordan slowly put down his glass, all his attention riveted on his sister. His jaw tightened and he stood up. 'Charlotte! What are you talking about?'

Charlotte's head swivelled round to her brother. 'Judith was born in India. She lived there until she was almost fourteen years old—until her parents were murdered and she had no alternative but to come to England.'

Jordan stared at Charlotte, her revelations pounding in his brain like hammer blows. 'What? In God's name, why didn't she say anything?'

'Because she saw her parents killed and everyone else at the cantonment in India where she lived—yes, Alicia,' she flared, directing her gaze at that haughty young woman once more, 'women and little children, too. She was the only one to survive the massacre. She suffered terribly and still has nightmares about it—and she never talks about it to anyone—never. It's much too painful for her to remember.'

Frowning with disbelief at what he was hearing, Jordan looked at his mother. 'Did you know?'

Lady Grant shook her head slowly. 'Only that Judith was born in India and that she came to England when her parents died.'

'Then why the hell didn't anyone think to tell me?'

Charlotte moved towards the door. 'I'll go to her.'

'No,' Jordan said in a voice that brooked no argument. 'I'll go.'

Alicia quickly stepped in front of him. 'Jordan, you can't. Listen to me...'

When he looked at her, his brows lowering and his features as hard as granite, she shrank from the blast of his freezing gaze. 'My compliments, Alicia. This time your tongue has achieved its aim. Now get out of my way.'

The tone of his icy command almost sent her scuttling for cover. Automatically she stood aside and watched him stride out of the room, her face devoid of emotion, but hate was beating a bitter note in her heart. She recalled the ride they had taken in the park several days earlier and the way Jordan had pandered to Judith, concerning himself with her comfort and well-being, and how his gaze had strayed to her repeatedly during the ride.

Inwardly she seethed. The hatred and scorn she felt for that dark-haired witch was all over her contemptuous face. Judith Wyatt had inveigled her way into the household and everyone's affections in a way Alicia could not forgive. She lowered her eyes to hide the feral gleam in their depths, her thoughts upon revenge.

Jordan knocked on Judith's door. When she didn't answer he entered anyway. The room was in semi-darkness. Judith was standing in front of the window, gazing out at the night, and with her back towards him she was just a dark, slim figure silhouetted against the light. He walked towards her and still she didn't turn, but he knew she was aware of his presence.

'Judith. Why didn't you tell me about India and your parents?' he asked quietly.

'Because it would have led to questions,' she answered, her voice barely above a whisper. 'I didn't want to talk about it.'

'Have you ever? To anyone?'

'No—not really. To speak of what happened would be like reliving the experience—when all I want to do is forget.'

'And have you?'

She shook her head. 'No.'

'Then it might help if you were to talk about it.'

She turned and gazed up at him. His face was all angles and planes and shadows, and a heavy lock of dark hair fell over his forehead. In the subdued light he looked mysterious. His expression was firm, his eyes glittering and faintly troubled. 'To you?'

'Why not?' he murmured, looking down into her huge, clear hazel eyes, which were always steady and direct, giving her a waiflike innocence. 'Because I know India, because I know its customs that seem strange to people not acquainted with that country, because I've seen what happens to people when cantonments fall into rebel hands, I'm willing to listen.'

'It isn't your problem.'

'Then I'll make it my problem.'

She looked deep into his eyes. He really did seem disposed to listen.

'Share it with me, Judith,' he persisted gently. 'Hasn't anyone ever told you that a trouble shared is a trouble halved, that two can bear a cross more easily than one?'

She smiled. A softness entered her eyes and a haziness that suggested tears. 'Yes. My mother—once.'

Jordan was relieved to see her smile and her shoulders relax a little. It was a start. 'What was she like, your mother?'

'Gentle, warm, loving. She adored my father and me, and they both loved India passionately.'

'Was your father connected to the army?'

'No. He was an Assistant Collector and a linguist. Having been educated at Cambridge he was extremely clever—if a little eccentric. He wasn't ambitious or any of the things that drove others who went out to India with the East India Company—which was probably why I was forced to accept my aunt's charity when I came to live in England. My father's love of India was such that he would have given it anything— love, loyalty—and he ended up giving his life and my mother's. But he was where he wanted to be, and he wanted to be left alone to live and work in peace.'

'Where was he stationed?'

'For a time he was in Madras—which was where I was born and spent most of my childhood, but then the Company posted him to Calcutta. We'd been there five years when he was moved again, and we went to live between Bombay and the Maratha states in central India. Have you been there?'

Jordan nodded. 'Having passed through the Carnatic I am familiar with the area. But much of my soldiering was done among the hills of the North West Frontier, and the Nepal border.'

Her eyes lit with interest. 'Did you see the Himalayas?'

Jordan nodded. 'A great deal of my time was spent among the foothills on horseback with my regiment. We slept under the stars, with nothing to hear but the night birds and the hum of the cicadas, and the purring of panthers in the trees—all sounds that became as familiar to me as the traffic and the cries of the cities. I remember how invigorating it was to feel the first flush of dawn, and to feast my eyes on the glens where there were seas of columbines and forget-me-nots. I don't deny that one had to be tough to survive as a soldier in those northern territories, but it had its compensations.'

'I would like to have gone there. The Hindus are very superstitious about the hills. They believe the Gods live there. Did you know that?'

'Yes. And who is to say that they don't?'

'No one, I suppose. Mother wanted to stay in Calcutta, but father was happy to go anywhere the Company sent him if it meant seeing more of India. We lived at one of the military stations, which scattered the Company raj and its boundaries. It was quite small compared to some. Unfortunately there was lawlessness and constant disturbances from the feared Pindaris, who roamed at will.'

Jordan knew all about the Pindaris. They were mercenaries of the old Maratha armies who had split up into small groups and penetrated Company territory back in '16, even going so far as to threaten Bombay. Plundering and massacring was their livelihood. To deal with this menace Lord Hastings—the Governor-General of Bengal—had assembled the largest British force seen in India, and it had turned out to be the most difficult campaign they had ever conducted in that country, lasting two years. The incessant marching and broiling heat had made it a wearisome business, but the Pindaris were eventually destroyed.

Judith had paused in her telling, and although Jordan appeared calm, he waited in a state of tension for her to go on. She wasn't looking at him, she was looking out of the window into the dark, back over four years to the time when she had been afraid, as if the images of the past were marching with each shifting shadow. With an effort he restrained the urge to move closer, to take her in his arms and soothe her as he would a frightened child.

'What happened then?' he asked gently, loathing himself for adding to her torment by forcing it from her.

Judith looked at him long and hard before turning away. She wrapped an arm around her waist as if to contain the horrors, pressing her free hand to her forehead in an attempt to relieve her over-burdened mind. Jordan's scrutiny unnerved her, and no matter how she tried to push the memories from her, they returned, lapping inside her head like an ascending sea. Still she hesitated, but in the end she turned to face him once more, and a flicker of sanity lit the chaos of her thoughts.

'You are right. Maybe I will feel better if I tell you.' She held his eyes a moment, and then her gaze slid away. 'Almost every day we heard of fresh outbreaks of lawlessness, but they were always far away and, being protected by the military, we never thought we would be involved. But one day most of the soldiers marched out to settle a dispute on the border, and the next day we awoke to find all the servants had run away. Something was about to happen. We could feel it.' She paused and looked up at Jordan. 'One can smell it in the very air in India—you must know that.'

Jordan nodded. Watching her, he clenched his hands into fists, having to struggle to stop himself from dragging her into his arms. Her voice tore through him, but he couldn't make it easier for her. He had to let her go on.

She bit her lip, her face strained, her body tense. Wringing her hands in front of her, she turned away and hugged herself again. He saw a shudder pass through her. As she shook her head tears formed in her eyes and spilled over her lashes, running unheeded down her cheeks, and he could only guess at her wretchedness.

'It was towards midday—when the sun was at its hottest—when the Pindaris came, armed with talwars and guns. I had gone to the river that ran outside the station to walk in the cool water—although I remember the river being as calm as a lily pond that day and like a warm bath. I was thirteen years old and had disobeyed my parents by wandering off—which I realised afterwards saved my life.

'When I was about to return to our bungalow all the birds on the river rose in a cloud. That was when

I heard gunfire and people screaming. I was too frightened to run so I hid in a thicket of thorn and elephant grass beside the river and waited, lying down with my hands over my ears to shut out the sounds. I stayed there all night—but I can't remember when the screaming stopped.'

She wiped her face with her hands, her eyes registering horror as she realised that the door in her mind, kept closed and locked at such great cost for so long, was wide open, and she was about to let all the horrors spill forth. Very slowly she took hold of her emotions, controlling herself with will.

'Eventually I felt brave enough to leave my hiding place. When I entered the cantonment, what struck me most was how quiet everything was. I could not believe what the Pindaris had done. Everyone—forty families and the remaining soldiers—had been killed—although I think butchered would be a more appropriate word to describe what I saw. Bodies had been left where they had been struck down, others thrown into the well or burned in their bungalows. I—I found my parents on our verandah. My mother's head had been shattered by a talwar—and—and my father...' She swallowed, shaking her head, the memory too shocking to tell.

Her toneless monologue was a story of pain and a tremendous sorrow so great that if she told it with emphasis she would surely break. Jordan listened, feeling a pity begin to melt his heart as she went on with her tale of horror.

'An orgy of burning and looting had taken place and there was dried blood everywhere. It was quite extraordinary really because at the time I felt nothing. I was numb inside. It was as if I stood outside myself. I remember looking at the shattered flagpole and wondering what the Pindaris had done with the British flag. But what I remember most when I look back is the smell, the flies and the carrion.

'The smell was not the familiar smell of charcoal and burning cow-dung, but of scorched wood and earth and baking flesh. The scene, with its bloated bodies of people and animals, was like a vultures' table, and they were already devouring the spoils. It was horrible. I'll never forget it.'

'And then?' Jordan gently prompted when she fell silent.

'I went back to the river. Not knowing where the Pindaris were, I was too frightened to move on. Besides, the nearest station was nearly twenty miles away and I knew I would never make it on foot—all the donkeys had been slaughtered, you see. We had some bullocks and two elephants at the station, but the Pindaris had taken them. So I waited until the soldiers returned.'

'How long was that?'

'Three days. After that—when my parents had been buried—along with all the other bodies, I was taken to Bombay and sent to England.'

'And the rest I know.'

She nodded. 'Yes. I left India when the monsoon had begun and the whole country was under a deluge

of rain, but I will never forget how beautiful it was—
and how sweet its fragrance. I have since discovered
it is a fragrance unique to India—of spices and garlic,
musk and sandalwood, heat and dust.' Her eyes had
gone a softer colour, remote with memory. 'My parents loved it so much—me too, and despite what happened and the bitter memories, I shall always feel like
a person divided. I am tied to India by affection and
will for ever consider it to be my home. It runs
through my life like the blood in my veins.'

Jordan placed his hands on her upper arms and scru-
tinised every detail on her pale face upturned to his.
'Thank you for telling me, Judith. Unburdening yourself to someone who can fully understand the com-
plexities of your situation was necessary. Perhaps it
will bring you peace and help rid your mind of its
ghosts.'

'I hope you're right. I often wake in the night
dreaming about what happened, but when morning
comes and the dark hours have receded, all the demons are back in their box.'

'When a person has experienced the worst that can
happen to them, they can never be so afraid again. I
believe that, and so must you.'

Judith tilted her head to one side, her look curious.
'Did something awful happen to you, too?'

'Yes. So I do understand what you've been
through.'

She smiled softly, a playful glint in her eye and an
adorable little dimple appearing in her cheek. 'Would
you like to tell me about it, Captain?'

Her puckish humour brought a warm gleam to his eyes and he returned her smile, confounded by the spirit of this young woman. 'It's a long story. I think we'll save that for another day.'

His voice was so soft it made Judith's blood run warm. The pull of his gaze was too strong for her to resist and her whole being melted with its impact. It was as though his clear silver eyes, shining with the brilliance of diamonds, were looking into the very depths of her heart and soul. She felt the touch of his empathy like healing fingers soothing her pain like balm. She had seen in his eyes the reflection of her torment and she knew he understood. She had told her story without knowing how he would react, and in opening up to him he now shared the secret of her past with her. She had included him in something very personal, and that was what counted.

'Thank you for listening. After four years of silence, being able to speak of what happened has given me reassurance—and the best thing of all is the knowledge that I have told it to someone with whom I can talk freely of India, to someone who has been as closely linked to it as I. You were right when you said it might help to talk about it. It has brought me an enormous feeling of relief. But what must you think of me?' she laughed a little nervously. 'I must be so different from most of the women you are acquainted with.'

'You are indeed—which is one of the reasons why I find you so attractive.' Reaching out he gently touched the fine line of her jaw, and he smiled at her with something half-rueful in his expression. 'You know, when I told you that you remind me of the moonflowers that grow in India, I meant it—particularly when I look into your eyes. Their petals are so white and pure, free from moral taint or defilement, and so translucent that the light shines right through. You will have seen them.'

She flushed, flattered and deeply touched that he should liken her to such a beautiful thing. 'Yes. They fascinated me. I used to watch them. The popping noise they made when they opened was always magic to hear. I pressed some in a book, and now they resemble crumpled silk handkerchiefs. But they're still lovely and remind me of home.'

At that moment they were interrupted by a knock on the door. Without being told to do so, Charlotte came in full of concern. She paused and looked at them both with some consternation—the fact that Jordan still had his hand on Judith's cheek not escaping her notice.

'Oh! I'm sorry to interrupt, but I had to come and see if you were all right, Judith. You seemed so distraught when you ran from the room. I know how much Alicia must have upset you.'

'I'm fine now, Charlotte, really,' Judith said, smiling in an attempt to rid Charlotte of her concern. 'Jordan has been very kind and understanding and I feel much better.'

Looking up at her brother, Charlotte saw in his expression admiration and something else when he looked at Judith, something that was more than polite regard and brought a slow smile of understanding to her lips.

'If you'll excuse me, ladies, I will bid you good-night,' he said, crossing to the door. 'Unfortunately I have some pressing meetings in town tomorrow so I have to make an early start.' Before going out he turned and looked back at Judith. 'You'll be all right?'

'Yes—thank you.'

When they were alone Charlotte gave Judith a side-ways smile. 'So, my brother has been both kind and understanding, has he?'

Judith found herself blushing. 'Yes. He was very nice.'

'And what where the two of you talking about when I interrupted?'

'Nothing in particular.'

'And?'

'And nothing, Charlotte,' Judith said with a nervous laugh.

'Come now, even you don't walk around in blink-ers. Half the female population in London has imag-ined themselves in love with Jordan at one time or another.'

'Have they indeed? Then I applaud their judge-ment.'

Charlotte's eyes widened. 'You do?'

'But of course. It would be ungenerous of me to do anything else after his kindness to me just now.'

'So you *have* noticed after all that my dear brother is probably the most handsome, virile man around?'

'I am human and I have noticed. He's also a gentleman and I am a nobody and therefore quite beyond the pale. His friendship is welcome, but anything else would be out of the question.'

'We'll see,' Charlotte said, flouncing to the door where she paused and turned round, mischief written all over her pretty face. 'But I must warn you that if the two of you carry on like this then you are in danger of making Alicia insanely jealous.'

Rolling her eyes in helpless dismay, Judith went and shoved her out of the room.

Chapter Seven

When she was alone she sat on the cushioned window seat, and with her knees drawn up to her chin she gazed up at the full moon and the myriad of stars that hung in the clear sky. The distant horizon to the west was awash with a deep pink flush, heralding another fine day.

She sighed, resting her cheek against the cool glass, thinking about what had just transpired and the man who had sought her out to comfort her. Her rampaging emotions and imaginings where Jordan was concerned were of a personal nature and were beginning to disturb her greatly.

Ever since their first meeting she had tried to ignore them, but they invaded her mind constantly, beckoning like mischievous imps playing a teasing game, flitting to and fro when she was least expecting it. Over the past few days he had established himself firmly in her thoughts, and she was becoming painfully aware of him as a man, of his blatant sensuality, and of the excitement that coursed through her with his every glance and each spoken word.

She didn't regret telling him about what had happened to her in India. It was something she had never shared with anyone else—not even Charlotte knew the details—and it formed a bond between them. But she could not quell the warmth that suffused her body whenever she thought of him and she trembled slightly, feeling the blood pumping strong through her veins when she remembered the unique power of his silver eyes whenever they settled on her, as if reading her innermost thoughts and marking her down as his victim.

With no knowledge of men of the world like Jordan Grant, she was afraid and yet strangely excited by the melting she felt within her when dwelling too long on his image, and she knew she would very soon be out of her depth if she did not take care.

Journeying to town the following morning, as Jordan lounged against the padded upholstery of the carriage, for the first time since returning to England his concentration wandered away from matters of business. Ever since he had left Judith's room the previous night she had filled all his thoughts.

He thought long and hard about what she had told him, and he was caught somewhere between torment and tenderness. He remembered her agonised face when she had told him what the Pindaris had done— they were the kind of images that were familiar to him also, images that had once turned his own life into a living hell. But he was a man and he had chosen the life of a soldier. He had also known that the Asian continent was careless of human life, so he had expected to witness such barbarities, whereas Judith had been a thirteen-year-old girl who should have been spared such trauma.

Ravaged and raw and alienated from the country she had come to look on as her own, she had come to England. How confused, alone and threatened she must have felt; but she was resilient and had survived better than most young girls would have done.

Whenever he was with her he was physically stirred by her closeness. In fact his growing attraction to her was disquieting. When he had sought her out in her room and seen the soft look in her eyes, shining with recent tears, he had thought how vulnerable she looked, with a sweet, wild essence that would always belong to her, reminiscent of the fragile Indian moon-flowers.

He felt a consuming, unquenchable need to know her better, but for the present he had an important meeting with the directors at India House and he immediately immersed his thoughts in that. But then a face with a pert, round chin, a lovely expressive mouth, and thickly fringed hazel eyes crept unbidden into his mind, teasing him, beckoning him. A slow smile curved his lips, and when the carriage was about to turn into Leadenhall Street, with a gleam in his eyes he immediately instructed the driver to head for Bond Street instead.

When a large box elaborately tied with a broad silk ribbon arrived at Landsdowne during the afternoon,

Judith was absolutely amazed when Lady Grant laughingly handed it to her, and she was stunned when, having taken it to her room accompanied by Charlotte, she opened it and discovered among the tissue paper an exquisite white silk, star-spangled dress and matching slippers.

There was also a shawl, which had rapidly become a fashionable and practical accessory to any outfit, and it was not made of serge or cotton or wool—which would have been the case had it been manufactured in England. The shawl that Judith feasted her eyes on was one of the best—a luxurious cashmere, which had been imported from India.

'Oh, Charlotte!' she gasped, gently fingering the material of the dress and guessing at once who had sent it. 'It's exquisite. But—there must be some mistake. It can't possibly be for me.'

'Yes, it is. Here, see for yourself,' Charlotte enthused, handing her a card that had been attached to the box. 'Now you have no excuse for not going to the Penroses' ball.'

Glancing down at the card in her hand Judith's flesh warmed. It simply read—Yes, you shall go to the ball. J. 'It's from Jordan. But—I can't possibly accept such a gift.'

'Why ever not?'

'It's much too grand—and far too expensive. I'll be afraid to wear it for fear of spoiling it.'

'That's a ridiculous objection.'

'Not only that, there is Alicia to consider. She will be hurt when she finds out.'

'Livid, you mean. Alicia will turn green when she finds out—and I hope I'm there to see it. You may be sure you'll outshine even her in this dress,' she said, lifting it out of the box and gasping when the tiny spangles caught the light and gleamed, sending tiny dancing shapes around the walls. 'But it's an unusual dress. I can't remember seeing one quite like it. It's most unlike Jordan to choose anything so—so extraordinary.'

Judith didn't think so and smiled secretly to herself. She knew that as soon as Jordan saw it he would have been reminded of the moonflowers, the beautiful white Indian blooms he had told her she reminded him of. On seeing the dress he would have known instantly that she would like it.

Charlotte, who had looked forward to the ball like a child anticipating Christmas, could hardly be contained on the journey to town two days later. Jordan hadn't returned to Landsdowne so Judith had as yet been unable to thank him for the dress. She accompanied Lady Grant and Charlotte in the carriage. Emily and Edmund had travelled on ahead with Alicia, whose reaction, when Charlotte had lost no time in telling her of Jordan's gift to Judith, had been to smile thinly and say 'How nice.' But her eyes when they had rested on her rival had been quelling.

The house Jordan rented when in town was in Piccadilly. It was huge and very grand and stood back at the end of a short, tree-shaded drive. Jordan was absent when they arrived. When they had eaten,

Charlotte took Judith's hand and dragged her up the stairs to show her the rest of the house.

Between meetings at India House and the daily demands of his other business commitments, Jordan's life was full. When Charlotte learned he was to visit the East India docks at Blackwall immediately after breakfast on the morning following their arrival in town—on a day when the East India fleet was outward-bound, because it was one of the greatest sights to be seen passing down the River Thames, she begged him to allow herself and Judith to accompany him.

Jordan, who had just strode into the breakfast room, his sister and Judith being the only occupants, refused outright. 'No, Charlotte,' he said, helping himself to some coffee on the sideboard. 'It's out of the question. The very idea is preposterous. The dockyard is no place for you—what with the noise, smell and the workmen—whose language is unguarded and not fit for the ears of gently reared young ladies.'

'Oh, please, Jordan,' she begged, her eyes enormous with longing. 'We promise not to be a nuisance. We shall remain in the carriage at all times. No one will even know we're there.'

'Have you forgotten that Edmund is to take you to visit the gardens at Vauxhall today?' he reminded her brusquely.

'No, but we can go another day. Besides, Alicia has a headache and is to remain in bed, so we could save that until another day. I know Judith would like to see the fleet prepare to sail, wouldn't you, Judith?' she said, looking to her friend for support.

Jordan's gaze shifted to Judith, where she sat folding her napkin. Her face was animated and brilliant with hope, her eyes fixed on his with ardent expectancy as she waited with bated breath. Of course she would like to witness the great ships setting sail for the east, he thought. It was only natural. They were a link to her past. But he was reluctant to take either of them to the docks this morning, which would be teeming with all kinds of humanity. He shook his head, a denial working its way to his lips, but as he continued to look at Judith he could feel himself wavering, and in no time at all his resolve slipped away.

'Would you like to go, Judith?'

'Oh, yes please. I'd love to.'

'Then you shall,' he conceded. 'Edmund will accompany us. Run along and get ready, the two of you. But I want your word that you will remain in the carriage at all times.'

'You have it,' Charlotte cried gleefully, disappearing upstairs in a swirl of taffeta and lace with Judith in tow to prepare for the outing.

It was a spectacular sight that met them at Blackwall. The dockyard had been built to Company specification in '06, with a masthouse enabling an Indiaman to be fully rigged in a matter of days rather than weeks. The number of heavily armed Company-owned vessels at anchor in the deep water, the workshops and warehouses—all within half a mile of India

House—storing all kinds of exotic commodities from the East that stirred the imagination, and all employing thousands of people, gave an individual a very respectful idea of the Company's worth.

Hundreds of people had turned out to see the fleet set sail. The bustling wharves were a seething mass of noisy humanity—sailors, workmen and onlookers. Some were rough and unkempt, and ladies held onto their skirts to avoid contact. Company shareholders stood in groups, their faces wearing identical expressions of pride as they conversed with each other. Crew and passengers were swarming all over the scrubbed decks as the heavily laden vessels shifted restlessly with the rising tide, the charcoal grey water lapping at the great hulls, lying low in the water.

The ships carried additional surgeons, sailmakers, smiths, tailors, barbers, caulkers and joiners, making sure they were run efficiently and maintained like a small town. The holds were packed with all manner of goods—food and drink, tar and oil, powder and ammunition for the guns in case of attack from pirates, and a hundred other things—not counting the precious cargo.

Sandwiched between Emily and Charlotte in the carriage on the edge of the crowd, Judith feasted her eyes on the vessels, watching the tall masts and webs of rigging swaying with the motion of the water. Remembering her own journey from India on one of these vessels, she breathed in the familiar, comforting smells of hemp and pitch, which welcomed her like old friends. Those great ships represented home, and the elusive faces of her mother and father passed wraithlike through her memory. The memories of her last days in India were all too fresh, and the breeze blowing off the river suddenly seemed very cold.

Jordan glanced across at her. He could see the dark memories crossing her face as she looked at the scene, and that her hands were clenched tightly in her lap, as if by dint of will she could hang on to the remembrances associated with India.

'Are you all right?' he questioned anxiously.

Slowly she brought her gaze round to his. She looked at him intently as he silently reached out to the part of her she had laid bare to him not so long ago, when he had touched and lightened a dark corner of her mind. She smiled, feeling a faint, unexpected drift of happiness. 'Yes, I'm fine. Truly. My mind was assailed by memories, that is all.'

He nodded, understanding. 'Then if you ladies will excuse Edmund and me, we will leave you for a few minutes.'

When the two brothers had climbed down to mingle with other Company shareholders, Charlotte moved across to make more room, her eyes sparkling with excitement out of a rosy, flushed face.

'I wish we could get out and mingle with the crowd. It would be so exciting to get a closer look. I think the whole of London must have turned out to watch the fleet get under way.'

Judith's eyes followed Jordan and Edmund as they made their way to a group of gentlemen who were gathered on the quayside, influential, too, by the richness of their dress and the attitude of those around them. After a few moments she watched a man approach and speak to Jordan. He lowered his head to listen to the man, who was pointing towards a warehouse some distance away. After excusing himself to Edmund and his acquaintances, Jordan accompanied the man in the direction of the warehouse.

Judith could see nothing unusual in this and was about to look away, but a man, following closely in their wake and who looked like a beggar, caught her eye. He was wearing a heavy coat, too heavy for the hot day. The sleeves were far too long and concealed his hands, and the wide-brimmed hat hid his face. The crowd was thick, the man inconspicuous to Jordan. His gait had a measured, almost sinister steadiness that set alarm bells ringing in Judith's head. Her gaze slid to his hand by his side, and she froze, for she caught a glimpse of steel—evidence of malign intent. A cold hand gripped her heart and she gasped, sensing that Jordan was in grave danger. She must warn him.

'Emily—go and fetch Edmund and tell him to go to the warehouses over there,' she said breathlessly, pointing towards them. 'Jordan is in danger—I'm certain of it. Please hurry.'

Both Charlotte's and Emily's eyes snapped wide open with astonishment, and they watched in some consternation as, in a flash, Judith was out of the carriage and pushing her way through the throng, her heart beating so hard she thought it would burst. Without attempting to call her back, sensing the urgency of the situation, immediately Emily went in search of her husband.

Entering the dim interior of the warehouse, the man accompanying Jordan melted into the shadows. Jordan couldn't have said what it was that alerted him to danger—it might have been the sound of a footfall or a passing shadow, but there was a sense of evil on the air, and he felt a prickle of warning on the hairs at the back of his neck. Hard and motionless as a rock, every muscle in his body became tense, but pulsing with raging energy, ready to explode into action. Quickly and concisely, his mind worked in an icy calm, severed from the emotions that could cloud his judgement. These were the responses that had carried him through a thousand similar situations that had kept him alive so far. He always travelled fully armed, and slipping a small pistol from his pocket, he whipped his head round just in time to see a man closing in on him, his hand half raised to expose a sliver of metal.

The beggar's hand reached towards him. Down the knife came and like a cat Jordan leapt aside. The blade cut harmlessly through the air, finding no soft flesh to flay, only the fabric of his jacket sleeve. Reluctant to fire his weapon, Jordan crossed the intervening distance and there were frenzied movements between the two of them, as they became locked in a devilish embrace. Jordan managed to grab at his assailant's hand and wrest the knife away from him, sending it clattering to the floor.

Clutching a coil of rope, the man who had brought him to the warehouse leapt out from the shadows be-

tween the packing cases, at the same moment that
Judith entered. When he saw her pressed against the
door, momentarily rendered speechless by amazement,
he panicked and dropped the rope. Regaining his
senses quickly, he drew a knife and advanced towards
the still struggling pair.

Judith's eyes opened wide to see the man lunge forward with his arm raised ready to strike. His eyes glittered hard in the dim light, and his teeth showed in a
ragged snarl. Her gaze became riveted on Jordan, who
had his back to this new danger. Anguish and desperation can be a powerful opiate against fear. It wasn't
a conscious decision that propelled Judith forward, but
suddenly she was running towards him wildly. A cry
broke from her lips, a high, deadly shrill.

'Jordan! Watch your back.'

Heeding her cry, Jordan spun round just as this new
threat was upon him, and he was unable to prevent
the man from sinking his knife into his accomplice's
back, before running out of the door and becoming
lost in the crowd.

Feeling the man go limp, Jordan stepped back and
looked at him, his chest heaving breathlessly. His assailant gagged and suddenly clawed at his back, from
which the hilt of a knife protruded. He fell to his knees
before slumping forward onto his face, his body jerk-
ing violently with convulsions before becoming still.

Immediately Jordan glanced round at Judith. She
was frozen, staring at the corpse, her eyes wide with
horror, her arms wrapped round herself. He strode
swiftly towards her.

'You saved my life,' he said quietly. 'Thank you for that.' His tone held a moderate note—of gratitude, pride, and perhaps awe, that made Judith lift her face to him. Jordan drew a deep breath. With her face as white as death, her eyes wide and staring, something in his chest tightened. Placing his hands on her upper arms he drew her close. 'Judith, are you all right?'

She nodded, gulping hard. The relief of knowing that Jordan was safe and unhurt made her legs go weak. 'Yes. I—I thought—I was afraid you would be killed.'

Whatever it was that Jordan saw in her face at that moment made him utter hoarsely, 'Dear Lord!' and pull her against his chest.

Judith gave up all pretence of courage and clung to him, burying her face in his solid warmth. Having just been subjected to several dreadful moments of fear, the realisation that he was actually holding her nearly broke her fragile grip on her control. 'I was so scared,' she whispered. 'I thought—I feared—I was terrified they were going to kill you.'

Remembering the devastating moment when he had heard her cry out, and realising the danger she had put herself in, made Jordan take hold of her arms and gently push her away. Holding her face between his hands he looked intently into the wavering depths of her eyes. 'Don't you ever,' he breathed harshly, 'disobey me again. What you did was both reckless and foolhardy. I made you promise to remain in the carriage and not do anything foolish. Are you crazy? The light in here is so bad I might have mistaken you for an assailant and blown your brains out.'

'I didn't think,' she whispered. Content that he was safe, she felt the terror of the last few minutes and the fears of the future fall away. Pulling herself together she said lamely, 'I—I'm sorry. I—I saw the man following you. When I saw the knife in his hand I knew he was some miscreant intending harm. It was clear to me that you were in danger—but I was too far away to warn you—so I followed you in here. How could I do otherwise?'

'What the hell's going on?' a voice shouted from the doorway. It was Edmund. After sending Emily back to the carriage to sit with Charlotte, he had come to see what all the fuss was about. Glancing at the dead man on the floor, Jordan's dishevelled appearance and Judith's trembling form, he took in the situation at once. 'Good Lord! Are you all right?'

Jordan nodded. 'Our unappealing friend here,' he said, turning the corpse over with the toe of his boot, 'has just tried to kill me—or kidnap me, I'm not sure which,' he growled, his eyes going to the coil of rope on the floor. 'His accomplice lured me in here on the pretext that someone concerned with the Company wished to have a word with me.'

'Do you recognise him?'

Jordan looked down at the upturned features, at the glazed eyes and the matted brown hair revealed by the discarded hat. Satisfied that the man was dead, he shook his head. 'Never seen him before—or his accomplice.'

'How did you manage to stab him in the back?'

'I didn't.'

'The man who lured him here killed him,' Judith said, stepping forward.

'Jordan, why would anyone want to kidnap you— or kill you for that matter?' Edmund inquired.

'I believe it was kidnap they had in mind—but as for the reason, you would have to ask our assailant,' he replied grimly. 'I think they hoped to take me by surprise. When it became clear I had the upper hand, no doubt his accomplice waiting in the shadows considered it best to remove him altogether. Captured alive, there is no knowing what he might have disclosed under interrogation.'

'I think we should get out of here,' Edmund said, looking uneasily into the dark corners of the warehouse, which smelt strongly of spices and tea. 'I'll get someone to take him away.'

When Edmund had gone Jordan turned his head towards Judith. His expression was grave and serious as his relentless gaze locked with hers. 'I apologise, Judith. I should not have spoken to you so harshly just now. You must understand that I did so out of concern.'

There was no mistaking that he spoke in earnest, and Judith felt a sudden warmth in her heart at his kindness. The numbness was melting from her limbs and she moved towards him, conscious of the dead man lying at a grotesque angle a short distance away. 'That's all right. You had every right to be angry with me.' Dropping her eyes she saw the damage that his assailant's knife had done to his jacket. 'Your—your sleeve is torn,' she whispered.

Jordan drew back and barely glanced at the tear. His teeth flashed in a sudden, unexpected smile. 'I've been through worse. It would take more than an assassin's blade to finish me.' Her eyes must have clouded suddenly, for his smile vanished. 'I'm grateful for your concern, Judith. Truly. I can only consider that with what my assailants had planned for me, your arrival might have saved my life.'

'Someone must have a very deep grievance against you.'

'It looks like that.'

'And you meant it when you said you don't recognise either of your assailants?'

'Never seen either of them before in my life. But then, when someone is out to do you harm, they don't have to commit the act themselves.'

'Are you saying the man was a hired assassin?'

'It's possible.'

'Isn't that a bit extreme? What would anyone gain from having you killed—or kidnapped?'

'Revenge—and something else, perhaps.'

Judith was deeply concerned by what had happened. Since her encounter with Jehan Khan at Landsdowne they had not spoken of it. At the time it had seemed important, in so far as it represented a threat from that direction, and now she could feel the threat tightening.

'You told me not so very long ago that I should fear Jehan Khan and Lord Minton. Have you reason to fear them?'

'I don't fear either man—but I have reason to be wary of them.' He put a gentle hand beneath her arm, looking down at her face in the dark shadows that surrounded them. 'Come, Judith—let's get out of here. It's all over now. One of the villains who set this pretty trap for me is dead and I am lucky to escape. I will have Emily take you back home. Edmund and I will stay and clear this mess up with the authorities.'

When they reached the carriage and Jordan instructed Emily to return to the house, Charlotte looked at him with enormous disappointment and murmured something about unfairness under her breath, but when she caught a searing glance in return, she had the good sense to shut up.

Jordan was consumed by a cold, violent rage as he strode off in search of his brother. If Judith's abduction and this attempt on his life were anything to go by, as it turned out, he was completely wrong in one judgement he'd made when he'd returned to England. The effect of his close friendship with the Rajah of Ranjipur was not nearly so insignificant as he'd imagined, though just then he had no way of foreseeing the extent of its profound, violent consequences in his life. It all implied something he hadn't wanted to think about, but found he could no longer avoid.

The powers of Prince Chandu were far-reaching, although here in England the man was virtually untouchable. His ability and his vast wealth, and those he could hire with it, put him above the law and beyond reach—or so he thought. Not unless Jordan himself was willing to settle with Prince Chandu on a personal basis. Jordan reminded himself who he was, and the family he represented, and he didn't want to be accused of conducting his affairs the way Prince Chandu conducted his. But if he wanted to preserve the lives of those closest to him, and his own, he had to be realistic.

Chapter Eight

Judith was deeply troubled by what had occurred earlier. The incident had taken the shine off her preparations for the ball, but Charlotte, not one to let her concern for Jordan dampen what was to be an exciting event, soon put her into the spirit of things.

'When I have finished with you you won't recognise yourself,' she told Judith, almost bursting with enthusiasm as she took Jordan's gift off its hanger.

And every word she said was true. When she stood Judith in front of the long mirror to inspect her handiwork, Judith could not believe what she saw. The gown was of a fine white silk and spangled with tiny stars that caught the light. The skirt was full and flowing, and on Charlotte's advice she had declined the wearing of a hoop. The bodice was modestly cut and silver Brussels lace hung from the elbow length sleeves so that the material draped softly over her forearms. Lady Grant's maid had curled her thick wealth of hair into a mass of ringlets that fell in gentle tiers from the crown of her head to the nape of her neck.

Judith stared at the elegant figure in the gorgeous gown and white satin slippers, more than a little bewildered by her reflection. But then her lips parted in pleasure and a delicious sensation welled up inside her.

'Oh, Charlotte. Is that really me?'

'Every inch.'

'It—it's rather like an ugly duckling turning into a swan.'

'No, it isn't. You were never an ugly duckling, Judith. You just didn't make the best of yourself. You really should take advantage of your attractive looks upon occasion. You look spectacular. You'll eclipse every other woman at the ball—even Alicia in her lemon and gold.'

However, it wasn't Alicia Charlotte was concerned about but her eldest brother, and she dearly longed to see if Judith, in her exquisite gown, would have a noticeable effect on him.

When it was time to leave for the ball Judith tried to compose herself as she left her room, trying to stem her nervousness about what would be her first and last experience of a society ball—and about meeting Jordan and praying that she wouldn't make a fool of herself. She descended the stairs with Charlotte. Apart from the butler hovering in the hall everyone was in the drawing-room, but suddenly Jordan emerged to see where the carriages had got to.

His eyes became riveted on the young woman accompanying his sister. Completely transfixed, he was rendered speechless for the first time in his life.

Judith's appearance could not be faulted. The material of her dress was so thin that it did not disguise the wearer's slenderness and grace. It complimented her lustrous hair—a vibrant, glorious colour. The large hazel eyes, pert nose and perfect, soft pink mouth were gentle against the honeyed skin. She was lovely, more than Jordan had imagined.

They paused when he moved to the bottom of the stairs. He was impeccably groomed. Judith took note of this proud and darkly handsome man, magnificent in a claret-coloured coat and white trousers, ivory silk waistcoat and pristine cravat. Slowly they continued their descent, and when they reached the final step, Jordan reached out and took Judith's hand. She felt his fingers, strong and firm, wrap themselves around her own. There was a twinkle in his silver eyes, and a slow appreciative smile worked its way across his face as his gaze leisurely roamed over her body. The unspoken compliment made her blood run warm.

'Now what do you think of our prim little school teacher, Jordan?' Charlotte asked, laughter bubbling on her lips.

Prim? Jordan thought. There was nothing prim about Judith that he could see at that moment. 'You look entrancing, Judith,' he murmured. 'I'm happy to see you have agreed to go to the ball after all.'

'The dress persuaded me—as you knew it would. Thank you, Jordan. I should have thanked you earlier—but somehow we became distracted by other matters. No one has ever given me anything so beautiful.'

'It was my pleasure.'

Unable to tear her eyes away from Jordan, Judith was blind to Charlotte's satisfied smile, and to her look of smug triumph when Alicia—accompanied by everyone else in the party—emerged from the drawing-room. On seeing Judith looking so stunning, compliments tripped over each other from everyone's lips, which she accepted gracefully, but when she looked at Alicia her happiness dimmed. Alicia's face hardened and her eyes burned with a jealous malevolence as her gaze passed insolently over her dress, before she turned away. At that moment a footman announced that the carriages were waiting and they left.

The streets outside Penrose House in Mayfair were congested with private equipages carrying the distinguished and sophisticated members of society. Dignified footmen arrayed in crimson livery were kept busy opening carriage doors to allow the guests to spill out. Judith existed in a state of breathless unreality and was overcome by an almost childish excitement as she drank everything in. She stepped into the hall, which was so big it reminded her of a cathedral. The whole house was a blaze of light and a sea of shimmering hooped gowns, sparkling jewels, dancing plumes, and alive with a cacophony of vivacious chatter. The scene was like a brilliant, joyous pageant, elaborate and bizarre, magnificent and strangely unreal.

The scent of flowers spilling out of baskets and vases hung like an intoxicant on the warm air. Penrose House was extremely grand. Two marble staircases swept up from either side of the hall, coming together at the first landing to form a gallery, and one huge crystal chandelier hung in the centre.

'Lord and Lady Penrose certainly have a taste for the erotic,' Judith commented in a conspiratorial whisper to Jordan as they slowly inched their way towards their hosts, indicating with her eyes the nude statues in every niche and balancing on every pedestal around the hall and up the stairs.

Jordan's eyes twinkled down at her and a seductive smile formed itself on his lips. 'Are they acceptable in your opinion?' he murmured, for her ears alone.

'Oh, yes. They're beautiful objects. They look so elegant.'

'I agree. Lady Penrose chose them herself. You will note that Aphrodite and Adonis make up the main— their purpose being to stimulate the pleasures of the imagination.'

Feeling her cheeks burning at what he implied, she looked away.

Jordan chuckled softly, absolutely enchanted by her innocence. 'I think you misinterpret my meaning, Judith, and if so I apologise for confusing you.'

She favoured him with an irrepressible sideways smile, her eyes telling him she did not believe him. 'Did I? You are certain of that, are you?'

'Of course. The pleasures I speak of I associate with taste. They are not the same as the gratification of appetite.'

'And what is your definition of taste? Do you believe it is a matter of feeling—or scientific knowledge?'

'The issue is not straightforward and few can say what it really is, but I think taste is a matter of feeling—and sense—and must be distinguished from lust.'

'Now I am truly confused,' she laughed. 'Please explain to me what you mean.'

'When a person views a work of art, I believe they should do so directly and unencumbered, and not be distorted by lower forms of sensuality and desire.'

'Then I can see that must pose a problem for a great many gentlemen.' At that moment they were passing a particularly alluring statue of Aphrodite. 'Beautiful, is she not? Aphrodite, the Greek equivalent of the Roman deity of Venus, representing all the qualities of love and beauty,' Judith quoted from her studies. 'I fail to understand how a man can look at her objectively and not desire her?'

A slow, roguish grin dawned across Jordan's features. 'I agree. In fact, I would say that is virtually impossible,' he replied quietly.

Judith looked at him, her eyes full of mischievous laughter, and she was unable to stifle the smile that tempted her lips at the complete absence of contrition on his handsome face. 'I was right, wasn't I? I did not misinterpret your meaning in the first place.'

His eyes twinkled wickedly. 'You did not,' he confessed unashamedly.

'You are quite impossible,' she said, laughing under his amused gaze.

'I know. Infuriating, isn't it,' he chuckled, placing his hand under her elbow and guiding her in the direction of their hosts.

Jordan found this delightful young woman truly amazing. At one and the same time she managed to be an innocent young girl and a beautiful, alluring woman, full of beguiling contrasts. To discuss a subject with such jaunty impudence—a subject most young ladies of his acquaintance would find either boring or beyond them, he found utterly exhilarating.

When Lord and Lady Penrose and the betrothed couple had received them, they passed on into the ballroom, filled with men and women already dancing to the strains of an orchestra. There was a host of people waiting to meet Jordan. He was accosted at every step. It seemed as if he knew nearly everyone present.

The ball began in grand style. Calmly watching Judith as the evening progressed, Jordan noted how the reflection of hundreds of candles and the Venetian mirrors became accomplices in illuminating her gentle beauty. Despite her inexperience at social gatherings and polite repartee, she seemed to find her feet admirably. She became a laughing, beautiful young woman, in possession of a natural wit and intelligence that soon had a crowd of admiring young swains eagerly vying for her attention and the chance to add their names to her dance card. It was soon full, and she had one after another of them sweeping her off her feet into the dance.

As she dipped and swayed to the music, her slender form floating with a fluidity and grace over the floor in a swirl of white skirts, the tips of her satin slippers visible as her feet darted to and fro, the more Jordan watched her the more irritated he became at all the attention she was receiving. He could not bear to see other men vying for her attention, coveting her, to watch the appreciation in their eyes as they devoured her upturned face, smiling and flushed from dancing. He guessed their thoughts were not so very different from his own, and he despised them for it.

For the first time in his life Jordan experienced an acute feeling of irrepressible jealousy, which twisted his heart and caught him completely off guard. It was a feeling he found decidedly unpleasant.

The lively music and fast steps, the thrill of being swept around the dance floor in the arms of handsome young men, filled Judith with an unaccustomed gaiety. She could not escape if she'd wanted to from the zealous swains who gave her no respite. She felt wonderfully alive, and even Alicia's cold glowers could not penetrate the aura of excitement that surrounded her.

There was a respite in the dancing when everyone descended on a room next to the ballroom, where a most extravagant supper had been set out. Fortunately for Judith, unlike most of the ladies present, her slender body was not encased in a whalebone corset, so she wasn't prevented from savouring most of the mouth-watering dishes.

Later, when one of her partners returned her to Lady Grant, finding the room had become warm and stuffy and feeling the need for some air, she slipped out of some tall French doors onto a small balcony situated a few feet above the level of the ground. Lanterns hanging in the trees lighted the darkness.

Suddenly she was startled when a black-garbed gentleman appeared through the doors and stepped in front of her and bowed. When he spoke his voice was a gravelly baritone.

'So here you are, Miss Wyatt—and all alone, which is most unwise. Why, any disreputable scoundrel could whisk you away without anyone knowing. I'd be failing in my duty if I didn't take you indoors.'

'Oh! And your name, sir?' she asked as she allowed him to lead her back inside, thinking it an odd thing for him to say.

'Lord Jeremy Minton—and this is our dance, I believe.'

The name hit Judith like a cold blast. Lord Minton! This was the man Jordan had told her about, whom he disliked intensely. And now here he was, expecting her to dance with him! There must be some mistake. How could it have happened? How could his name have appeared on her dance card without her knowing?

Gracious rejection was already on her lips. 'Oh— but you must be mistaken. I—I don't recall—'

'Check your card, Miss Wyatt. You will see there is no mistake. It is mine by right.'

Quickly she scanned the names on her card and her heart plummeted when she saw his name was indeed entered for the next waltz.

His smile was one of smug satisfaction. 'There you are, you see. At the time there were so many gentlemen flocking around you that you appeared to be in a state of some confusion. I will forgive your oversight.'

Feeling a small frisson of alarm, Judith glanced around hoping to see Jordan. She recognised his tall figure across the room immediately, but he was in conversation with a group of gentlemen and had his back to her.

The musicians had already started playing when Lord Minton took her hand and led her out on the dance floor. She tried to disengage it, but arching one dark eyebrow he looked at her imperiously, appearing not to notice. As they danced Judith was conscious of the hard bulk of his muscles beneath his coat, and the strength and power of the shoulder that flexed beneath her hand.

She had already noted that despite the hard line of his thin lips, and the cruelty she saw in his weathered face, he was quite good-looking, but it was marred by too heavy a brow and penetrating, pale blue eyes set too close together. He was surprisingly nimble on his feet and his limbs moved with impressive tensile power, despite having a large build, and she had the momentary notion that she was dancing with some well-regulated machine. Suddenly she felt the contact with him quite revolting.

'You look divine, Miss Wyatt,' he murmured, watching her face closely. 'Are you enjoying the ball?'

'Yes—very much.' Judith had collected her thoughts sufficiently to respond with grace, but her reply was stilted, and she was praying the dance would be of short duration. Her brows drew together in a puzzled frown when a thought occurred to her. 'Tell me, Lord Minton, how did you know where to look for me?'

He smiled, but the smile did not reach his cold eyes. The scented nearness of her body, coupled with his delight at his success in getting her alone so that he could speak to her, combined to lift him to a pitch of heady excitement, and an old ache revived itself in his loins. He looked down at her, at her straight shoulders rising above her firm breasts, observing how the dress highlighted her collarbones perfectly—so fine, so breakable.

But where she was concerned his lust must be held in check for the time being. The target of his interest was Jordan Grant, and it was necessary for his own survival to get even for past differences and obtain something that did not rightfully belong to him. He would give ten years of his life to see Grant lying dead, and he was convinced that with a little persuasion—tender or otherwise, it mattered little to him, Judith Wyatt could be coerced into aiding him to achieve that goal.

'I was watching you,' he said at length. 'I saw you slip through the French doors onto the balcony. I didn't expect to find a lady disappear outside alone. I made up my mind that you either had an assignation or you must have a taste for the air.'

'And as you have discovered, sir, it was the latter—especially when a room is stuffy and warm.'

His eyes locked on hers and he said meaningfully, 'After living in India for most of your life, you will have become accustomed to the heat.'

Judith stared at him, her eyes widening in amazement. 'You are extremely well informed, sir? To the best of my knowledge I've never seen you before in my life.' Suddenly, something about his deep voice stirred the ashes of an unpleasant memory and her brow creased in a puzzled, questioning frown. 'That is so, isn't it? We have never met before?'

A small smirk appeared on his lips. 'If we had, I should be mortally offended that you could forget it. However, I do know a great deal about you, Miss Wyatt.'

Judith listened in stunned disbelief as he went on to recite her life's history, wondering how he could possibly know so much about her, but before she could question him, suddenly something caught her eye. Someone had appeared in the ballroom and was causing quite a stir among the throng. It was the turbaned figure of a man exotically dressed in a long tunic of saffron-coloured silk sashed with turquoise. Accompanied by two white robed servants, he came forward into the pool of light that embraced the dancers and stopped, his face expressionless when his eyes settled on Lord Minton and his partner.

It was Jehan Khan.

Quick as a flash Judith remembered that unnerving moment when she had met him on her way back from church, and that when she had spoken to him in Hindustani she had seen his eyes register surprise. She also recalled Jordan telling her that the Indian was residing with Lord Minton. Had Jehan Khan told Lord Minton of their encounter, and had the latter, on learning that she was familiar with the language, made enquiries about her? She stared up at him, two bright sparks of anger showing in her eyes.

'I am concerned why a gentleman I do not know should show so much interest in me. It is none of your business.'

'I was exceedingly curious to learn more about a young woman who speaks Hindustani like a native. How could that be? I asked myself, unless she has spent some considerable time in India.'

'What do you want from me, Lord Minton?'

His hooded eyes levelled on hers. 'I want you to remember at all times that you have reason to fear me, Miss Wyatt. I find you are in a position to help me acquire something I want. We have things to discuss, you and I.'

When the waltz was halfway through and Jordan standing beside Alicia, had calmly observed the arrival of Jehan Khan, his eyes did a broad sweep of the dancers in a search for Judith. He saw her image in a maze of bodies. Never had he seen her look so provocatively lovely, and he had a sudden urge to beat a path to her feet and send all her persistent suitors packing. His eyes shifted to her partner and the shock of recognition blanched his features. His emotions shattered from all rational control and fury seared through him like a knife.

Unbidden, a small mountain retreat in the foothills of the Himalayas seeped into his mind. Against a backdrop of these majestic mountains he remembered the smell of pine trees, and that the glens were full of snowdrops and lilies. But he also remembered the dust and the heat of one particular day, the flames—reaching, dancing, leaping and devouring—and more, much, much more. It was a sight that would haunt him for the rest of his life.

Hearing Jordan utter a low, savage curse, Alicia looked at him. His eyes were glacial, his jaw taut, and his mouth drawn into a ruthless, forbidding line. Curious as to what could have brought about this change in him, she followed his line of vision, her eyes lighting on the man dancing with Judith. 'Why, Jordan, you seem determined to harass that poor gentleman. Who is he?'

'Lord Jeremy Minton, and I have a thousand reasons for disliking him.'

The dark frown that accompanied his statement surprised Alicia. This black side of Jordan's mood was new to her. She realised that the gentleman who held all his attention had unleashed in him all the concealed forces of his passionate nature, all the more terrible because he was a man who was normally in control and able to master them.

'Excuse me,' he ground out. 'There are one or two things I have to say to that blackguard.'

Having expected him to claim the next dance, Alicia's mouth opened to vent her displeasure, but he was already moving across the room towards the couple on the edge of the dance-floor with the stealth of a panther. She glared at his retreating back but then shifted her gaze to his quarry, interest beginning to stir in their depths.

Without warning, a hand reached out and snatched Judith out of Lord Minton's arms, startling the couples closest to them.

Jordan's features were tight as his narrowed eyes swept over his implacable enemy like whiplash. He looked at him from his superior height with such a cold and barely contained rage that for a moment Judith thought he was going to murder Lord Minton right there and then. The look that passed between them crackled with hidden fire.

'If you have a shred of sense, or if you have learned anything from the past, Minton, you would know better than to approach anyone remotely connected to me or my family,' he said in an explosive underbreath.

'I beg your pardon?' the other said, without emotion.

Jordan's fists clenched in a visible effort not to drive them into Lord Minton's face. 'You heard me the first time,' he ground out between his teeth, in that same deadly voice. 'Let me give you a piece of advice, Minton. Get out of here before I give way to my inclinations.'

'Which are?'

'To throw you out myself. It would not be good for your dignity, your friend watching you over there,' he said, gesturing towards Jehan Khan with a brief nod without removing his eyes from the target of his hatred, 'or your health. So get out.'

Lord Minton's muscles tightened visibly, and a hot flush had risen from his white stock. His eyes were glittering with unspeakable rage, and for a moment something savage and raw stirred in their depths. It was clear that he was tempted to throw himself at Jordan, before the fury was replaced with icy contempt and he had the sense to step back. He bowed stiffly to the young woman. 'It has been a privilege to meet you, Miss Wyatt. I trust you will enjoy what is left of the ball.' To Jordan he said, 'We will meet again, you and I, Captain. Soon.'

Jordan took a step forward. He was standing quite still, showing no more expression than a stone. Whatever lived behind those silver eyes was hidden. 'Beyond the requirements of formality you will never speak to me, to Miss Wyatt, or to any member of my family again, Minton—not until you are on your knees begging for your life at the barrel end of my pistol or the point of my sword. Then I will give you leave to address me as you please—for they will be the last words you utter.'

Too anaesthetised by shock, Judith listened. She was trembling in every limb. Lord Minton turned and made straight for Jehan Khan, and after speaking quietly to each other, together the two of them quit the room. Fortunately the unprecedented altercation had passed unnoticed by anyone. Only Alicia, who had moved closer to hear what transpired, was aware that anything was wrong, and she turned and looked at the retreating figure of Lord Minton and his companion with a curious interest, not at all fooled by their apparently harmonious departure from the room.

Chapter Nine

In a moment Jordan turned to Judith. Still trembling from her encounter with Lord Minton, she saw that to her utter disbelief he was still livid, and that this time his anger was directed at her. Never had she seen such savage, scorching fury as that emanating from Jordan at that moment.

He bent his head and said in an ominously calm tone that belied the leaping fury in his eyes, 'Come with me.'

His hand moved as rapidly as a striking snake and clamped on her forearm. He steered her towards the French doors which she had disappeared through earlier, but before he stepped outside he took two glasses of champagne from the tray of a passing footman and handed one to her. It was a gesture designed to add to the charade of two people wishing to partake of some intimate conversation in private. When they were alone Jordan drank the sparkling wine in one draught and placed his glass on the stone balustrade. Judith put hers down untouched.

His look cut through her. The anger and rage were gone from him. What there was instead was ice.

'You little fool. After I'd spelled out the vicious nature of Minton's character, I thought you'd have more sense than to add his name to your dance card. Damn it, Judith!' he snapped, raking his fingers through his hair and beginning to pace the narrow balcony with angry, frustrated strides. 'Are you so simple that you didn't know what you were doing?'

Stung by the unfairness of his attack, Judith's fists clenched by her sides and her cheeks flamed as she glared at him. 'How dare you say that to me? The least you could do is consider my position in all this.'

'That is precisely what I am doing.'

'I honestly don't know how it happened and I deeply regret the unfortunate incident. I didn't want to dance with Lord Minton and I know I should have made my excuses the minute he approached me, but I had no idea who he was until it was too late. Besides, he's not an easy man to say no to.'

'I do know that.'

'Then you should try and understand how difficult it was for me instead of berating me so unjustly. Through no fault of my own I have been dragged into something I know nothing about and cannot even begin to comprehend. I don't mind admitting,' she whispered, with a shiver of revulsion when she recalled the cruelty Lord Minton's snake-like eyes had revealed, and how she had recoiled against his arm which had been like an iron thong about her waist, 'that I'm scared.'

Jordan stared down at the tempestuous young woman in the gorgeous white dress, her face both delicate and alive with her emotions. The fury within him died, and as he looked down into her glorious eyes, his stomach clenched.

'I'm sorry, Judith. Above all things I want to shield you from hurt, not be the source of your anguish. It was not my intention for you to become involved in any of this.' He perched his hip on the balustrade and folded his arms across his chest, his look one of extreme gravity. 'As yet I do not fully comprehend it myself. Since returning to England I've had no contact with either Minton or Jehan Khan—in fact I've only seen Minton once and that was from a distance. I have my suspicions about what is behind all this—that it concerns something that occurred in India some time ago.'

'Then please tell me so that I can at least understand some of it.'

'I told you that I spent much of my time on the North West Frontier, but before that—back in '15 and for more than a year afterwards, I was engaged in the Gurkha War in Nepal. You will have heard of it.'

She nodded. 'Yes, and the treaty which followed, bringing the Company large tracts of land in the foothills. It was shortly afterwards when our own troubles with the Pindaris began.'

'It was at this time that I first met the Rajah of Ranjipur. The Rajah and I became friends and I did him a service for which he was deeply grateful at the time. He was a man for whom I held the utmost admiration and respect, a man who was fair and just in all his dealings with his fellow Hindus and the British. Jehan Khan—who was one of his retainers—was weaned away from his service by the Rajah's cousin, Prince Chandu, and elevated to the high position of adviser to the Prince himself. Chandu is the Devil's own. He is cruel, utterly ruthless and selfish, and he turns others into murderers to suit his own ends. I have already told you that the Rajah died without a direct male heir from his body shortly before I left India, and that the Company annexed his estate, which is the usual practice in such cases.

'Prince Chandu, who found British rule intolerable and was constant in his wish to rid India of these foreigners, accusing them of plundering, injuring and disgracing the people, considered it his right to inherit his cousin's estate and was vicious against the Company. But all the time Chandu had only one motive and that was to serve himself. He rules his land as despotically as his forebears have done, and his people live in fear of him. If he wants something he believes it is his right to take it.'

'But where do you fit into all this? You are no longer connected to the army so why are you being pursued?'

Jordan stood up, his face tense and wrapped in secrecy. His tall figure dominated Judith, and his eyes fixed compellingly on her lovely features. 'I cannot divulge that until certain facts have been made clear.'

'I thought you would say something like that. Why won't you tell me?' she persisted.

His face became grim. 'Because you are safer not knowing,' he said, which was true. If she was abducted again and she knew too much, she would soon tell her assailants what they wanted to know. She would be unable to resist their methods for long.

'What I will tell you is that I became involved in a long-standing quarrel between the Rajah and Chandu. It was of a highly sensitive nature, involving the Rajah's beloved daughter. It was a long time ago and I thought the matter ended—but maybe it isn't—at least, not where Prince Chandu is concerned.' Suddenly Jordan's forehead creased with concern. 'Tell me, Judith, did Minton threaten you in any way?'

'Yes, I believe he did,' she answered, trying to piece together the fragments of the puzzle of all Jordan had told her—and what he'd left out. Resting her hands on the balustrade, she gazed out from their small circle of light to the garden beyond, hearing the silvery notes of a fountain somewhere amongst the trees. The warm, honeysuckle and rose perfumed air lapped around them, whispering that it was a night made for lovers, but dark storm clouds were already gathering in the distant heavens.

'Lord Minton told me that I have reason to be afraid of him, and that we had things to discuss, but I was not fated to learn how far his words would have carried him because that was when you interrupted—and thank God you did.'

'What else did he say to you?'

'He—he knows all about me—everything. He knows how old I am, that my father worked as a clerk for the East India Company, and that I was born and raised in India and came to England when my parents were killed. He knows that when I am not at the academy I live with my aunt in Brighton. He also knows that at present she is abroad and that I am residing at Landsdowne as your mother's guest. How did he find out?'

'It wouldn't be too difficult. What puzzles me is why he should want to.'

'He also told me that he became curious to learn more about me when I spoke to Jehan Khan in his native tongue when I encountered him that day.' She smiled softly. 'I don't suppose it's every day you meet people in London who can converse fluently in Hindustani.'

Jordan looked at her in amazement, his admiration increasing the more he got to know her. 'You speak Hindustani?'

She nodded. 'And Urdu and a smattering of other languages, of which there are many in India—as you know yourself. There's nothing unusual in that, so you needn't look so surprised. When I was growing up I spent most of my time with the natives.' She paused and looked up at him, saying on a more serious note, 'I—I think it was Lord Minton who abducted me.'

'Why do you think that? Has he said anything that might imply that he did?'

'No. It was his voice. I'm sure it was the same. At one point in our conversation there was a sudden change in his tone that caused shards of fear to prick my spine. It brought back the nightmare of my abduction, and I didn't know who or what the person who had spoken to me had been. Lord Minton, though,' she said, her expression becoming thoughtful, 'his voice... But that was impossible, I declared to myself, and too fanciful by far. Absurd, even—but could it be the same?' She looked at Jordan. 'I don't think the similarities are coincidence.'

Jordan nodded, his expression grave. 'I believe you are right. I've thought that all along, but until I have proof we'll just have to be patient—and on our guard in case he tries something like that again.' Suddenly the musicians began playing another waltz and he smiled down at her. Taking her hands he drew her towards him. He was standing very close and she had to look up to him. His gaze dipped lingeringly to her soft lips.

The focal point of his gaze did not escape Judith and she felt herself melting.

'I think this is our dance,' he murmured.

Automatically Judith pulled her hands away and consulted her card. 'No. I have already promised it to a gentleman by the name of Sir Babbington Smythe.'

Jordan's grin was tigerish. 'Blast Babbington Smythe! I'm claiming it for myself.'

'But—I can't let him down. It wouldn't be proper.'

'Yes, it would,' he said, and taking her hand he propelled her through the French doors, where he drew her into his embrace and swept her into the waltz.

Like the man himself, Jordan's movements were re-laxed and bold as he gently swirled her in graceful circles, with none of the mincing steps her other partners had demonstrated. Meeting his engulfing silver gaze with warmth, Judith relaxed against his arm, feeling that he was holding her closer than was seemly. But she told herself she didn't care as a glow of warmth and happiness surged through her. The gentle, spicy cologne he wore, mixed with his own manly smell, touched her senses and filled her head.

Catching the admiring looks of other women both on and off the dance floor, she smiled to herself. Jordan was by far the most handsome man present, and no doubt many of them yearned to be in her position, to bask in the aura of his powerful masculinity, and have his bold eyes capturing and imprisoning theirs—which was exactly what they were doing to hers at that moment.

A glow warmed her, and she realised she was falling victim to the curious power of attraction he possessed over all other human beings she knew, an attraction which was already beginning to blaze into something more profound. It was mad, impetuous, abandoned and sensual—impossible to deny or halt.

Where Jordan was concerned her mind was a battleground of conflicting emotions. She couldn't ignore the treacherous leap her heart always gave at the sight of one of his enthralling, intimate smiles, and the softness in his eyes when he looked at her, the smiling tenderness she heard in his voice, were both utterly shattering to her self-control. There was nowhere she could hide from the truth, for the truth was that she wanted him, and she could well imagine the pleasure that he could give a woman. With a mixture of quiet acceptance and nervous anticipation, she realised that what she felt for Jordan was actually out of her hands.

Judith could have no comprehension of what was going through Jordan's mind as he looked down at her glowing face, of where his imaginings were leading him. He was thinking what a glorious sight her shimmering mass of dark hair would be, brushed out of its ringlets, draped over his pillow and spilling over his bare flesh, and how pleasurable her supple young body would feel writhing in ecstasy beneath his own. The meanderings of his mind amazed him, but the path along which they travelled was not displeasing.

Judith Wyatt had somehow found her way into his blood. He was drawn to the sincerity in her eyes, her smile warmed his heart, and feeling her slender form pressed against his in the most innocently provocative way sent desire raging through his veins. Her charms were subtle, her personality unlike other women he knew. There was a sensuality about her, a natural sophistication and inspiring liveliness that drew him to her. He wanted to hold her against him away from prying eyes, to mould her body to his, and he wanted all the Babbington Smythes here tonight to know that she belonged to him.

'Oh dear!' Judith said, when her eyes lighted on a thin, uninteresting-looking gentleman with red lips and a po-face, who was glaring at them from the edge of the dance floor. 'I've just caught a glimpse of Sir Babbington Smythe, and he looks fit to commit murder.'

'Then I shall permit him to call me out,' Jordan teased, grinning, 'after the dance and not before.'

'You would fight over me?' she asked, laughing delightedly, finding the idea of two grown men fighting a duel over her extremely flattering.

'But of course. I would take on a whole regiment of men if necessary. You, my beautiful little moonflower, are captivating.'

His term of endearment warmed her heart. 'That's why you bought me this particular dress, isn't it? Because it reminded you of our conversation about the moonflowers. I am right, aren't I?' she asked, enjoying the feel of his hand on the small of her waist. It seemed to pulsate with life, sending shock waves through her entire body.

He nodded, his eyes locked on hers.

'And you would really fight over me?'

'You are a very rare specimen indeed, and worth fighting for,' Jordan murmured, his eyes openly and unabashedly displaying his approval as his gaze ranged over her face upturned to his.

'And you, Captain Grant,' she replied, giving him a coy smile, 'say the nicest things.'

'Only to those I like,' he told her, his eyes glinting with amusement. 'But where Sir Babbington Smythe is concerned he has every right to be angry. You have humiliated him by overlooking his name on your dance card, and I have compounded it by taking his place. So, you see, it would be most impolite of me to end his life when he has done nothing wrong and must be wretchedly bemoaning his loss. My sympathy is with the poor man entirely.'

'Then it is obvious to me, that he is better off humiliated and alive, than dead and proud,' she said, laughing softly, enjoying herself enormously and falling in with his mood.

'My sentiments exactly,' Jordan said, spinning her round until she was almost breathless. 'Are you enjoying yourself, Judith?'

'Absolutely—and I know I have you to thank for that. Unfortunately, I don't think Alicia is enjoying herself very much,' she remarked, having caught Alicia's eye where she was standing next to Charlotte. Alicia was glaring at her with an expression that could have crushed rock, and for one brief moment Judith sensed her overpowering jealousy and rage. She had the impression that Alicia would not let Jordan out of her sight for a moment, in which case she must have seen them disappear onto the balcony. She suddenly felt her spirits sag, deriving no pleasure at flaunting the close relationship that was developing between Jordan and herself before the other woman's gaze. 'She's standing with Charlotte and looks extremely put out about something.'

'You really shouldn't worry about Alicia. Perhaps her dancing partner has let her down,' Jordan said lightly, knowing this was the case, because he was to have partnered her in this waltz. 'Do you think we should introduce her Sir Babbington Smythe?' he suggested teasingly. 'Maybe they can inject some humour into each other.'

'Jordan—that is a cruel thing to say,' Judith rebuked, but she was unable to stop herself from smiling back at him. She found something irresistibly comic about Sir Babbington Smythe and Alicia dancing together. But then on a more serious note she said, 'I'm afraid Alicia doesn't like me. You must have noticed.'

'Alicia can be extremely trying and vexing at times.' He paused, frowning thoughtfully, and then he said, 'I shouldn't have said that. She has many attributes to her credit. Alicia is beautiful and vivacious. She is also fun to be with and popular with everyone—and I am not unaware that she has aspirations where I am concerned. I am not insensitive to her overtures,' he said, having recognised the bold gleam in Alicia's eyes on more than one occasion issuing an invitation. He also knew she was no innocent, and that she'd had at least one affair in the past. There was a sultry promise which emanated from her like a sexual aura, but it failed to fire his own need.

'Then—why do you not respond?' Judith asked impulsively, realising too late that it was the height of bad manners to ask a gentleman such a personal, intimate question, but it had tripped off her tongue before she could stop it.

He grinned. 'Because I have a well-developed instinct for self-preservation.' After a brief pause he continued, his arms tightening and his lips nearly brushing her hair. 'When I marry,' he said, his smile fading, his voice softening and his eyes shining down at her with a caressing, purposeful light, 'I want my wife to have more than women like Alicia can give me. I want her to be the most special woman of all.'

The slow curve of his firm lips and the sparkle in his translucent eyes that followed his statement, combined to a disarming degree to sap the strength from Judith's limbs. She didn't know what it was, but there was an inflection in his voice and a warmth that seemed to suggest that he was talking about her, as if he had already made up his mind that she was the one he wanted. She lowered her eyes and stared at his shirt front, much too conscious of the magnetism of the man and the uneven beat of her heart. She flushed with confusion—and regret, for her common sense raged, and she knew she could not allow that to happen.

But she refused to have her happiness ruined—not when there was another hour or more of the ball left to enjoy.

Jordan's feelings for this unassuming woman were indeed serious. Although Alicia was undoubtedly beautiful, her features were not as fine and delicate as those of the young woman in his arms. Nor was her skin as fair. But then, it would be difficult in his eyes for any woman to surpass those features of the maid he had decided to make his own. His eyes feasted on the creaminess of her neck and shoulders, and the gentle swell of her breasts. A strong yearning to hold her tighter, a yearning that cauterised his mind with his physical need, seized him.

Now he was home his plan was to take a wife, which was something he had put on hold in order to pursue his military career. He had stayed a bachelor long enough—but to look outside his own circle, to marry a girl of the lower class... An amused smile touched the corners of his mouth at the thoughts that were filling his mind, and of the shock that would explode upon society if he did marry a girl of Judith Wyatt's pedigree. He smiled inwardly. It would be worth marrying her for the reaction—not that he cared a damn what anybody thought.

Taking a respite from the dancing, standing beside Charlotte, who was chattering away in fierce animation, Alicia let what she said pass over her with no interest. Her eyes were fastened on Jordan whirling Judith in the waltz—their second waltz, and the last, for to dance more than two dances with any one lady would be quite improper and commented upon, and not even Jordan would flout convention so brazenly. But then, she thought angrily, the mood he was in tonight, he just might.

'They dance beautifully together, don't they, Alicia?' Charlotte said, following Alicia's scowling look and purposely rubbing salt in the wound with her casual comment.

Alicia ignored her remark, continuing to glare at Jordan. His look was one of complete absorption as he gazed down at the woman in his arms, which made Alicia both furious and frightened. He had never looked at her that way, and she was unprepared for this insult, this humiliation. Suddenly she wanted to hit out at them both for his rejection of her—casting her aside for a nobody. No one treated her like that.

Nobody! Not even Jordan Grant, no matter how rich and powerful he was.

Rage almost consumed her. Her beautiful face was convulsed with it, and she was filled with a loathing that brought out everything cruel and fierce in her. Her whole being was filled with a fierce hatred for the woman Jordan was smiling at with so much lovesick passion it made her feel sick. So much the worse for you, Judith Wyatt, she thought as her jealous heart hungered for revenge. I'll get even with you some day, she vowed. I swear it.

Turning sharply, she left the ballroom to go in search of her sister, who had gone to sit in an ante-room with Lady Grant. She was finding the excitement, the oppressive heat from the candles and the large contingent of people, all too much. Alicia came to an abrupt halt when she saw Lord Minton in conversation with Lord Penrose. Suddenly a malicious smile curved her lips and she looked at him with keen interest. He was handsome enough, she thought, but there was a coarseness about him.

Deciding that it might be to her advantage to make it her business to get to know this gentleman who had roused Jordan to such fury, slowly she began moving towards him, watching him closely when he paused in his conversation with their host when he became aware of her approach. His eyes narrowed, and something that went beyond interest ignited in their depths. His lips curved in appreciation of her beauty, but Alicia was not deceived, for when she drew close and looked into those cruel, pale blue eyes, she recognised that which was in herself. She knew in that instant that they could never be friends, and she realised that Lord Minton would make a dangerous enemy.

Two hours later, after Jordan had released Judith from his arms and allowed her to dance with someone other than himself, the party assembled on the steps of Penrose House to return home just as the first flash of lightning streaked across the sky, and thunder rumbled over London.

Having just returned from the room which had been set aside for the ladies to retire to, Judith had been both surprised and puzzled to see Alicia conversing with Lord Minton with the ease and confidence of long acquaintance. And yet she could swear that neither had known of the other's existence until tonight. It was plain that Lord Minton had not been intimidated by Jordan's threat on the dance floor, although he had been prudent enough to keep his distance and not provoke another unpleasant incident.

From Judith's point of view she could not think of a more disagreeable man than Lord Minton for Alicia to attach herself to, but it was no business of hers who Alicia chose to associate with. Neither Alicia nor Lord Minton had seen her pass by on her way to join the others to await their carriage, but the cold calculation she had seen in Lord Minton's eyes when they had looked into those equally calculating eyes of his companion had made her shiver, and she was interested to know what they had discussed with such intensity.

Bringing her thoughts back to the present, she was disappointed when Jordan excused himself and climbed into his own carriage, which he had arranged to have brought to Penrose House when the ball ended. He explained that he had an engagement to keep and would return home later.

Secretly he intended visiting a certain establishment close to the river, where he knew some of Jehan Khan's servants could be found when they were not dancing attendance upon their master. It was his intention to glean as much information as he could from them regarding the purpose of Khan's visit to London, and also to confirm his suspicions that Minton and Khan had been behind the attack on his own person at the warehouse at Blackwall that day. But as his carriage left Mayfair, he was unaware of the closed, black equipage following in his wake.

Chapter Ten

Jordan alighted from his carriage a short distance from the tavern. The thunder was passing over but the wind had risen, and he raised the collar of his redingote to shield his neck from the slanting rain. Knowing a multitude of dangers lurked in the dark alleyways, he told the driver not to wait, that he would find his own way back.

Approaching the tavern, he stepped aside to let a trio of inebriated sailors pass by, their arms slung around the shoulders of a couple of whores. Momentarily distracted, he failed to see the coach that halted in the shadows a short distance away, or the two men in white robes who climbed out and darted across the street, crouching low among coils of rope close to the tavern to avoid being seen.

Jordan entered the tavern and pushed aside a beaded curtain. He was a stranger to the place, but he knew of its popularity. The Crescent Moon was no ordinary tavern, nor was its presiding tavern-keeper any ordinary tavern-keeper. His name was Ali Shah. His short body was cushioned in fat, his voice as sweet as a maiden's, and his eyes and hair as black as a raven's wing. He had left Bombay and sailed to London on one of the Company's vessels twenty years ago, never to return.

The air inside the main room was thick with the smell of spiced food, burning sandalwood, tobacco smoke and human sweat—and the all-pervading smell of opium. The ceiling was low and heavily beamed, the walls hung with a strange mixture of English artefacts and traditional Indian mosaics and murals. Pipe-smoking, somnolent figures lounged at scratched tables, while others sat cross-legged on heaps of velvet, golden-tasselled cushions—in fact Jordan could have been in a Joyhouse anywhere in India.

Ali Shah's rich Indian background and his long association with the British made his tavern and his manner of entertainment rather different from the usual. Night after night business was brisk. Every kind of traveller flocked to his tavern—mainly sailors and employees of the East India Company who, during their travels in the East, had developed a fondness for the Joyhouses and the dancing-girls.

From as far afield as Goa, Kashmir and Calcutta, these dusky-skinned girls—whom Ali proclaimed were the choicest jewels of India—with large dark eyes heavily rimmed with kohl, their hair sleek and oiled, their bodies clad in glittering, diaphanous fabrics from the East, swayed among the customers, performing their slow, rhythmic, ritualistic dances to the sound of the sitar. They were also expected to pleasure Ali's customers in the age-old way, and when their bodies lost their beauty and they were no longer desirable, they would disappear like others before them into London's seething metropolis.

The travellers who found their way to the Crescent Moon had also developed an unbelievable passion—for many an addiction—for opium, the strong narcotic dulling their senses into languor and forgetfulness.

When Jordan was seated at a table with a clear view of the beaded curtain, with a nod from Ali one of the dancing-girls attached herself to him. She leaned close, and even before he looked at her, the cloud of her perfume—which smelled heavily of seduction and musk, enveloped him. Her black hair was parted down the middle and hung in a heavy plait to her waist. He met her kohl-rimmed, velvety eyes and smiled. Her soft, fully-fleshed mouth, darkened with red salve, parted in response, exposing small, perfect white teeth. She was young and decidedly lovely.

Eager to oblige the handsome customer, she poured him some wine when he declined a pipe. He gave the impression that he was there to relax and watch the dancing, but inside he was tense and alert as he watched for Khan's servants to appear. He saw Ali disappear through the beaded curtain and return a few minutes later, but thought nothing of it.

Looking around he saw no familiar faces. His eyes were drawn back to the beaded curtain when it parted to admit three more customers. Ali beamed a welcome and told them how delighted he was to offer them the hospitality of his establishment. After glancing around the tavern one of the newcomers grinned broadly when his eyes lighted on Jordan. Immediately he detached himself from his companions and weaved his way through the somnolent bodies and the haze to Jordan's table.

'Jordan! Good Lord! Good to see you, but I never expected to see you here of all places.'

Jordan rose and put out a hand, his lips smiling a welcome, genuinely glad to see him. The man's name was Thomas Parry, and he was one of the Company's representatives in the Spice Islands. He was home on leave for the first time in eight years. The two had become acquainted in Calcutta and had travelled from India on the same vessel, getting to know one another well.

'After all I've heard about this place I thought I'd take a look close at hand,' Jordan replied sociably. 'Didn't expect you to be here either, Tom.'

Tom shook his hand and slipped easily into a chair across from him, already well-oiled. Tom liked Jordan Grant. He was a fine figure of a military man who didn't parade himself like some of the British in India. He got on well and was highly respected by the native troops. It was said that during the Anglo-Nepalese war back in '14–'16, when more territory had been won in Nepal for the Company, Captain Grant and his regiment of bearded Sikhs had put the fear of God into the Gurkhas—who were known to be a formidable fighting people—and later into the rebels on the North West Frontier.

'Are you here alone?' Tom asked, summoning Ali to bring him a drink.

Jordan nodded, retaining the lounging indolence of his long body as he picked up his glass and took a sip of the dark red wine.

'Then you must stick with my companions and me. The streets hereabouts are riddled with corruption and vice—some of the roughest damned streets in London. A man's life isn't worth that after dark,' he said snapping his fingers into the air. 'Many a cut-throat will do you in for a nickel-plated brandy flask or a silk handkerchief.'

'And what of you, Tom? Are you here for a pipe— or the female company?'

'Nothing wrong with both, is there?' Tom chuckled, his rugged, good-humoured face splitting into a grin as he eyed appreciatively the girl who had served Jordan and was hovering within his reach. Leaning over, Tom stretched out his arm and traced his finger along her naked abdomen. She responded with a sultry smile and teasingly danced out of his reach, inviting him to follow.

'You don't change, Tom.'

'They do say something like that,' he replied, lounging back in his chair and continuing to watch the dancing-girl from beneath lowered lids. 'They also say the flesh is weak—and I'm not ashamed to confess mine is weaker than most.'

'A fact I have observed for myself.'

'Ah, Jordan. I've seen enough pallid redheads and fair-haired maidens with their giggles, their simpering and dissembling to last me a lifetime. My mother's been parading them before me for the last few weeks—in the hope that I'll marry one of them and settle down in England. May God preserve me from such a fate.'

'From that, Tom, I take it you are no admirer of European beauty.'

'Damned right I'm not. The indolence of the English women—and their preoccupation with matters of fashion, etiquette and rank—is enough to drive a man into an early grave. Give me the dusky, exotic wenches of the East any day. It's true what they say— the East gets into your blood,' he said on a sigh of nostalgia. 'Even at home a man has to go looking for it. What the hell does a man do in London for six months?'

'Are you telling me that's a problem for you, Tom? I thought you were looking forward to your vacation.'

'I was, but it's beginning to lose its charm damned fast.'

'Then I suppose when one is obliged by society to live by society's rules, the promise of unconventional amusement offered by our host in this exotic establishment tends to give rise to the most irregular stimulation. Is that not so, Tom?'

'Absolutely. And you must agree with me, Jordan, otherwise you wouldn't be here.'

Jordan's expression remained bland, giving no indication that his reason for visiting the Crescent Moon was entirely different from that of his friend's.

Tom's lips curved into an ironic smile. 'My imaginative solution to the problem created by society would definitely not appeal to my dear mother. But unfortunately this is not the East, where my friends are aware of my pattern of living, and it would be expected of me to visit an establishment such as this in the early hours.'

Jordan laughed. 'I've always admired your standards of morality, Tom, which are wonderfully uncomplicated.'

Tom's eyes narrowed as he dragged them away from the swaying hips and coolly surveyed his friend. 'Your own, too, Jordan—at least they were,' he said meaningfully and with unusual gravity.

Jordan's smiling face had set itself into an implacable mask. It was the face that had won him many a battle or a game of chance. It was cool, self-controlled, and without a flicker of emotion, and like his face his manner gave no indication of the way he felt. 'I'd like to think they still are,' Jordan admitted. 'I'm the last man to judge another man's morals.'

'True. Those who live in glass houses should never throw stones.' Drinking deep of his wine, Tom turned his attention back to the girl. 'Dear Lord, what a beauty. Feast your eyes on that, Jordan. Look at those eyes—and that mouth. A man would give a year of his life to place his lips on that.'

'I doubt the All Mighty would ask that of you, Tom. I think you will find that a few shillings will suffice,' Jordan drawled with mild cynicism, amused by the look of complete absorption on the other man's face as his eyes did a slow, salacious sweep of the girl. To Tom she was simply an object, her body having the requisite firm-fleshed litheness and provocative movements of a dancing-girl, her languid grace awakening all his carnal needs.

It wasn't too long ago that Jordan would have thought like that, when he thought each day might be his last. Then, he had refused to think of the women he made love to as people—it was so much easier to regard all women that way. It worked. Life is never made easier by complicating it.

Tom introduced him to his companions, who joined them at their table. Jordan began to relax, despite beginning to feel hot and having to loosen his neckcloth. In jovial spirits one of them insisted on toasting India, the Company and friendship, and as one toast followed the other, all the time one of the servants was there to replenish their glasses. This was not the case with Jordan, who was determined to remain alert and kept one eye fixed on the beaded curtain, scrutinising everyone who entered. He had no intention of becoming inebriated and sipped the deep-coloured liquid slowly. His glass remained almost full, and was topped up only once by a grinning Ali himself.

Lounging back in his chair, the voices of his companions becoming somewhat distant and the haze beginning to thicken around him, he looked at the girl who had served him and was dancing among the customers in more detail. Swaying to the music, she was a living, breathing embodiment of all those voluptuous women of India, as sleek, beautiful and predatory as a cat.

Small and well-rounded and possessing an abundance of sensuality, she was dressed in a silver choli and diaphanous, voluminous trousers, caught in round her hips by plaits of beads and at her ankles, above tiny tinkling bells, bangles and her gold sandalled feet. Becoming mesmerised by the bright jewel in her navel, which darted before him like a one-eyed firefly, Jordan tried tearing his eyes from her, but time and time again they were drawn back like metal filings to a magnet—in fact, he couldn't keep his eyes off her.

He shook his head. What the hell was the matter with him? The haze was thickening around him and voices came to him from down a long reverberating tunnel. And still the dancing-girl writhed before him, teasing and tantalising, and each time he reached for her she laughed and nimbly evaded his questing hands. Suddenly there was something strange in his sensations and indescribably new. He seemed to lose all identity and suffered pangs of dissolution. He wanted the dancing-girl—he must have her. He was unable to focus on anything else. She had become an obsession.

He was conscious of distorted sensual images running in his fancy, and an unknown freedom of the spirit and soul that delighted him like a heady wine. He hastened to partake of the pleasures flitting and dancing in front of his eyes, feeling soft hands touching his face like the fluttering wings of an exotic butterfly. He stretched out his hands to capture it, but it deftly slipped away.

As he travelled on these excursions of the mind, he was plunged into a kind of wonder at his depravity. This situation was peculiarly apart from the ordinary run of his mind. Normally he would stand aghast before the acts he was imagining committing with the dancing-girl, but his conscience slumbered.

Taking his glass, when he looked into the deep red liquid something stirred. He must have stared at it for a full thirty seconds before sanity struggled to the fore as sudden and startling as a crash of cymbals.

The wine! The heat, the giddiness—it was drugged. It had to be. He shook his head to try and clear it, and looking up, through the haze he saw that Ali was watching him closely, his dark eyes hooded and hiding all expression. Tom's face swam before him and he heard his voice coming from somewhere far away.

'Jordan? Are you ill? What in God's name is wrong with you?'

'Get me home, Tom,' he managed to gasp, his words slurred. 'I don't care how you do it—but get me home. The—the wine—drugged.'

Tom was incredulous. 'But, how?'

'Not now, Tom—not enough time. Just get me out of here.'

Immediately Tom and his companions helped him to his feet. He reeled and lurched but they managed to get him out of the tavern, unaware of the two silent figures lurking in the shadows, disappointed that their plan to abduct Grant-sahib had failed.

It was probably a combination of the excitement of the ball, the rain whipped by the wind lashing at the window-panes, or thoughts of Jordan, that prevented Judith from sleeping. Tired of tossing and turning in the warm darkness, she climbed out of bed and padded over to the window. Pulling back the drapes, she looked out on the dark watery world. When the rain fell with so much ferocity it reminded her of the rainy season in India. She loved the fury of the storm. It never failed to touch a chord inside her.

Hearing the rumble of wheels and seeing the soft orange glow of a light suddenly appear beneath an archway of trees at the end of the short drive, she peered out, straining her eyes to try to make out what it was. On seeing the bulk of a coach and that the light was its lantern, she realised it must be Jordan returning from his club or wherever it was that gentlemen went to until the early hours. She watched two blurred and indistinct figures alight, noticing that the taller of the two was being held up by the other.

'Oh, my goodness—it looks like Jordan! He must be drunk,' she gasped in alarm, unable to think of any other explanation why he would return home in this condition. Immediately she reached for her robe, thrusting her arms into the sleeves at the same time as her feet found their way into her slippers.

But then she paused. What was she was doing? Ladies didn't go wandering about the house in their night attire, and she couldn't possibly go down at this hour and bring Jordan in off the street. Besides, it might shame and humiliate him to find he was being helped inside his own house by one of his female guests. But then, she knew he wouldn't want any of the servants to see him in this condition, or his family, and with Lady Grant having retired to bed feeling most unwell, to see her son tumbling about in a state of inebriation would only distress her and make her feel worse.

She did consider waking Jordan's valet or Edmund, but Edmund and Emily's room was on another floor at the back of the house, and his valet's room was somewhere in the attics. By the time either of them appeared Jordan could have woken the whole house.

In a state of acute indecision she glanced outside. Seeing him stumble and sink to his knees, the decision was made for her. Leaving her room, she sped noiselessly along the dark landing and down the stairs to the hall, hoping everyone had gone to sleep hours ago and wouldn't hear a thing. Opening the heavy door she stepped into the drive, glad to find there was a respite in the rain if not the wind. It took hold of her hair, whipping it about her face, and tugged at the hem of her robe. Finding its way underneath, it cheekily touched and caressed her bare legs.

She ran down the drive and confronted the two men, able to make out that the smaller and more sober of the two was staring at her in amazement.

'Captain Grant, I believe,' the man said, his eyes taking in her dishabille in one sweeping glance that seemed to penetrate through her night robe.

'I know who he is,' she said shortly, having to raise her voice above the noise of the wind. She was embarrassed that this stranger should see her in her night attire, and infuriated with Jordan for putting her in this position in the first place.

'I'm Tom Parry, friend of Captain Grant. On finding him in this unfortunate condition in an establishment I wouldn't dream of offending your delicate ears by mentioning, I thought I'd better do the sensible thing and bring him home.'

Suddenly Jordan started forward, unintelligible words tumbling from his lips. The light of the lantern showed his face drawn and ashen. He looked like a man so drunk he was about to pitch forward. Tom caught him and slung his arm about his shoulders to keep him upright.

'Oh, this is quite shocking,' Judith said in a furious whisper. 'I would have thought Jordan to be man enough to hold his liquor.'

'He can. Jordan has the capacity to consume colossal quantities of alcohol without losing an ounce of dignity.'

'Then what's wrong with him? Is he ill?'

'No. He's been drugged.'

Judith stared at Tom aghast, her fear for Jordan overriding all else. 'Drugged? But—but—how? And why would anyone want to?'

Tom shrugged, unable to come up with an answer. But he was curious, especially since the Crescent Moon was frequented by people from the subcontinent, and one of them might hold a grudge against Jordan. But he gave away nothing of his mystification to the young woman, who was clearly so concerned about Jordan's condition that she had thrown decorum to the four winds and come rushing out in her night attire to assist.

'The only explanation I can come up with is that someone put it in his drink. Why, I don't know. What I do know is that it took effect so quickly he was unable to tell me anything. Take it from me, Miss—?'

'Wyatt,' she replied in an aching whisper, swallowing past the awful lump that had risen in her throat. 'I'm a friend of his sister and I'm staying with the family for a few weeks.'

Tom nodded, digesting this. 'Well—in my experience it'll be useless trying to talk to him while he's in this state. He wants putting to bed to sleep it off—but he'll have one hell of a head in the morning, if you'll pardon me saying so.'

'I'll pardon anyone anything if I can get him inside and to his room without waking anyone,' Judith replied, looking at Jordan's handsome face with his hair tumbling in disarray over his brow. At that moment she had no wish to dwell on how he came to be drugged, or the sinister implications of it. Time for that later, when she had got him safely to his room.

'Would you like me to take him inside?' Tom offered.

Judith shook her head. 'Goodness, no—but thank you, anyway. His mother, Lady Grant, is unwell and would be most upset to see Jordan in this condition. I'll try and manage him. At least he's upright and seems able to walk—if a little unsteadily.'

Tom took in her slight figure, unconvinced that she'd succeed in getting him up the stairs, but he could see by the firm set of her chin that she was determined to manage. He took Jordan as far as the door, and after draping the drugged man's arm around the slender shoulders of the girl and saying goodnight, he closed the door noiselessly behind him.

On her own with Jordan, Judith knew it was going to be no easy task getting him to his room. 'Now just you help me as much as you can. And don't you dare go to sleep just yet,' she whispered, knowing as she said it that he didn't hear her.

Staggering precariously beneath his greater weight, which seemed to get heavier with every step she took and almost sent her crashing to the floor, with super-human strength she managed to cross the hall to the stairs, where she paused, leaning against the newel post to get her breath.

Jordan stirred and looked down at the woman in white. Her image was indistinct. Through his con-fused, drug-clouded mind his thoughts strained for clarity, but continued to meander through fantasy. Everything struck him as odd and his brain refused to register certain things. He had a peculiar sensation of standing in the middle of a slowly turning sphere, and he could find no explanation for the girl to be there. But memory and a swaying, tantalising vision of a dancing-girl floated through the caverns of his mind like a butterfly and penetrated his torpor.

For the sake of his health he had not been the kind of man to visit the whorehouses in the East—to slake his lusts with any female who could be bought for a few rupees. But since he had admitted this girl to his home he assumed he must have invited her, which

seemed a perfectly reasonable explanation for her being there, so he accepted the situation and could see
no earthly reason why they shouldn't proceed to his
bedroom—which was what he must have intended in
the first place.

He grinned down at the white apparition in the dim,
swirling light. Her hair was a cloud of darkness, her
eyes large, dark-lashed and lustrous, and he welcomed
the idea of some intimate, female companionship—
even though he could not place a definite image to
identify the one only inches away. When he thought
she was about to move away, he suddenly reached out
and caught her to him like a small bird captured in a
storm, placing her back against the hard balustrade
with his full weight pressed against hers so that she
couldn't move.

'Oh, no—my lovely dancing-girl,' he murmured,
his voice slightly slurred. 'Truly you are as beautiful
as a star. But—to my torment—you flit and twirl in
my sight and then dance away to tease me. But
enough, I say. I will not be turned away until this
craving hunger still gnawing at the pit of my belly has
been relieved.'

In a shivering trance, Judith stared up at him.
Clearly Jordan was still not himself. His eyes had a
fixed, unnatural brightness and were without expression. She knew then that although he saw her, he
didn't know who she was—that she was no more to
him than a pretty dancing-girl he had met somewhere
earlier.

Before she could react, his mouth had swooped down and locked onto hers with a desperate urgency, parting her lips in a deep languorous kiss that took her breath. To struggle was useless, for his enveloping embrace entrapped her, and it was impossible to protest when his mouth slanted fiercely over hers.

At the back of her mind she told herself that this was only a performance, and to keep Jordan quiet she had no alternative but to participate in the performance and behave like the dancing-girl he believed she was. She could see no harm in the subterfuge if it meant getting him to his room without waking the whole house. And so she yielded to his kiss, tentatively returning it and relaxing against him. But she could smell his skin, his hair—and his presence, like a magnet, was drawing her to him and doing strange things.

Suddenly she felt a throbbing heat creeping into her body, and everything began to change. She felt as if the whole world had gone mad. His lips became more insistent, his tongue sliding and probing, his hips hard and demanding against hers.

Sensing her capitulation, Jordan's ardour increased and he kissed her with a hunger he saw no reason to control. The lips beneath his were soft, the body he clasped supple and yielding, her perfume intoxicating and unmistakably real.

Dazed by the confusing messages her body was sending to her brain, and afraid that if she didn't stop him he would make love to her there and then on the stairs, with a shaky breath and a frantic throbbing of her heart that would not be calmed, Judith placed her hands against his shoulders and exerting pressure pushed him back, but it was weak at best. Raising his head Jordan gazed down at her, his anger at being interrupted apparent. Passion had turned his face hard and intense, and Judith felt a stirring of panic when his eyes, translucent in the ghostly dark and holding a fierce glitter, moved restlessly over her inadequately clad body.

'Shush,' she breathed near his ear, placing her hand over his mouth when she thought he would say something, thinking nothing of resorting to mindless bribery in an effort to get him upstairs. 'Not here. Someone might see. We must go to your room. Help me get you upstairs, Jordan. Please. Do you understand?'

She thought he must, because he turned his head and looked up at the flight of stairs. Hauling his arm once more about her shoulders, her free hand gripping the balustrade for support, she began to stagger up the stairs, tripping over the hem of her robe halfway up, banging her shin and almost falling in the process. Physically she was quite strong, which was a good thing considering she was supporting a man twice her weight.

On reaching the top she uttered a sigh of relief. Without respite she proceeded with her burden along the landing, all the time aware of his closeness and his virile masculinity. Whether it was the promise of what they would do when they reached his room, or because somewhere in his subconscious he was concerned about disturbing his mother, Jordan seemed to sense he must accomplish his goal quickly and with the minimum of noise, and ceased to be the dead weight he'd been. Judith uttered a silent prayer of thankfulness when they passed Lady Grant's door without making a sound.

Chapter Eleven

When they entered Jordan's room and the door was firmly closed on the world outside, Judith exhaled a profound sigh of relief. Jordan seemed to sense where he was and immediately struggled out of his redingote and threw it on the floor. He shook his head in an attempt to bring some semblance of normality to his thoughts, but nothing was as it should be. He saw the shape of the bed and his mind and body reached out to it for sleep. But there was still a compulsion inside him that told him to hold on to the vision of the woman hovering in his sights, not to let her go until he'd satisfied his burgeoning need.

The storm had passed over and the moon had risen, casting its silvery light over the furnishings. Jordan sat on the bed and began pulling off his shoes and un-buttoning his waistcoat and shirt with amazing speed, and casting them aside.

Judith watched him in trembling disquiet, mesmer-ised by the uncovering of his magnificent male body, aghast at the way her gaze caressed his shoulders and the tapering, furred chest. It was lean and broad in all the right places, strong, proud and savage. Suddenly his nakedness embarrassed her, and when he began fumbling at the buttons on his trousers, the merest thought of what he was about to uncover brought hot colour racing to her cheeks, even in the privacy and semi-darkness of the room. That was the moment she knew it was time to make her escape before it was too late.

With her heart thumping in rapid beats, she began edging towards the door, but his eyes were fastened on her, his lips smiling about his white teeth, and when she reached out for the handle, as quick as a striking python he was on his feet, blocking her escape. Nimbly she bolted past him and scampered across the room, her only thought to avoid him, but impatiently he flung himself after the pale, darting shape of her and caught hold of her arm, pulling her back against the hard rack of his chest.

'Oh,' she gasped, unsuccessfully trying to wrench her arm from his grasp.

'Ah,' he said exultantly, turning her round in his arms and lowering his face to her hair, breathing deeply of it, his fingers tangled in the luxuriant tresses. 'I have your full attention now, my sweet. No more flitting about, no more teasing. This is what it's all about—a man and a woman—with nothing between us.'

'No,' she cried, fighting him wildly, twisting and writhing in an attempt to gain her freedom, but his iron-thewed arms held her fast.

'Be still,' he murmured, cupping her face in his lean hands and brushing her lips with his own. 'Why do you fight me? Is it because I haven't paid you? Is that it?'

'Yes,' she gasped, latching onto this in the hope he would realise his mistake and release her.

But that was not what Jordan intended. Mindlessly driven by a strong compulsion to have this tantalising creature, holding onto her wrist, he fumbled in his jacket pocket and produced a small key. With great difficulty he opened a drawer in a large armoire and removed a box. Snapping it open with one hand, he removed something and slipped it over Judith's head. Feeling a hard, cold object come to rest in the little valley between her breasts, she realised it was a pendant of some kind.

'There, that should be payment enough.' Immediately his mouth came down hard on hers once more, sending jolt after jolt of wild sensations pulsating through Judith and silencing any objections. They were standing close to the bed and Jordan pushed her back onto it. Placing his arms on either side of her like two strong pillars, he lowered his weight until he lay upon her. His dark hair tumbled over his brow, and his eyes gleamed down into hers.

Judith knew that physical resistance was useless against his unswerving passion. Feeling his hard, thrusting body pressed against hers, and knowing her own vulnerability, she seriously doubted that she could hold him off—and she was no longer sure that she had the will to resist, nor that she wanted to.

Drained of strength and beset with nerves—almost with a kind of terror, at the speed with which events were taking over—Judith felt his lips upon hers once more, moving hungrily, twisting and demanding, warming her to the very core of her being. His tongue passed between her lips to probe and taste the honeyed sweetness within with a ferocity that drew a moan from her throat, breaking her resolve and lacerating her will, causing every one of her senses to erupt in a ball of flame, arousing her to heights she couldn't yet imagine.

She knew she could not withstand his persuasive, unrelenting assault for long—and she also knew that what he was doing to her could be a prelude to other pleasures. And why shouldn't she experience them? She confessed to herself that she wanted him so much. Why shouldn't she continue to play the dancing-girl for an hour or so? Slowly, encouraged by his mouth and his caress, the thought took root and began to grow and to blossom into something wonderful. When his lips left hers and travelled to the warm, pulsating hollow at the base of her neck, her chaste body came alive beneath his questing hands. Desire swept through her, warm and hungry, gathering force until it became a storm of passion.

The thought of what she was about to do flashed through her mind, but she rejected it quickly. And yet beneath the waves of pleasure she was aware of a faint sense of shame. This was not how she had wanted to experience her first night of passion. There had been no vows said between her and Jordan, and because she was a nobody and quite penniless there never would be. Despite the tender words he had spoken to her at the ball, she wasn't going to fool herself into believing he was going to make any undying declarations of love. She was unhappily aware that he had made love to countless other women, and that he simply needed her now because he thought she was a dancing-girl—clearly a dancing-girl he wanted desperately to possess, and in his drug-induced mind he believed she was that person.

She had always sensibly believed in the teachings of her mother and her tutors at the academy, that it was a sin for a woman to give herself to a man in carnal lust outside wedlock, and that she must learn to exercise the strictest discipline over the demands of the flesh. Indeed, her ideals had always dictated that for her there would be no frenzied coupling with a lover, that would engage body and mind but not the heart. Her self-respect demanded more. Not only must she love, but she must be loved equally in return. She had always regarded her virginity as something infinitely precious, wanting to keep it for her husband for their wedding night, and if there were to be no husband then she had intended taking it with her to her grave.

But she hadn't realised that love when it came would be so powerful and all-consuming. She loved Jordan with all her heart, and if she could just have this one night of happiness to remember, to savour and memorise in the years ahead, then surely God would forgive her this one weakness. She realised that tomorrow the pain of what she had done might be intolerable, but regardless of this and what came after, tonight she wanted to belong to him completely.

When his fingers began fumbling with the fastenings on her robe and he tried to tear away the encumbering garment, gently she pushed him away.

'Wait,' she whispered. 'Don't be in such a hurry.'

Kneeling up on the bed, she slipped the offending robe off her shoulders and whipped her nightgown over her head in one single, glorious stroke. An almost wicked smile tempted Jordan's lips as his silver gaze followed each of her movements. Judith felt his eyes on her—on her breasts, on her legs, and she rejoiced in the sensation as if it were a caress. How she would like to light the candles, to have as much light as possible shine on her body, her face, when he made love to her, so he would know she was the girl he called his moonflower and remember. But she couldn't do that. Best to let him go on believing she was the dancing-girl.

Her senses reeling and lifted by a love that was stronger than modesty or reason, proud and unashamed, believing she was in control, she leaned over and kissed his mouth, slipping her arms about his neck and letting her hands caress the hard, smooth, rippling muscles of his back, but Jordan took control away from her. Bending his head, he flicked the tip of his tongue over the hard, rosy peaks of her firm breasts, letting it wander with tantalising slowness over her flat stomach, before tipping her back onto the bed to explore in detail the more intimate secrets of her body. He did so posses-

sively, with the sureness and expertise of a knowledge-
able lover, deliberately and slowly rousing her to diz-
zying heights.

There was a moment when Judith thought she heard
a sound—a low, creaking sound of a door being
pushed open or of someone treading on a loose floor-
board. She listened for a moment, but when Jordan
raised himself above her and caught her mouth in another drugging kiss, she could not deny the hot,
sweeping excitement that gripped her, the throbbing
need that was building and growing with such intensity she thought she would die of it. Reality no longer
mattered as her mind ceased to function and her body
became soft and pliant, taking on a will of its own.

Unable to resist any longer the erotic demands, the
heat, the pressure of him, when he moved between her
trembling thighs, no longer able to retreat from the
course she had set herself, she opened them willingly
and allowed the boldness of his rigid manhood to enter
and fill her aching void. In that one irretrievable moment, when the pain of her shattered maidenhead had
subsided and been replaced by something new, something infinitely wonderful, when she began to move as
he moved and answered his demanding, thrusting hips,
that steadily increased in power and force, in joy and
a beauty that became unbearable, driving her to a ter-
rifying precipice, Judith knew what it meant to become as one with another human being.

Jordan took her in a wild, ravenous passion, curving
his hands around her hips and forcing her into a tempo
to match his own. Wild spasms drove his fullness

higher and deeper within her, their bodies moulded together, as he slaked himself with her like a man offered water after a prolonged thirst. Her arms and body welcomed him, and she arched to meet him, with her head thrown back and her hair a stream of tangled silk. With his name on her lips she allowed herself to be possessed, clasping him and caressing him, abandoning her body with all her heart and soul and a hurricane of love.

It was near dawn when Jordan rolled away from her and fell into a deep sleep. As sanity slowly began to return, summoning the remains of her energy, Judith left her lover's lair and quickly donned her nightgown and robe, her skin still throbbing and tender from his caresses.

There was something almost childlike about his naked, masculine frame outspread across the turbulent bed, his tousled head almost buried amongst the pillows. The bed was huge, but when he was lying down it looked too small to hold him. He was truly magnificent and she felt a great, aching love for him. Bending over, she softly placed a kiss on his brow.

'I love you,' she breathed, letting her eyes linger on his profile for one blissful moment, before she slipped silently from the room and down the landing to her own.

Like Judith, Alicia had been unable to sleep. In the small hours she heard a sound and went to investigate. Seeing no one, she realised Jordan must have come home and had gone to his room. She paused outside his door when she heard a voice. It was the voice of a woman. Unable to stifle her curiosity, softly she opened the door. Apart from the moonlight the room was in darkness. Straining her eyes she saw the naked bodies of a man and woman entwined on the bed making love. The woman's sighs and groans of pleasure reverberated in her ears. It was Judith, she knew it. As she watched the shameless pair she was consumed with a primitive desire to kill—to be avenged.

The slut! The bitch!

Silently she stepped back. Closing the door, she returned to her room, her only conscious thought being that one day she would be avenged. She had no idea how long it would take, where or how. That didn't matter. All that mattered was that one day she would take her revenge on Judith Wyatt and make her wish she'd never accepted Lady Grant's offer to spend the summer at Landsdowne.

When the dawn was beginning to lighten the sky and the house was stirring to life, Judith perched on the window seat with her knees drawn up to her chin and hugged her secret to her. Was it possible to feel such happiness, such elation shimmering inside? Daydreaming, she went over in her mind the splendour of Jordan's lovemaking, unable to believe it had happened, but it had—her body, still pulsating from his caresses, gave evidence to that. When she'd returned to her room and looked at her face in the mirror, she had wondered if she would see a difference. There was a sparkle in her eyes and a gentle flush on her cheeks, and her expression was one of perfect tranquillity, but otherwise she looked the same.

The fact that her future could not be shaped and shared with the man who had wakened her body to divine, sweet torment, that her happiness wasn't destined to last, didn't seem to matter just then. It wasn't until the door opened and someone entered her room that she was forced to face the enormity of what she had done.

Turning her head she expected to see one of the maids or Charlotte—although she would be most surprised to see her friend up and about at this hour, in fact, she would be surprised if Charlotte surfaced before midday following her exertions at the ball. She saw Alicia with her back pressed against the closed door, a sneer on her lips and a cruel gleam in her green eyes. Never had she looked so vicious. Judith felt the colour drain from her cheeks, but she managed to control the shaft of dislike that twisted through her at the sight of her. In no mood for a confrontation, she stood up, sensing that the other woman's presence boded nothing but ill.

'What do you want, Alicia? What are you doing in my room at this hour?'

Alicia stood with her hands on her hips, eyes slightly narrowed, surveying her rival's pale face and taking in her unbound hair, which tumbled about her shoulders in a luxuriant mass. 'I've come to salute you. You're a cunning one and no mistake. You certainly know how to worm your way into a man's arms—and his bed.'

Judith stared at her in blank astonishment, taken off guard by her accusation. In alarm she made a great effort to steady herself. 'How—how did you...?' Suddenly she remembered the sound she had heard when Jordan had been making love to her. All the years of schooling her features into a polite mask were forgotten. The disgust she was feeling showed clearly on her face. 'So—that was you—the sound I heard. Snooping, were you, Alicia?'

'You slut,' she hissed, moving forward, her pretty face disfigured by anger and spite. 'You miserable little tramp. I could strangle you with my bare hands. I know your sort. I knew what you were the moment I set eyes on you—a scheming, jumped-up nobody who came to believe you could suddenly better yourself. You couldn't keep away from him, could you? What a proper little snake in the grass you've turned out to be.'

'It wasn't like that.'

Alicia smiled a thin smile. 'Wasn't it? I know what I saw. I saw you. It appeared to me that you were submitting with the greatest enthusiasm.'

Judith lifted her chin. Alicia believed she had her exactly where she wanted her. She expected her to cringe and cower. Judith looked at her coldly, showing not the least sign of shame for what she had done as she attempted to explain a little of what happened. Not that she felt she should—especially not to Alicia, but it would not go amiss for her to know the condition Jordan was in when he'd arrived home.

'I was still awake when Jordan came home. When I looked out of my window I saw he was with an acquaintance, who was holding him up. Seeing him lurching and staggering, the general impression I got was of an inebriate rolling home from the tavern, so I went downstairs to help him inside. I was afraid he would wake the whole house, you see.'

'How considerate. And he wasn't drunk?'

'No. Through no fault of his own he had been drugged. When his acquaintance left, my only thought was to save him from embarrassment, and to get him to his room without waking Lady Grant. As you know, she wasn't feeling at all well after the ball, and I had no wish to add to her distress by letting her see Jordan in that condition. I swear that what happened was not what I intended to happen. I only wanted to get him to his room without disturbing anyone.'

'You succeeded admirably,' Alicia sneered.

'I know how you feel about Jordan, Alicia, but no matter what you think I did not do it to spite you.'

'I don't believe you.'

'You are entitled to believe what you like. I never thought—never dreamt—Jordan would lay a finger on me in that way. But—he is strong—and very persuasive.'

'Are you saying he forced himself on you?'

'He didn't rape me, if that's what you mean.'

Alicia arched her brows. 'Rape! That's such an unpleasant word to hear from you, Judith. Gently bred ladies would know not to use it,' she jeered.

'Normally I am the very model of respectability and it is not a remark I would make to just anyone,' Judith replied, in no way defensive. 'But I am sure you don't need me to explain its full meaning.'

Refusing to play the part of a broken victim, Judith considered the word and what it meant. Jordan had not taken her by force—he didn't have to. Her only reservation lay in the fact that his thoughts had not been of love, but of a primeval fulfilment—the desires of the flesh. To him their coupling had meant nothing more than the mating act. When he awoke he wouldn't remember any of it, and it was for this reason that he must never know she had shared his bed for that brief time, even though her whole being hungered to repeat their turbulent consummation.

'What I am saying is that I couldn't get away from him—and I confess,' she said softly, 'that after a while—I had no desire to. But if it makes you feel any better, Alicia, being under the influence of a narcotic, he didn't know who I was. When he wakes he won't even remember what happened—and if he does, I promise you he won't remember who shared his bed.'

Alicia's eyes narrowed, and for one exquisite moment she began to fondle her dreams of revenge. What was to prevent her using the situation to her advantage? Only Judith would know, and she would have to live with it for the rest of her life.

'I don't think we have anything further to say. I think you'd better leave, Alicia.'

'With pleasure. And I think you'd better start packing. After this I imagine the whole family will be outraged by your unacceptable conduct. I can't see Lady Grant wanting you to remain in her house. It's hardly the way to repay her hospitality.'

'If you have one iota of consideration for Lady Grant, Alicia, you will not tell her,' Judith snapped. 'There is no need.'

Alicia looked at her, her eyes steady. 'What are you saying?'

'That I have no intention of confronting Jordan with any of this. Regardless of what you may think of me, I am not a fool. Socially I am beneath him, and the last thing I want is for him to feel that he is obliged to marry me—that I have tricked him into it. There would be a terrible scandal.'

'Jordan is a natural survivor. He'll live it down.'

Judith shook her head. 'I don't want him to know—he must never know.'

She sounded as if she meant it, and Alicia was certainly not going to argue about it.

'I told you,' Judith continued, 'he won't remember any of it so what's the point? It would serve no purpose. I will bear the burden of what happened between us. Do you understand what I'm saying, Alicia?'

In answer, Alicia's mouth settled in a thin line and she looked at her scornfully. 'Oh, yes. I understand more than you realise.'

'What do you mean?'

'That I am quite prepared to follow your example. Don't worry,' she said, and with a haughty toss of her head she turned and strode back to the door. 'Your oh-so-sordid little secret is safe with me.'

When Alicia had marched from the room in a swirl of white lace, Judith finally allowed her defences to crumble. Engulfed in a well of misery and loneliness, she sank onto the bed, her shoulders slumped, her euphoria of the moments before Alicia had come in shreds. There raged within her the full realisation of what she had done, and there was no way she could deny the dreadful truth. Last night she had been completely irrational, and it was equally obvious that she'd let emotion drive her to do something that was incredibly impulsive. In one desperate moment to share Jordan's love, she had sacrificed her virtue, her morals and her principles, and it left her with a mass of shame.

As brief as it had been, it was over. She would return to the academy and pick up her life and pretend last night had never happened. But she would never forget.

A sob rose in her throat, and for the first time in four years she felt despair fill her soul completely. She felt emotionally drained and afraid. With tears streaming down her cheeks she covered her face with her hands and wept out her misery, which seemed to have no end. She was branded by Jordan, and she would ache with love for him every waking hour. But she would have to leave Landsdowne. Her actions had left her with no choice. The decision was hers to make, and she had made it the moment she had let him make love to her. Besides, she had no way of knowing how he felt about her, except that he had implied he enjoyed being with her, and their Indian backgrounds gave them much in common.

Unconsciously her hand rose to fondle the necklace he had placed round her neck as payment for her services. He had believed her to be a whore, and never had a whore made love to her client as willingly as she had.

She raised the pendant and looked at it closely for the first time. She knew very little about jewels or their worth, but even her inexpert eye could see it was a magnificent design. It was of a rare beauty. There was a huge central diamond, roughly cut with a yellow glow in its depths, and smaller diamonds and rubies were set around it. The gold mounting and chain alone would be of great value.

It was certain that Jordan would miss it and search for it, but would he remember giving it to his companion of the night? She didn't think so. Still, she couldn't return it to him otherwise he would demand she tell him how it came to be in her possession. It looked extremely valuable, and she decided it would be safer kept around her neck than concealed in a drawer, until she could make up her mind what to do with it.

Her eyes alight with concentration, her mind coldly calculating, formulating and deciding, Alicia left Judith's room and went directly to Jordan's. She pushed the door open quietly. Naked and lying on his stomach, he was stretched out across the bed, his head buried in the pillows, fast asleep.

Feasting her eyes on the absolute perfection of his masculine body, she felt something warm kindle in the pit of her stomach. She had no doubt whatsoever that being made love to by Jordan would be a far different matter from the adolescent fumblings and pawings of Philip Mason. Philip was her father's steward, whom she had taken as her lover for just one short week last summer when boredom had set in, as it often did when she was forced to spend any length of time in the country. The affair had meant nothing to her and they had been very discreet, for if her father ever found out about it he would take a shotgun to his steward.

Closing the door, she padded across the carpet, her eyes taking note of the rust-coloured stains on the sheets. Her smile was one of pure malice. Judith didn't know it but she had done her a favour. The evidence that intercourse had taken place would explain away the fact that she was no longer a virgin, which was something she had always known she would find difficult to explain to her husband on their wedding night. When Jordan awoke and found her lying beside him, he would believe the entire responsibility for her first intimate encounter with a man was solely and exclusively his.

Stripping off her robe, she lay down beside his inert body, nestling close, feeling immensely smug and pleased with herself. Getting Jordan to the brink of matrimony had been a lengthy process, but she was certain it would be well worth the wait.

Chapter Twelve

Wandering in and out through the depths of sleep, something formless and as black as the hounds from hell was sitting on Jordan's head and preventing him from moving. It was mid-morning when it lifted and he floated out of a flickering, golden haze comprised of bright sunlight and fragments of memories. Completely disoriented, he lay without moving, watching the play of light on the floor, pain stabbing through the sockets of his eyes and embedded in his brain. He tried to lift his head, but there was a regiment of soldiers at full charge at work inside his skull.

Closing his eyes, he tried to remember the events of the night before that had made him lose all contact with reality. He recalled what happened at the ball, going to the Crescent Moon and his meeting with Tom Parry and his companions, but he couldn't remember anything after that. There had been an exceedingly pretty dancing-girl, but her face was a blur to him now. He tried to remember more of the details, but the tableau etched inside his brain was a blurred, ominous vignette.

He forced himself to concentrate on a certain face—Judith's face, when she had been in his arms, gazing up at him as they danced. He focused on that one special thing, tracing every detail of her delicate features, feeling the throbbing on the perimeter of his mind begin to lessen—to become bearable. It was a technique he'd used frequently in the past, a technique that had been as successful then as it was now.

But there was something else, something far more important that he had to resurrect. He lay there trying to bring to mind the memory, which was competing with the regiment when it began pounding once more. Opening his eyes he saw the clothes he had worn for the ball strewn on the carpet, but something was amiss. One of the garments was white and gossamer thin. He stared at it for what seemed like an eternity, slowly becoming aware of a warm body pressed to his back. More sharply than he intended, he raised his head. It began swirling dizzily and he put a hand on the top, since there was every possibility it might explode.

Rolling onto his side, he leaned on one elbow and stared at the naked woman lying beside him. A cloud of auburn hair was spread out on the pillow, and the face was indisputably one he recognised. Reality struck him with enough force to set off a further explosion of pain in his head.

'Good God! Alicia!'

Her eyes fluttered open and she smiled up at him, stretching languorously like a cat in the sun, unashamed by her nakedness. 'Good morning, my love,' she crooned, trailing a finger over the crisp mat of hair on his chest and over his brown, muscular shoulder. She yawned behind one slender white hand and snuggled into him, placing her lips in the warm hollow of his throat. 'Mm. You were wonderful last night, Jordan. I'm already looking forward to a repeat performance.'

Jordan was incredulous. He couldn't figure it out. He couldn't accept that he'd spent the night with Alicia and was unable to remember their animal coupling in the dark—empty of tenderness or joy—and nor did it do anything for his masculine vanity.

'Alicia,' he repeated sharply, once he'd recovered from the initial shock. 'Kindly explain what happened.'

She bent her head back and looked up at his thunderous countenance, pouting her soft lips, making a pretence of being hurt. 'Really, Jordan! If I had any hope that you might be pleased to see I am still here, your tone of voice would have taught me otherwise.'

'That is beside the point. I wake up and find you in my bed—without being aware how you got here—and you are surprised when I ask you to explain?'

'Do you not remember? Cast your mind back.'

Jordan tried, but all he could conjure up were misshapen images of an enchanting creature—part angel, part spirit—who had writhed beneath him and made his blood stir hotly. The image did not fit the woman lying beside him. He froze at the mere thought of having made love to Alicia, and the abjection and passion of the attachment.

Pushing her away, he swung his long legs over the edge of the bed and pulled on his trousers, feeling less at a disadvantage with his clothes on. 'I would be grateful if you would refresh my memory of the entire night. I don't mind admitting that it is extremely hazy and I really cannot recall a damned thing,' he gritted furiously. 'Did you come to my room of your own accord?'

'Why,' she cried, his words bringing her to her knees on the bed. 'I would never enter a gentleman's bedroom uninvited. How can you think that, Jordan?'

'Then what the hell are you doing here?'

'I—I heard you come home—very late—but I didn't know it was you at the time. I left my room to investigate—and you were in the hall—shockingly in your cups, I might add. In fact, I had to help you up the stairs to your room.' She smiled softly. 'That was when you became extremely amorous and one thing led to another and—well—I'm still here.'

'Don't look like that, Alicia,' Jordan snapped when he saw her simpering smile and the enticement in her look, his tone carrying anger and frustration. 'I have no intention of ravishing you again—if that's what did happen. It's precipitated an infernal mess, and I'm not about to repeat it.'

Jordan gave her a hard look, his mouth tightening as he stared down at her, at the pink mouth and long-lashed green eyes. He found it strange that he got no pleasure in perusing her naked form, that she no longer had the power to attract him—the only emotion she was capable of rousing in him now being revulsion. She might look soft and fragile, but he was beginning to suspect she was as strong as steel inside. He felt disgusted with himself—and with Alicia, for allowing it to happen.

Running an impatient hand through his dark hair, he turned away, rubbing his brow, when a moment of flame and vision rushed over him, and for one single second he was of clear sight. He saw Ali Shah, and the knowledge that he had been drugged by some act of evil at the Crescent Moon crashed through his mind like the report of a cannon.

'Jordan—I hope you remember our conversation—our agreement.'

With an awful sense of foreboding and dread in his heart, Jordan growled, 'I don't. Remind me.'

'Why—you said we would be married.'

'Then I am more of a fool than I thought.'

'But—you must. You cannot refuse—you will not. If I've learned one thing about you since we became acquainted, it is the fact that you are a gentleman, and gentlemen do not renege on their word.'

'Thank you for your trust, Alicia. I shall try and take heart from it,' he replied with dry sarcasm, which Alicia prudently ignored.

'You have compromised me and now my reputation is completely ruined. How do you think it will look—cohabiting in your bedroom while your mother is sleeping almost next door?'

'Leave my mother out of this.'

'You can't possibly expect me to weather the scandal alone.'

His dagger gaze pinned her to the bed. 'Why? Is there to be one?' He took a deep breath, trying to stay calm.

'I sincerely hope not. You made love to me, Jordan. You—you were the first.' She lowered her eyes at that blatant falsehood, lest he should see it.

Jordan's patience snapped. 'Blast it, Alicia, stop badgering me. Have you nothing to say about your sordid affair with your father's steward—Philip Mason, I believe his name was?' he reminded her brutally, speaking sarcastically, with a kind of cold contempt in his voice. 'Bearing that in mind, it seems to me incredible that you accuse me of robbing you of your virginity.'

Alicia paled. How could he possibly know about Philip? 'I—I don't deny that Philip and I were close— for just a short time—but we were never lovers,' she lied. 'I would never stoop so low as to let one of my father's employees do what you did to me.'

'Don't feign innocence with me, Alicia. You know as well as I do that it's true.'

'Then what of this? You can see by the evidence that I speak the truth,' she said, her eyes burning with green fire as she indicated the small bloodstains on the white sheets. A silence fell between them, and with a surge of triumph Alicia realised she had hit her target. She saw Jordan blanch, and when he lifted his gaze from those tell-tale marks, his eyes were watching her with an expression that was at last attentive.

Jordan had been convinced that Alicia had disposed of her virginity long before he returned from India, and he had a peculiar, humiliating feeling that some-how she had cunningly forced his hand. But he could not call her a liar when the evidence of their mating was emblazoned on the sheets.

Alicia watched him closely. His profile was harsh and forbidding. She knew he was thinking madly of some means of escape from marrying her, and she also knew that behind that taut façade boiled a terrible, violent rage. But she had no intention of letting him off the hook.

'Oh, Jordan,' she sighed. 'Why—last night you were so enthusiastic about being a bridegroom.'

'I don't remember,' he growled, gritting his teeth in frustration. 'Now—I think you should leave. Get dressed and return to your room before my valet or one of the servants comes in.' He turned away as she slipped her clothes on, but he didn't miss the flare of temper in her eyes, or the fright that he might not comply. 'You must forgive me, Alicia, but I have much to think about,' he said curtly. 'We'll discuss this later.'

Alicia shrank beneath the icy gaze he levelled at her, but she persevered nonetheless. 'You mean you want to wait for the ceremony to take place?'

The thought of being joined in holy wedlock to Alicia was one that froze Jordan to the marrow. 'I have no wish for the ceremony to take place at all—ever—but it seems I am left with no alternative.'

Jordan watched her go, shaking his head to clear his senses as a multitude of emotions marched to war within him—confusion, anger—and a bitter regret that his actions, through no fault of his own, had brought about this intolerable situation. He was unable to deny what he had done—and then again, because he couldn't remember, he was unable to admit it. But the proof on the sheets was damning.

Dear Lord! he exclaimed silently, bowing his head and massaging his temples, which were beginning to ache. Why couldn't he recall what had happened? There was a vague memory of making love, and a smiling face, and a great wave of feeling surged through him as he began to remember dimly that the woman writhing beneath him—so soft and warm and smelling of roses, had not been of the common kind. He tried to focus on her face, but it shifted like a thing in a mist, and his reason wavered. But it did not fail him utterly, for again his memory was beginning to stir among deep layers of cloud, and he was following his companion of the night down a sensuous path in his mind.

He had an inability to distinguish between Alicia and the passionate woman he had made love to. However, if she answered his passion with such zeal and unforgettable pleasure if he made her his wife, then perhaps marriage to her would have its compensations, he thought bitterly.

His feelings were nebulous, chaotic, and much as he would like to avoid doing so, he knew he must give some thought to the problem that faced him. Already he could feel the noose of matrimony tightening around his neck—a noose he would gladly have placed there himself if he were marrying the woman of his choice: Judith. He recalled how happy she had looked at the ball in the dress he had bought her, and the memory pierced his heart.

He clenched his fists, fury sweeping through him like a whirlwind that he was being pushed into a marriage he had no stomach for. He was caught in a trap, knowing full well that Alicia would make it known what they had done—out of spite, if nothing else— should he turn his back on her. The scandal that would ensue would destroy his mother, and he would not allow that to happen. Besides, if, as Alicia claimed, she had shared his bed, then it was not beyond the bounds of possibility that a child could result from the union.

Already resigning himself to his fate, he turned when his valet entered and ordered the man to bring coffee and prepare a bath. Even though his heart was still full of rage, it was steadier and more resolute.

On edge about her first meeting with Jordan, with careful grooming, Judith dallied over her toilet as long as possible. She would have preferred to stay in her room until the following day, but her absence would be commented upon and someone was bound to come looking for her. When she was ready she went in search of Charlotte.

But she need not have worried about encountering Jordan. When they entered the drawing-room they found Lady Grant, who was feeling much better, seated on the chaise-longue reading. Raising her head, she smiled and informed them that Jordan was out and

Alicia was still sleeping off the effects of the ball. She also told them that they would be leaving for Landsdowne within the next hour or so. Jordan would not be accompanying them. He was to remain in town with Alicia, Edmund and Emily.

When they drove away from town, it seemed that Judith's heart would break, but she was stubbornly determined to get through that day and the next. She refused to cry. She would go on. She would survive. Time would help, but she did not believe then that it would heal.

On their arrival at Landsdowne, Judith was surprised to find a letter waiting for her from her Aunt Cynthia. Her aunt had written to inform her that she had come back from the Continent early due to ill-health, and Judith could travel down to Brighton if she so wished. Judith was surprised that her aunt had taken the trouble to write, but she was glad she had—even though she suspected Aunt Cynthia had an ulterior motive: that she wanted someone to look after her. Just when she felt as if there was no way to save herself from drowning, she had been thrown a lifeline, and she was determined to grasp it.

She would hate leaving Landsdowne, but it would solve her immediate problem. In the light of what had transpired between herself and Jordan, she didn't dare stay, not close to him, in the same house. She had considered returning to the academy, but she knew Lady Grant and Charlotte would think this strange following her enthusiasm to spend the summer away from it.

Understanding Judith's concern for her aunt, Lady Grant accepted her decision to go to Brighton, but Charlotte was less than happy. Her face fell as Judith explained that she was leaving.

'You can't go to Brighton, Judith.'

'I think I must, Charlotte. If Aunt Cynthia is unwell then I have a duty to go and see her. When I return to the academy there's no telling when I'll be able to go down. Besides, there are some things I want to bring back with me—clothes and a few books I'm going to need.'

'But you haven't had a chance to get to know Jordan properly,' she argued.

'I think I know him as well as I am ever likely to,' Judith replied softly. 'He did ask me to dance at the ball—twice, in fact. And he bought me that lovely dress. I have much to be grateful for.'

Judith sounded faintly regretful, which was not lost on Charlotte. She gave a sigh of exasperation. 'Oh— he really can be extremely vexing at times. Why on earth he had to remain in town escorting Alicia here and there baffles me. Anyone can see he doesn't care about her in any romantic sense. Can't you stay at Landsdowne for another week or two?' she pleaded. 'That will still leave you with enough time to visit your aunt before you have to go back to the academy.'

'No, Charlotte. I'm sorry, but I would like to leave within the next few days.' Seeing Charlotte's look of despondency, she smiled reassuringly. 'Don't worry. When I return to London I'll come and visit you at the earliest opportunity. I promise.'

'Oh, very well. If you insist then I suppose you must go. But life will be extremely dull without you.'

'You won't feel so deprived when the others return from town.'

'No—I suppose you're right.' Suddenly Charlotte smiled and took Judith's hand affectionately, then frowned, concern showing in her eyes. 'There I go again—thinking of myself as usual. You are right to go to Brighton, Judith. Truly you have not looked yourself since the ball. You are quite pale. Perhaps some sea air will not come amiss.'

'I'm fine, Charlotte—really, so you must banish all fear for my health. Don't fuss.'

Charlotte was not convinced and she gave her an inquiring look. 'Did something happen on the night of the ball you haven't told me?'

Uneasy under the unwavering gaze, smiling broadly in an attempt to allay Charlotte's concern, Judith said, 'Something did happen. I had a wonderful evening. I enjoyed it so much and met so many nice people. Everyone was very kind.'

'That wasn't what I meant. It's just that you seem—well—different, somehow. You would tell me, wouldn't you, if something was wrong?'

'Of course I would,' Judith replied, wishing she could unburden herself and certain she would find a willing listener in Charlotte. But it was a knowledge she could not share with anyone. Why, the whole of London would ridicule her if they knew what she had done—and that she had thought she could make a man of Jordan Grant's standing love her.

* * *

After four days, Jordan and the rest of his party arrived at Landsdowne. During the time Jordan had spent in town he'd returned to the Crescent Moon—not only to question Ali Shah, but also to try to recall something of what had happened to him that night—all to no avail. The tavern-keeper was nowhere to be found. He had even gone to the home of Tom Parry, but his mother, a flamboyant lady who adored her only son, had informed him that Tom was out of town for a few days visiting friends.

It was mid-afternoon and Judith was reading in the library. She waited fifteen minutes before putting her book down and going to join the family in the drawing-room, where everyone seemed to be in good spirits. Unobserved, she stood in the doorway, a small, isolated figure clutching a hand over her pounding heart as her eyes were drawn to the man she had not laid eyes on since she had left his bedroom.

He stood in front of the hearth facing the room, with one arm casually draped across the mantelpiece, his gleaming booted foot resting on the hearth, his long legs encased in superbly tailored fawn trousers. The lean, hard planes of his cheeks looked harsh and for-bidding, his jaw set and rigid. Her pulses quickened and her cheeks grew warm, for she could still see the sprawl of long, powerful limbs, and the tumble of dark hair against the white sheets.

The growing ache in Judith's heart attested to the degree of her love. Seeing Jordan in the luxurious splendour of the drawing-room, so very much at home and every inch a gentleman of wealth and quality, never had he looked as handsome—or as unattainable, to Judith as he did just then. And to make matters worse a positively glowing Alicia, dressed in a gown of shimmering gold silk, was clinging to his side. In an attempt to calm her nervousness, she let out a slow, steadying breath and went in, bringing Jordan's eyes to focus on her. His face was a pleasantly smiling mask that hid all thoughts.

Edmund immediately got up from where he was sitting beside a smiling Emily and went to the sideboard, where he poured some wine into a crystal glass. Judith accepted it with a little smile. Assuming it to be champagne, her mind began to register that something was happening she knew nothing about. Cold fingers of apprehension traced her spine.

'It's a little early in the day to be drinking champagne, isn't it, Edmund?'

'It's for a toast,' he explained, putting on his most engaging smile. Arching a brow at his brother he touched the rim of his glass to hers.

When his mother had returned to Landsdowne after the ball—on Jordan's instructions taking Charlotte and Judith with her, Edmund had been concerned and puzzled by his brother's condition and his behaviour. Having no knowledge of what had happened to Jordan when he'd left them to keep an engagement after the ball, when he'd seen him the following morning, his face so deeply etched with lines of strain and fatigue, it had struck genuine alarm in Edmund. In fact, his brother had looked like hell.

Like everyone else, over the weeks since his supremely self-confident, invulnerable older brother had arrived from India, Edmund had quietly watched a closeness develop between him and the hazel-eyed girl from Miss Powell's academy, so he had been both surprised and puzzled when he had dispassionately told him that he was to marry Alicia. Considering it wise not to involve himself in Jordan's personal life, he had not queried his reasons, but he sensed that this young woman, who was looking at him with wide-eyed apprehension, was about to be battered by the announcement.

'What's the occasion?' Judith asked, looking directly at Jordan. An expression she couldn't recognise flickered across his face, and his silver eyes seemed extremely bright beneath his dark brows, but there was no smile, no word of affection. Perhaps he felt nothing for her after all, she thought bleakly. He looked at her coolly and inclined his head slightly.

'Judith! I trust you are well?'

Thrown off her balance by his cold, almost ceremonious tone, with a painful effort to dominate her disappointment she managed to say, 'Perfectly. I hope you all had an enjoyable few days in town.'

'Oh, absolutely,' Alicia enthused. 'Why, we've hardly had time to pause for breath, have we Jordan?—what with a visit to the opera—and last night there was a lavish party at Sir Matthew Joseph's house in Grosvenor Square.'

As Alicia continued to prattle on, Judith looked at Jordan again. All of a sudden she wanted to cry. She couldn't understand it. Could this cold, polite stranger be the same man who had danced and spoken so light-heartedly to her at the ball, who had made love to her with such tender passion in the dark, secret hours of the night?

'Jordan and Alicia have some good news to impart,' Emily said.

'Oh?'

'Jordan and I are to be married,' Alicia burst out, unable to contain herself any longer.

Judith stared. The pronouncement was beyond her worst imaginings. Alicia's green eyes gleamed taunt-ingly, glorying in her victory. Her lovely features were transfigured with joy at flinging the announcement in the face of her hated rival, but to the others listening it seemed no more than the exuberance one would expect from a bride to be.

When Judith caught Alicia's stare and saw her green eyes gleaming with triumph and malice, she thought she was going to be sick. So, this was Jordan's destiny! Glancing up at him she saw that his dark, hard-featured face showed little pleasure. That wretched woman had done her utmost to snare him, and she had succeeded—and Judith had an awful sus-picion that this situation had come about because of the night she herself had spent in his bed.

Shock drained away what colour she had as she realised how complete her humiliation was, and that her own position was irredeemable. Suddenly she didn't want to be there, and in a state of suspended anguish she secretly began counting the minutes until she could politely excuse herself from this family gathering and end her ordeal. Displaying a calm she didn't feel and managing to bring a smile to her lips, she said, 'Congratulations. When is the happy event to be?' She knew it was a mundane, inadequate thing to say, but she had to say something and there was nothing else she wanted to say.

'Of course it isn't official yet—and when it's formally announced, I know all the ladies in London will envy me. Jordan has to speak to father—but that is only a formality, of course. The wedding will take place as soon as it can be arranged. Jordan doesn't want to wait,' Alicia said, linking her arm possessively through the prospective bridegroom's and looking up at him adoringly. 'That is so, isn't it, Jordan? So, Judith, what do you say to that?'

The tone, haughty and lightly contemptuous, made Judith's hackles rise. A slight surge of anger momentarily diverted her thoughts from her own shock, grief and bitter hurt, which helped her to regain her self-command. 'What can I say?—except that I hope you will both be very happy.'

Excusing herself, she went across the room and sat beside Charlotte, who was not looking at all pleased about the situation. Setting her untouched glass of champagne carefully on the small table beside her, Judith refused to let anyone see how Jordan's presence or the unexpected announcement affected her. She looked down at her lap, for she could feel Jordan's scorching gaze on her, and she could only control her feelings as long as she didn't look into his eyes.

'It's hardly a love match,' Charlotte whispered to Judith when the others began conversing among themselves. 'Jordan looks more like a man going to his execution than his wedding. He doesn't want this engagement, I can tell. I'd like to know what Alicia's done to coax him into it. And no matter how brave a face mother is putting on, she looks quite despondent. In fact, she looks as if she's about to dissolve into tears at any minute. Alicia is not right for Jordan and mother knows it. So does Edmund,' she said, looking to where he sat on the sofa beside his wife. 'He doesn't look overjoyed, either.'

Judith smiled, agreeing with Charlotte, but she wouldn't dream of saying so. 'Love matches are rare in the society-conscious world of the *haute ton*, Charlotte. Why—who knows? They might deal well together,' she replied quietly. 'They may not be much alike, but many couples start married life together with less in common than Alicia and your brother.'

'Less? They have absolutely nothing in common at all, Judith, as well you know,' Charlotte whispered fiercely. 'But I love Jordan so much that I'm not going to make any unwelcome comments. I just hope he knows what he's doing and comes to his senses before it's too late.'

Me too! thought Judith sadly.

'And what are you young ladies whispering about?' Edmund asked, looking around to where they sat, and getting up to help himself to another glass of champagne.

Judith glanced towards him and smiled, managing a look of innocent confusion. 'Why—Charlotte was just wondering if she is to be a bridal attendant—is that not so, Charlotte?' she said, observing Charlotte's indignant features with a look of glowing amusement.

Charlotte glared at her. 'I suppose it has crossed my mind,' she replied stiffly.

'Of course you will be my attendant,' Alicia told her in a rush. 'It would be such a blessing to me.'

'And you, Judith! I'm sure Alicia would simply love to have you, too,' Charlotte quipped mischievously, determined to get her own back on her friend.

Judith was amused that Charlotte's suggestion seemed to throw that ambitious creature across the room into a frenzy. She relieved the situation at once by saying imperturbably, 'Then I would have to decline, naturally.'

'Naturally,' Alicia agreed icily.

Judith was relieved that she wouldn't have to become involved in the complications and details of Jordan's wedding. 'I'm sure Alicia will have bridesmaids enough without me. Besides, that is simply not possible anyway, and you know it, Charlotte.'

'Oh? And why is that, pray?' her friend asked.

'I won't be here.'

Jordan's head jerked in her direction, all his attention riveted on her. 'You won't?'

'Sadly, Judith is to leave us,' Lady Grant explained.

Surprise flickered over Jordan's handsome face. Judith watched his tall figure disengage itself from Alicia's side and stride towards her. He stopped, looking down at her face, tipped back to meet his gaze. The sun slanting through the windows shone on her lavender dress and gleamed in the attractive arrangement of glossy curls about her head. Her eyes were wide and clear and watching him calmly, darker and more lustrous than he remembered, her skin more golden, softer. He didn't know whether to set the changes down to fault of memory or the days that had passed without seeing her.

Something stirred in his mind, something frail and elusive, but it was trapped beyond his recall. She seemed tense, he thought, as if keeping her emotions under control only by the greatest effort. To him, at that moment, her character was both strong and desperately vulnerable. She seemed young, a girl, almost, and yet it was a woman who was looking at him, with a woman's eyes—as if she concealed a secret. A chill settled deep in his bones, and he didn't know the reason for it. He thought he knew her, knew all he needed to know about her, so what could have happened to bring about this transformation?

He had an unbelievable longing to take her hand and pull her to her feet, to feel her body pressed close to his—and he had the absurd idea that he knew exactly how it would feel if he were to do so, but when he spoke, all that he said, in level tones, was, 'Leave? What foolishness is this?'

'It's not foolishness,' she answered quietly, wishing she knew what he was thinking. 'I've received a letter from my aunt informing me that she has returned from the Continent. Unfortunately she is not well. I'm leaving for Brighton in the morning.'

'I see. You feel that you must?'

'I—have obligations. It is my duty. If I don't go now, I may not have another opportunity for weeks— or even months—when I begin teaching at the academy.' She waited, searching his harsh, sardonic features, indulging in a brief, tormentingly sweet fantasy that he would beg her to stay, but he looked supremely unconcerned.

'That's settled then.' He turned on his heel and strode towards the door. 'Excuse me. There is something I have to do.'

Alicia made a move to follow him. 'But—Jordan—'

'Not now, Alicia,' he said with a look of sorely strained patience. Turning his back on her he walked out.

When the door had closed behind him, Judith had never felt so unhappy in her whole life. When everyone began discussing wedding arrangements, after listening to the conversation until she could bear it no longer, she stood up. 'If you will excuse me, I have to get my things together.'

'Of course, my dear,' said Lady Grant. 'Edmund will take you into town first thing tomorrow for the stagecoach. But you must not leave without first coming to my room to say goodbye.'

'I won't. But I—can quite easily go into town by myself. I don't want to be any trouble.'

'We can't allow that, Judith,' Edmund said. 'It's no trouble at all.'

'Thank you. I do appreciate all your kindness.'

'Nonsense!' Lady Grant said, smiling fondly. 'It's been like having another member of the family in the house. We're going to miss you.'

Chapter Thirteen

Judith was carefully folding her clothes and placing them in her trunk when the door opened. Thinking it was Charlotte, she carried on, and it wasn't until the person spoke that she jerked her head towards the door.

'I do hope you're not running away, Judith,' Alicia said calmly, her eyes aglow with smug satisfaction.

Judith looked at her, her face cool and exquisitely set. Yet inside her the anger that she managed to keep under ruthless control swirled around her in waves of heat. 'I never run away from anything, Alicia—and didn't your governess teach you that you should always knock on doors before entering anyone's room? What do you want?'

'Oh dear! I can see that the news of my betrothal to Jordan is not to your liking.'

'It doesn't matter to me,' Judith said flatly, directing her attention to placing personal items in her trunk. 'It really is none of my affair. I don't know how you did it, Alicia, but you succeeded admirably. Congratulations.'

'That's very noble of you, considering the circum-stances. Would you care to hear how I did it?'

'I'm not interested.'

'I'll tell you anyway. You were right when you told me that Jordan would have no recollection of making love to you that night. When he awoke and found me in his bed—with the evidence of our coupling and the loss of my virtue all over the sheets—he was left with no alternative but to do the honourable thing.'

There was a silence, a silence occupied by Judith examining this dreadful disclosure. The harsh reality of what Alicia had done when she'd left her room struck her with horror, and the look she cast her was one of profound disgust.

'Now I realise what you meant when you told me you were prepared to follow my example. What you have done goes beyond the bounds of immorality. It makes me feel sick to think that you could blithely climb into the bed I had so recently vacated and pre-tend you had been there all night—and you had the audacity to call me a tramp!' Judith seethed sca-thingly. Oh, what she would give to topple Alicia off her smug pedestal and tell everyone the truth. 'You do realise that I could expose what you have done, don't you, Alicia?'

'And I you,' Alicia countered calmly, her eyes nar-rowing and glittering viciously as she prepared to de-liver her trump card. 'What I have come to say to you is this. I shall enjoy being married to Jordan—and I shall also enjoy the prestige of being Lady Grant. I cannot allow the truth of that night to be known—not after I put my reputation on the line.

'I am not prepared to let anyone take my new life from me, so if you attempt to do any such thing, I will create so much unpleasant publicity that not one of the parents who send their darling daughters to be taught at Miss Powell's academy will allow you anywhere near them. Not only will the scandal destroy you, but also the much admired and highly esteemed Miss Powell. Do you understand what I am saying?'

Alicia let Judith's silence be her answer. With a toss of her head she turned to leave. 'I think you'll adhere to reason. In time—if you can spare it from the classroom, that is,' she mocked, 'perhaps you will find someone else—who belongs to your own station in life—to love.'

'Love!' Judith exclaimed with maddening calm, while quietly fuming beneath Alicia's blatant threat. 'What do you know about love? You have never loved anything beyond yourself. Yet *I* dare say that I have loved Jordan. I may not be a lady but I am a gentleman's daughter, and I have been Jordan's equal in love. However, perhaps I should remind you of what I told you when you came to my room after the ball— just in case it has slipped your mind. I don't want Jordan to know what happened between us—he must never know. So your threats are pointless, Alicia.'

When the door had closed on Alicia, leaving the ruin she had brought about, Judith sat down calmly on the bed to contemplate her situation. Her hand rose unconsciously to the pendant she still wore hidden beneath her dress. Removing it, she held it in her hands and gazed down at its exquisite beauty, running her finger across the bright diamond. She still hadn't decided what to do about it, but now she did consider giving it to Alicia.

The most painful, agonising part of it all was that she didn't have a choice. She had never dared to reach above herself, had never aspired to be a lady—but she had dreamed of being Jordan's wife. Sadly, she accepted that Alicia belonged to this life, more than she did, and if she did give the necklace to her she would be rid of it without raising Jordan's curiosity as to how it came to be in her possession. He would believe without any shadow of doubt that he had made love to Alicia that night—unless his memory of it returned. This was something she refused to contemplate, for the results to everyone concerned could prove disastrous.

However, on reflection she decided to keep it for the time being, for should she find herself with child, she would tell Jordan. She would want nothing from him for herself, and would not want him to feel under any obligation. But she truly believed that every child had a right to know its father, and every father his child. The necklace would be proof that she had been the woman in his bed that night, and that the child was his.

Briefly she did consider the dire consequences this would bring to Alicia if this should happen—that Jordan might refuse to marry her, but she couldn't help that. If there were a child, to avoid any embarrassment for all concerned, she would go away until after it was born. Unfortunately the child would not be spared the stain of illegitimacy.

Should there be no child, then she would have the necklace delivered in secret to Alicia with a note explaining how she had come to have it, and that she must return it to Jordan on the pretence that he had given it to her that night.

She fastened the pendant back round her neck and shoved it inside her dress. Then she placed the last of the items on the bed into the trunk, tightening the straps securely. What was left she would pack into a small valise in the morning. Feeling the need to stretch her legs, she went down the servants' stairs to avoid meeting anyone and out into the yard at the back of the house. With the threat of being accosted still hanging over everyone at Landsdowne—which was highly probable since Jordan's ordeal at the hands of someone unknown, she had no intention of wandering away from the house.

She strolled into the stable yard, relieved that there was no one about. With her noble head hung over the stable door, Tilly whickered on seeing her, blinking her big dark eyes. A fat ginger cat, with huge whiskers, was perched on top of the stable door keeping her company, but it jumped down when Tilly stretched out her nose and shook her mane vigorously on Judith's approach.

Judith did not, however, look to her right, and so she didn't see the open half-door to the tack room, or the tan-coloured jacket slung over it, or the solitary man who stood motionless in the shadows, watching every move she made, from her easy gait—which suddenly seemed to him both graceful and seductive—to the bounce of her luxuriant arrangement of dark curls.

Smiling broadly, Judith rubbed Tilly's velvet nose affectionately, wishing she'd brought a little treat to feed to her. 'Poor thing,' she whispered. 'I'm sure you'd much rather be galloping through the park or in the field munching grass, than cooped up in your stable on such a fine day as this.'

Suddenly a deep voice that seemed to leap out of the tack room next to her said, 'That could be arranged, if you'd care to accompany me on my ride.'

Judith turned in astonishment as Jordan's tall figure materialised from the shadows. He was watching her calmly, his hands thrust into his pockets, his dark hair gleaming beneath the sun's rays and falling over his brow. But she sensed he was keeping himself on a short rein, that he was wound as tight as a spring, and she feared the release. She panicked on seeing him, her eyes taking in his immaculate white shirt—casually open at the collar, his fawn riding breeches, and his gleaming brown boots. With a sublime effort she managed to bring her rioting nerves under control.

'Oh! I—I'm sorry. I didn't mean to intrude. I didn't realise anyone else was around.'

'There isn't. I thought I would take a ride before dinner. Shall we saddle Tilly and ride together?'

'No—we'd better not,' she murmured hesitantly.

'Don't tell me. Alicia would object,' he said with cynical amusement. 'Still, I'm glad you've come. I would like to have a word with you in private before you leave in the morning. Have you a minute?'

His features were hard and impassive, but Judith sensed danger. 'Of course,' she said, and then she added, 'I only came out for a moment. I—I have things to do,' as if it were some kind of protection.

'I won't keep you long. There's no need to ask what everyone else is doing,' he said, his eyes boring down into hers with cynicism, his jaw set and hard. 'No doubt they're all making plans for my wedding.'

'It's quite normal when two people are to be married.'

'And have you nothing to contribute to the conversation?'

'No. It—it's got nothing to do with me.'

He nodded. 'Since I can't persuade you to accompany me on my ride, perhaps you would allow me a few minutes of your time. Come in here.' Striding back into the tack room, he traced a path towards the opposite wall where saddles and bridles were hung. Feeling strangely reluctant to enter the quiet warmth of the building, Judith paused on the threshold, inhaling the smell of saddle soap, warm horse leather and hay. Seeing her hovering in the doorway, Jordan threw her an impatient look and strode back to her, taking her arm and drawing her inside.

'You can come in. You stand there looking at me like the deer that senses the hunter. Do not fear me. I don't bite.'

She flushed. 'I don't fear you.'

Through every fibre of her body she could still feel the touch of his hand on her arm when he released it. Watching Jordan, she wondered what was on his mind, what he was thinking. As she waited for him to speak, her eyes searching his granite features, she saw no sign of the passionate, sensual side to his nature. The expression on his face caused her an involuntary shiver.

'Do you remember the conversation we had on the night of the ball?' he asked suddenly. 'When we were dancing?'

'Yes—of course I do. It made a deep impression on me. Why do you ask?'

'Because I want you to forget it,' he said firmly, thrusting his hands deep into his pockets once more to keep them from clenching as he tried to bring under control a new onslaught of feelings that the mere sight of her had on him. It had the devastating impact of a rock crashing into his chest, and he strained to endure her closeness.

'May I ask why?'

'I said things I have since had cause to regret. I hope you understand what I'm saying.'

She stiffened, insulted, and her eyes flashed irately. 'Perfectly. When I asked why you did not respond to Alicia's overtures, you told me it was because you have a well-developed instinct for self-preservation,' Judith reminded him bluntly, so unbearably, agonisingly hurt that she wanted to test his discomfort to the limit. 'It would seem that your instinct for self-preservation has deserted you all of a sudden. I remember there were other things you said, but I will not embarrass either of us by repeating them.'

'Things are different now.'

'I know. You are to marry Alicia—and it is clear to me that you are not happy about it. Whatever happened between the two of you does not concern me. But was it necessary to go to such lengths?'

'Yes.'

'You don't love her. I can tell.'

'No.'

'Ever since I came here, Alicia has left me in no doubt that she would marry you. Whatever happened between the two of you after the ball, Jordan, she has certainly succeeded in accomplishing her goal.'

'When I returned home later that night, I was not myself,' he informed her irritably. 'I have no excuses to make and no recollection of what happened.'

'You were drunk?' she queried, wondering if he would tell her the truth. He didn't.

His firm lips twisted with cynicism. 'Something like that. I had no alternative but to offer marriage to the woman who...' he stopped, the words he had been about to say left unsaid.

Judith provided them for him. 'Who shared your bed. I know. Alicia lost no time in telling me,' she explained quietly when his eyes widened with questioning astonishment. 'You should be more careful, Jordan. You know the saying—he who plays with fire! You don't need me to tell you the rest.'

'Thank you for that piece of edifying information,' he ground out. 'I shall strive to remember it.'

'I can see the delicate situation you suddenly found yourself in must have been a difficult moral dilemma for you. However, your morals are entirely your own affair—and I am the last person in the whole world you have to explain anything to.'

Jordan looked down at the tempestuous young woman in the lavender gown, her face alive with her snapping hazel eyes, and he suddenly saw her as she had looked at the ball when they had danced—when he had decided to make her his wife. He was furious with himself and fate for having placed him in this untenable situation. His stomach clenched at the thought that he was going to have to let her walk out of his life.

When he next spoke his gaze settled on her with such iron control that she was deeply shaken. 'Alicia is to bear my name. She knows I am not in love with her—but she does expect consideration and respect, and I have every intention of giving the outward appearance of a happy and contented—if not a loving—marriage.'

'I'm sure you will.' Judith moved to stand before him, looking up into his eyes, rebellion drawing her out of her natural reserve. Her voice, so normal an instant before, was suddenly vibrant, filled with a restrained fury. 'You made a mistake, and you must carry it with you for as long as it takes, Jordan. A soldier you might have been—an adventurer, even, bold and brave enough to take any risk required of you. But I think I know you well enough to know you will never deal dishonestly with yourself or the woman you marry. So why have you brought me in here? If you wish to unburden yourself, why not to Edmund or someone else? Why me?'

'Because of all the people I know,' he said, mentally cursing himself for having felt the need to explain himself to her, 'I thought you would be the one to understand.'

'Well, I don't,' she flared, tears of humiliation burning the backs of her eyes and a lump of emotion clogging her throat. She wanted to run from the tack room without giving her feelings away, but knowing that was impossible, she turned and strolled over to the window in an effort to maintain her self-control. She was deeply in love with Jordan, but her love was unrequited. How she longed to share her confidence, but she must keep it to herself. How much easier it would be if it wasn't true, and she cursed herself for falling under his spell.

Tentatively Jordan made a move towards her, but unable to tell if she would want him near, he halted himself. He could almost feel the alert tension of all her muscles. Her very stillness was like a positive force. 'Didn't you hear any of what I was saying to you that night?' he asked quietly.

She turned as the threat of tears passed, and the lump of emotion in her throat began to dissolve. Without removing her eyes from that proud face, she gave a light, brittle laugh. 'I would like to tell you that my memory of that entire evening is extremely hazy,' she said, 'but I can't—and if I did, I am sure you would strongly doubt the truth of it. You see I do remember, and for a little while—with the beauty of the night—the champagne and the music, I allowed myself to dream. But that's all it was—a dream. Nothing more.' As she turned to go he strode after her.

'Judith—wait.' Taking her arm, he slowly turned her round to face him. 'I would have said more—as I could now, but I no longer have the right.'

'The right? No, Jordan, you don't. It's best not to say anything else.'

With the warm pink glow of the sun lighting up her lovely eyes, Jordan succumbed to the impulse which had been tormenting him from the moment he had seen her walk into the stable yard. With his hand still holding her arm he drew her closer. The warm scent of her body assailed him. He glanced down at her face, so near his that he could see the tiny hairs curling around her ears and the soft down on her cheeks. There was the most innocent expression on her face, and her bright eyes beneath the gentle sweep of her black lashes would not meet his. She tried to pull away from him for fear of what might happen next, and he could feel her fragrant breath on his cheek.

'Dear Lord,' he whispered, pulling her closer still, surprised when she came willingly and leaned against him, yielding her mouth to his with a low sobbing moan. His arms closed round her, crushing her to him as he kissed her possessively. The miracle struck like a spark from their embrace. His mouth gentled, parting her lips in a long searching kiss.

The achingly poignant discovery that it was as wonderful as she remembered was almost more than Judith could withstand. She felt all the old demons, dormant since the night of the ball, awakening inside her, clamouring hungrily for release. Allowing herself to be carried away, instinctively her hands crept up his chest and over his shoulders and round his neck, moulding her body to his. They kissed in mindless rapture while the dwindling afternoon sunlight slanted through the small windows.

As she responded with more ardour than he had expected, the effect on Jordan was devastating. Desire like scalding fire raced through his veins, and as quickly as he had caught her to him, so he cast her away. Half conscious, she opened her eyes and looked at him. Her face was so tragic that he was moved by it, but then his eyes hardened to icy flints and he spoke with chill precision.

'I want you to forget about me. Pretend that night never happened. Go to Brighton and see your aunt, and then return to London and take up your teaching post. That's what I want you to do.'

They looked at each other in a struggle that racked them both, and Judith clung to the sudden coldness between them as a shield. Drawing herself up proudly, she raised her chin. He would never know how much she was hurting, nor would he ever again catch the faintest glimpse of the happy girl she had been at the ball—his moonflower that had shrivelled up and died, like those once-living blooms she had pressed in her book. Fighting back her tears, she said with as much dignity as she could muster, 'You're right. That is exactly what I shall do. Now, you must excuse me. I have things to see to.'

Looking for diversion to keep his mind off Judith's departure for Brighton, Jordan went back to town. That same night saw him at White's in St James's Street, the most exclusive gentleman's club in England, to which he belonged, but no matter how hard he tried to relax, or how many brandies he drank, he had difficulty concentrating on conversation with friends and acquaintances and the game of cards.

His thoughts constantly drifted back to Judith and their kiss. He recalled the feel of her, the sweet scent of rosewater on her skin. He found himself lost in that memory, and it stirred others, but afterwards he was left with a lingering feeling of failure. He had fallen in love with her, and not known it.

Around midnight, when he was on the point of getting up from the card table and leaving, he was surprised when Tom Parry took the vacant chair across from him.

'Good to see you, Jordan,' he said airily, stacking a pile of chips in preparation for the next game of heavy play. 'Mind if I join you?'

'Normally I'd stay and take your money, but I'm leaving,' Jordan replied, giving him a sardonic look.

Tom looked across at him sagely. 'Why? Cleaned everyone out? Or have you lost your touch and allowed your partners to thrash you instead?' he quipped lightly, though he doubted it. To his cost, Tom had discovered Jordan's skill at cards in Calcutta, and he was just one of a large band of unhappy gentlemen to have lost considerable amounts of money to him.

'Neither,' Jordan replied coolly.

'Glad to find you in a better condition than the last time we met,' Tom remarked in a grinning undertone.

Jordan winced slightly at this, but nodded in wry agreement. 'Now you're here, Tom, I would appreciate a moment of your time.'

Tom nodded. 'I thought you might. Mother told me you'd called at the house, by the way, and I believe I know why. I knew when you came round after your visit to the Crescent Moon that you'd come seeking answers.'

'I am. After eight years fighting rebels and dodging shot and steel in India, it does nothing for either my vanity or my self-esteem to find myself taken in by a mere tavern-keeper in London's docklands,' he remarked dryly. 'Come, let's find somewhere less conspicuous to talk.'

Tom put down his cards and Jordan picked up the chips that represented his winnings. They retired to another table where they could converse in private, ordering a couple of brandies from a footman.

'I don't mind admitting that I'm experiencing difficulty remembering what happened that night, Tom. The full possession of my memory has not been restored. I was hoping you could throw some light on it.'

Tom shook his head. 'Can't tell you much. All I know is you were drugged.' He looked at his friend closely, exhibiting signs of cautious interest. 'Someone must have slipped it into your drink. Who would want to render you unconscious—and for what reason? Has it anything to do with your time in India?'

Jordan nodded, his face set in grim lines. 'I'm afraid it has.'

'Does it have anything to do with that Indian whose name is on everyone's lips—in particular the ladies? Jehan Khan, I believe his name is. Apparently he arrived in London shortly before we did—with Jeremy Minton of all people. I know he's staying at Minton's home—and I know there is no love lost between you and that particular gentleman.'

'You're damned right there isn't,' Jordan growled.

'Want to talk about it?'

Jordan shook his head in frowning concentration. 'No, Tom. Thanks anyway. How did I get home?'

'Under my escort.'

'And when we got there? How did I get into the house?'

'Just when I thought I would have to knock the whole house up, an angel of mercy came to my assistance—said she was staying with your family.'

'I see.' So, Jordan thought, gazing thoughtfully into his glass and gently swirling the amber liquid, Alicia must have seen him come home and the state he was in. But then another thought struck him and he frowned. The room she had occupied did not overlook the street, so it would have been impossible for her to see anything. 'What did she look like—this angel of mercy?'

Tom shrugged, lounging back in his chair. 'It was dark and difficult to get a good impression.' His expression became thoughtful as he recalled the young woman who had come running out of the house in her night attire, terrified that everyone inside was about to be shaken from their beds by a drunken master returning home from one of the dubious establishments gentlemen frequented until the early hours. 'She was small with dark hair—pretty face—in fact, come to think of it, she was quite lovely. Her first impression on seeing you was that you were in your cups and damned irate she was, too. But when I told her you'd been drugged—through no fault of your own, I did stress—she was full of tender concern.'

Jordan arched a quizzical brow at his friend. Tender was definitely not a word he would apply to Alicia. 'Tender?'

'Extremely—in fact I was quite touched, I can tell you. Insisted on taking you inside herself—although how she managed it is beyond me. You're about the weight of a small tiger, and unfortunately she didn't have any servants to hang you upside down from a pole and carry you to the slaughterhouse,' he chuckled. 'Oh, and she told me her name was Miss Wyatt,' he added as an afterthought.

A mixture of incredulity and amazement worked their way across Jordan's face. He stiffened and slowly came erect in his seat. 'Are you sure, Tom?'

'Absolutely.'

Jordan stood up. 'Thanks. I owe you for this. You've just cleared up one matter that's been giving me one hell of a headache.'

When he was in the carriage returning to his house, resting his head against the quilted upholstery, he closed his eyes and again tried to think himself away and back to that night—to commune with the invisible woman who was the very source of his vision, for it was along these lines that his mind always worked, and the habits of years as a soldier had become crystallised and were hard to break.

A vision rushed over him, and in a blinding flash he saw the woman he had held in his arms at Landsdowne yesterday as the woman who saturated and tormented his every waking moment, the woman he had struggled so hard to resurrect. He grappled with his memory, but all he saw was—what? Something hard and jewel-bright around her neck—something familiar. That ''something'' had also been pressed hard to his bare chest when they had made love.

As quickly as the vision had flashed upon him it was gone. He experienced a sudden sinking of the heart, accompanied by a deep sense of foreboding.

When the carriage drew up outside his house, he leapt out and went in, bypassing the startled butler without any acknowledgement. Taking the stairs two at a time, he went to his room. His eyes immediately went to a large armoire in which he kept several of his personal possessions. He kept one drawer permanently locked, and in this his valet had placed certain items that always travelled with him. He recalled thinking it strange when his valet had handed him the key the morning after the ball, telling him he had found it on top of the armoire. Thinking nothing about it at the time, he had thrust it into his pocket and not given it another thought.

Now he strode towards the armoire with the certain conviction in his heart that he would find the long leather case—in which he kept the sacred heirloom that was part of the state regalia of Ranjipur—devoid of its treasure. Taking the small key from his pocket and unlocking the drawer, he took out the case and snapped it open. He stared down at the bed of purple velvet, seeing the imprint where the necklace had lain, and the image of having placed it around a woman's neck was suddenly clear.

Once again he remembered embracing the young woman yesterday at Landsdowne in the tack room, the smell of her gentle perfume—of roses, and there flashed into his fogged mind, like a shaft of sunlight bursting through thick cloud and drenching the land with its heat, the realisation that Alicia hadn't been the one to share his bed that night, but Judith.

Judith!

His heart pounding with disbelief, he experienced a wrenching pain of unbearable guilt, and a profound feeling of self-loathing. Dear, sweet Lord! It had to be! Had she given herself willingly, or—heaven help him—had he forced himself on her? How could he have done that to her, when all he wanted was to love her, to be her husband and her friend, to share her hopes and dreams, her laughter and tears? In a drugged stupor he had robbed that beautiful, laughing, unforgettable girl of her most precious possession— her innocence.

And the awful shame of it was that he didn't even remember the joy of her.

But then he remembered their encounter the previous day, and he realised she must have forgiven him, otherwise she would not have walked into his embrace and kissed him with such tender passion. The sudden, startling vision of Judith's slender limbs, locked in wild abandon with his own, their two bodies twisting in ecstasy in his bed, was so shocking in its specificity that it left him trembling.

However, one thing did worry him about all this, and that was the fact that she must still have the necklace. If so, and should Minton or Jehan Khan get wind of it, then she was in grave danger. He frowned. One mystery was explained, at least, only to deepen another. He was puzzled as to why she had kept it. For what reason? Why hadn't she left it in his room when she'd left? Deciding that Alicia might be able to answer some of his questions, he immediately left for Landsdowne.

Chapter Fourteen

Alicia was both angry and worried when Jordan took himself off to London. She told herself that she was mistress of the situation, but underneath she felt fear. Jordan's lack of enthusiasm to be with her made her uneasy, and her unease deepened when he returned just twenty-four hours later and insisted on speaking to her alone in the drawing-room.

He was cool and calm—and he wasn't smiling. Something was different about him. What could have happened? His eyes were like steel flints, and the lines on either side of his mouth looked as if they'd been cut with a chisel.

Poised and beautiful, Alicia sat gracefully on the sofa with her hands folded in front of her. Jordan looked at her hard. Until Judith had appeared in his life he had enjoyed her company on occasion, but she lacked Judith's goodness, her humour and fresh and lively wit, and she didn't look at him with two adorable hazel eyes, and smile that wonderful warm smile.

'I must say that I'm glad your stay in town was of short duration, Jordan. I take it that your business was concluded satisfactorily?'

With his hands clasped behind his back, Jordan looked down at her, finding it virtually impossible to restrain his anger. 'Business was not my reason for being in town. The necklace, Alicia,' he said without preamble, watching her closely. 'Where is it?'

For a moment she floundered and then she said, 'Necklace? What necklace?'

'The one I gave you when you were in my room on the night you allege I seduced you.' His voice was low and even, and he was watching her like a fox watches a hen in a coop. 'Come, Alicia—don't tell me you've lost it. When a woman is given a gift of such rare beauty, it is not something she is likely to mislay. Allow me to refresh your memory. It's a rare diamond—priceless, in fact. It is of great value to me for sentimental reasons—but unfortunately there are others who are desperate and ruthless enough to kill for it.'

Alicia stared at him, her face as white as the petals of the huge daisies which filled the porcelain vase on the dresser. Her stomach churned as she gazed up at Jordan's relentless features. He looked so tall, so intimidating, and she wished he'd sit down. Unable to lie her way out of a predicament she had not foreseen, she said, 'I have never seen a necklace such as the one you describe. You must be mistaken, Jordan, and only think you gave it to me. After all, you said yourself that your memory of that night is extremely hazy.'

Jordan watched her face as several emotions struggled for supremacy in her. He could read her like a book. He knew what she was thinking and he stood there, fixing her with a penetrating, relentless silver gaze, all feeling ruthlessly extracted from his face. He had no intention of making it easy for her. He smiled, an absolutely chilling smile.

'I congratulate you, Alicia,' he said sarcastically, slowly pacing the carpet. 'That was quite a convincing performance you put on the morning after the ball.'

Her dark brows arched. 'I wasn't aware that I was putting on any kind of act,' she replied, trying to remain composed, yet at the same time assailed by a creeping fear that everything was going drastically wrong. Quietly alert and suspicious, she tilted her head and looked up at him. 'Are—are you beginning to recall things about that night?' she asked hesitantly.

'Unfortunately for you, yes. For reasons of my own, I will not bore you with the details of how I came to be in the state I arrived home in. I'd been drugged, and I was brought home by a friend who left me in the drive—not with you, as you would have me believe, but with Judith.'

Alicia's reaction to his words brought her to her feet. 'No!' she exclaimed heatedly, her own anger beginning to rise, but deep down she knew that when challenged she would be unable to come up with evidence to endorse the truth. 'That is a lie. I told you nothing but the truth.'

'Truth? You wouldn't know how to tell the truth if it leapt up and hit you in the face. Somehow Judith managed to get me to my room without waking anyone. It was Judith who occupied my bed that night, wasn't it, Alicia?' he demanded. 'Judith and no one else. It was Judith I made love to and gave the necklace to. Not, as you would have me believe, you.'

Alicia cringed at his tone. 'Really, Jordan! It is quite preposterous. You must stop this. I have no idea what you're talking about.'

'Don't insult my intelligence with your simpering denials,' he said harshly, looking down into her green eyes with a hard, murderous gleam, his lips curled over his teeth. 'I've known some dirty fighters in my time, but never have I known a woman who would stoop as low as you. Everything that happened to me that night was hazy, I admit it, but one thing I do remember is how much pleasure the woman who shared my bed gave me. That woman was certainly not you. So whatever you contrived, Alicia, you have no one but Judith to thank for its success—at the time, of course. Why did you do it?'

'Because I loved you, and I couldn't bear to think I might lose you,' she said, trying to put the softness back into her voice, and school her features into a tender look, but it didn't work on Jordan.

'If that is what you think, then you deceive yourself,' he told her scathingly. 'Not once have I given you reason to believe you are anything more than an acquaintance, but I always knew you were available—too ready to grasp everything I could give you. You bitch! And to think I almost made you my wife.'

With an indignant gasp, Alicia's eyes opened wide. 'Almost? What do you mean?'

'It's quite simple. There will be no marriage negotiations.'

'And what am I to do?'

'You should have thought of that before you stripped yourself naked and climbed into my bed like a London whore.'

'And you behaved like the vile, unprincipled lecher you are, Jordan Grant,' Alicia flared accusingly.

'Did it not occur to you that my memory might not be irretrievably lost—that when it returned it would shatter all your carefully constructed plans?'

'Judith told me you wouldn't be able to remember.'

'Did she, indeed? Then she was mistaken. Just how did you come to be in my bed, Alicia? Did you see Judith leave my room and challenge her? Is that what happened?'

'Yes—if you must know,' she admitted hotly. 'She also made it quite plain that she wanted nothing more to do with you—and that she wanted no one to find out what had occurred between the two of you.'

'And did you tell her what you intended?'

'No. Why should I?'

'And so you took advantage of her—and my own weakness. You tricked us both. You deceived me into believing I had made love to you.' His eyes raked her with an insulting glance. 'I never realised you could be so deceitful or conniving,' he said with biting contempt. 'Oh, I know how soft and persuasive you can be, how caressing your tone and beguiling your smile, but that does not overrule the hatred and treachery concealed in your heart—the hard, calculating core of you. Until now I would not have accused you of this, but at last I am beginning to understand you.'

Alicia's hands were clenched by her sides and her face so contorted with rage that it was almost ugly. She knew all was lost, that there was no longer any reason to keep up the pretence. 'Believe what you like. But if, as you say, you gave Judith a necklace that night, ask yourself why, Jordan. Could it possibly be because it was in payment for her services—the kind you give to a whore?'

Jordan's anger was pitiless and so powerful his eyes glittered, and he had to clench his hands by his sides to prevent them reaching out and throttling her. 'Be quiet, Alicia. Whatever happened between Judith and me was not some meaningless encounter with a woman of the streets.'

'Ha! So—the truth hurts,' she cried, plunking her hands in the small of her waist and leaning forward slightly, her bosom heaving with anger. 'Your ''Oh-so-pious little school-ma'am'' certainly showed her true colours that night, did she not? Little wonder she wanted no one to know about her sordid coupling with you, or why she left for Brighton in such a hurry— with such a valuable bauble dangling round her neck,' she sneered. 'No doubt she's already hocked it and will live off the proceeds for the rest of her life. It will be interesting to see how precious her teaching career is to her then—but no matter what she tries to aspire to, she will always remain what she is. A plain little nobody.'

The bluntness of her statement jarred every one of Jordan's nerves. He moved close, looming over her, and never had Alicia seen such an expression in any man's eyes. 'And you have a warped definition of how a well-bred young woman should behave. Judith could give *you* lessons in the art of being a lady. Dear Lord, how you must hate her.'

'Yes, I do hate her. I hated her the first time I laid eyes on her—with her hoity-toity manner and boasting a superiority of mind that was positively sickening. What do you think will happen when it gets out what sort of woman she really is? It will do her no good— the academy and Miss Powell even less.'

No human emotion could be traced on Jordan's face. In a silky, menacing voice, he said, 'If it is your intention to disclose any of this, or cause Judith any unnecessary suffering, then I advise you to reconsider. I shall have a word with Edmund to take you home. You will say nothing to my mother about why you are leaving. I do not want her upset. Of course, you may tell Emily what you like. I know she is sensible enough to be discreet—pity the same cannot be said of her sister.

'There will be no scandal. If you so much as breathe one word that will bring disgrace to either Judith or Miss Powell, I swear I will personally wring your neck.' These words were spoken in a cold, lethal voice, leaving Alicia in no doubt that he meant it. 'Is that clear enough?'

She drew herself up with nervous hauteur. 'You can't threaten me.'

'No?' he inquired. 'I meant every word. One thing you should know about me, Alicia, is that I'm a very determined man, and if any harm comes to Judith by your hand, I'll destroy you. Believe me when I tell you that you don't want me for an enemy.'

He turned from her and walked to the door. Opening it he looked back. 'Remember that being a woman you have much to lose. You must also remember you will have your father to answer to. He is an upright, moral man, and when he learns how you set out to entrap me into wedlock—and the sordid methods you used to do it—and not forgetting your little affair with his steward, I might add—a man he trusts implicitly, by all accounts—he'll not be lenient.'

Alicia watched him go. Embittered and with anger burning a hole in her chest, she paced the length of the room as she considered her predicament. She hated Judith, and she would never forgive her for the humiliation she had brought upon her. And what added to the injustice of it all was that after behaving like a slut, Judith Wyatt wasn't suffering for her wrongdoing.

Catching her reflection in the large gilt mirror on the wall above an ornately carved bureau, she stared at it hard. The slut would pay for her treachery—and Jordan for his rejection of her, Alicia. But how? There had to be a way. It was no good fighting Jordan, she wasn't strong enough, so she would have to outwit him. She recalled the necklace he had mentioned. He had told her it was priceless, of sentimental value to himself—and that others who wanted to possess it were ruthless enough to kill for it. The cogs of her mind began turning faster. Who had he been speaking of? Lord Minton? This was highly probable, if his irate encounter with this gentleman at the ball, and her own conversation with Lord Minton about his association with Jordan in India, was anything to go by—along with the bitter enmity that clearly existed between the two of them.

She smiled at her reflection, a satisfied smile and one of pure malice. Behind her, the fire gave the room a golden glow that suddenly seemed brighter. With purposeful strides she went to her room and immediately sat down to write a letter to Lord Minton.

Jordan had the impression that his mother shared his relief at Alicia's sudden departure for Kent, and that she was to be spared having Emily's sister as a daughter-in-law. She certainly looked happier and more relaxed than she had in days.

When Edmund and Emily whisked Alicia back to Kent, offering no explanation other than that she was missing her father, Lady Grant did not question this or try to persuade her to stay. Her own marriage had been a happy one, and so too was Edmund's. She could only hope that Jordan's would be equally so, and she felt that Alicia was not the right woman for him—although she would never dream of saying so.

She had been perplexed by the seeming contradictions in Jordan's life since his return from India. Something was troubling him deeply. She sensed it was of a serious nature and, not one to involve herself in either of her sons' private affairs, she hoped that it would soon sort itself out.

His moodiness and unhappiness over Judith's absence made her wonder, too, as did Judith's behaviour before she had left with undue haste for Brighton. Judith had come to her room to bid her farewell on the morning following the announcement of Jordan's betrothal to Alicia, and as the young woman had looked at her, Lady Grant had seen something in the depths of her eyes that could only be seen and understood by someone who had felt it themselves. Judith was in love with Jordan, of that she was certain.

Now there was a match she would approve of. Judith might have nothing to recommend her to society, and she might not have the kind of pedigree to rival Charlotte's, but she was warm and kind and extremely clever. She was the kind of woman who would make Jordan happy and be a credit to him, of that she was certain. And so, when he told her he was leaving for Brighton to ask Judith to marry him—his eyes glowing in a way she hadn't seen in a long time, she embraced him warmly and sent him on his way with her blessing.

Cynthia Wyatt lived in a solid, respectable house of three stories in the heart of Brighton, close to the Steine—a broad stretch of grassland that spread northwards from the promenade, on which the fishermen dried their nets. Up on the Downs, several windmills overlooked the town, where wholesale development of crescents, squares and terraces was taking place around a labyrinth of medieval streets called the Lanes.

Despite the discord that existed between Judith and her aunt, she loved to come to Brighton, so situated that a stagecoach leaving London in the early morning reached the resort by noon, returning to the capital during the afternoon. The town had grown rapidly from small beginnings as a poor fishing village. The arrival of the Prince Regent to live with his mistress in '83, and the restorative values of drinking and bathing in seawater, had set the seal on Brighton's development, making it the most thriving seaside resort in the country. Life there was chic, dashing and extremely enjoyable, its reputation as a centre of frivolity and fashion well established.

The Prince Regent had acquired a small house, which he had enlarged. Over the years bits were added onto it in all directions. People at this time were fascinated by China and India, and it was at this house, which became the Royal Pavilion, that the eastern fantasy was born. It was transformed into the most exotic and outrageous of all European palaces. Most people loved or hated it. Judith loved it, the onion-shaped domes and minarets that made up the skyline of the Pavilion reminding her so much of her beloved India.

Having been to her room to tidy her appearance after the journey, Judith joined her aunt in the drawing-room that overlooked the Steine. Cynthia Wyatt was forty years of age, with neat brown hair and plain though not unattractive features. Once slender, her bosom and waist had thickened and she now had a matronly look. Her air was not conciliating, and Judith always felt a sense of unease when in her presence. Seated on a gold and green sofa pouring afternoon tea, the older woman's face, paler than usual due to her recent illness, was one of deep concentration.

'How are you feeling now, Aunt Cynthia? Better, I trust,' Judith inquired with some concern, seating herself opposite.

Cynthia nodded. 'I am tolerably well. It was just a gastric ailment—nasty while it lasted, that caused me to cut my visit to France short.' She looked across at her niece, lifted one brow and frowned. 'You've dressed your hair differently, Judith,' she stated, in such a way that Judith wasn't sure if she approved of the softer style she had adopted or not.

Self-consciously she brushed a loose curl from her face. 'Yes. Charlotte persuaded me—she said it made me look less like a school-ma'am. Do—you like it?' she asked hesitantly.

'It suits you. It's certainly more fashionable and makes you look less severe.'

Judith almost dropped the teacup she was holding into her lap. Compliments from Aunt Cynthia were a rarity indeed. Taking a sip of the fragrant beverage, she studied her aunt over the rim. There was something different about her. Her expression was as cool as it always was when they were together, but there was an excitement behind it. She seemed to be suppressing some inner emotion. Judith didn't have to wait to find out.

'I'm glad you managed to get down to Brighton—although I hope I did not concern you unduly when I mentioned in my letter that I was unwell. It was considerate of you to cut your stay with the Grants short, and I hope you're not too disappointed. Still, I'm glad you came, for there is something I have to tell you that will affect you.'

Judith placed her cup on the small round table between them. 'Oh?'

'Mr Wakeman has made me an offer of marriage, and I've accepted. You are aware that we have known each other some considerable time, so it shouldn't come as any surprise.'

This was true, but Judith was surprised enough to look at her aunt with unaffected astonishment. Her thoughts were in such disorder that she couldn't say anything at all immediately. Aunt Cynthia had always dreamed of marrying a title and mingling with the real aristocracy, of wearing sumptuous gowns and dancing in marble ballrooms, but it wasn't to be. After all her years as a spinster—hoping for something better—she realised that marriage to Mr Benedict Wakeman, a lawyer who had a legal practice in Chichester, fifty, small and balding, who doted on her with excessive admiration, was the best she was ever likely to get. Quietly studying the look in her aunt's eyes, Judith could see they were filled with bitterness and something very like despair, and she found herself feeling sorry for her.

'This is not the first time Mr Wakeman has asked you to marry him, Aunt Cynthia,' Judith returned after a short silence, 'and you have always rejected his proposal.'

'Be that as it may, Judith, but I am not getting any younger, so this time I have taken his offer seriously. Benedict is a quiet man and will suit me admirably.'

'Then I hope you will both be very happy.'

'Of course it will mean selling this house.'

Judith's throat tightened and she had a strange, tremulous feeling inside. The pain of losing Jordan was so deep she didn't know how she would endure it, and to be told she was to be denied her visits to Brighton, too, was almost too much.

'Of course, now you are about to embark on your teaching career,' her aunt continued, 'you will be spending more of your time in London, but you must feel free to visit us in Chichester any time you wish.' Suddenly a thick gold chain exposed between the side of her niece's collar and her throat caught her attention. 'What is that you're wearing around your neck, Judith?' she asked. 'It looks far too heavy for comfort—or to have concealed beneath your dress.'

Judith hastily put a hand to her throat, feeling a loop of the chain holding the diamond. 'Oh—it—it's nothing, really,' she said nervously, trying to shove it back inside her dress.

'No, don't hide it,' her aunt said, leaning forward. 'Let me see.'

'It's nothing, Aunt.'

'I insist on you showing it to me.'

Reluctantly Judith complied. Moving closer, her aunt peered at it with wide-eyed astonishment, clearly impressed.

'Goodness! Where on earth did you get it?'

'It—it was given to me.'

'By whom?' she demanded.

Judith stiffened. 'If it is all the same to you, Aunt—I choose *not* to answer your question.'

Cynthia bristled, quite incensed. 'Really, Judith! Your insolence is not to be borne. You are being most unreasonable. Until you are of age I am your guardian—the nearest relation you have in the world. You cannot deny the claims of duty and gratitude. I am entitled to know what concerns you.'

'You are not entitled to know what I do not choose to tell you,' Judith answered resentfully, for to reveal how the pendant came to be in her possession was impossible. 'On this matter I have reason for silence and will not be explicit.'

Cynthia eyed her niece suspiciously as a dreadful thought occurred to her. 'It isn't stolen? You must give me assurance of that.'

'Of course it isn't stolen,' Judith gasped, offended that her aunt should ask such a question of her.

Cynthia reached out and took the pendant in her hand to give it a closer inspection. 'I'm no expert on these matters, but I have seen enough jewels around the throats of others to recognise quality when I see it. It could be valuable.' There was a very determined expression on her face and a sudden gleam in her eyes, and she smiled a thin, greedy smile. 'You must sell it.'

Judith gasped, appalled by the suggestion. 'No—I cannot. I wouldn't dream of doing such a thing. Besides, I have every intention of returning it.'

'You are talking in riddles, Judith,' Cynthia said, getting up, her taffeta skirts rustling crisply. 'Either it is yours or it isn't. I'll arrange for someone to examine it who will tell us its worth.'

Judith gave her aunt a sharp, resentful look, knowing she saw the necklace as the means of stepping into a different world, but said no more on the subject. That avaricious gleam in her eyes was even more apparent. She looked hard, very hard indeed, and Judith knew she would not give up the point. No doubt she would endeavour to coax and threaten until she got her own way.

Mid-morning the following day found Judith walking on the beach, her feet bare and her hair flowing behind her in the breeze blowing off the sea. She was trying to recover her spirits, and to dwell without interruption on the subject that was closest to her heart. Not even the warm sun on her face and the smell of the sea could relieve the deep sadness that engulfed her. Everything seemed so empty and meaningless without Jordan—hopeless, even.

Carrying her shoes, she strolled past the fishing-boats drawn up onto the shingle, and the bathing-machines, where the dippers were already hard at work submerging the bathers in the water. Eventually she came to a rocky stretch that was quite deserted. With her skirt and petticoat bunched in front of her, wistfully she clambered over the rocks, gazing down into the rock pools to see how many sea creatures the tide had left behind. Taking pity on a small kittiwake that appeared to have injured its wing, she put down her shoes and picked it up, cradling it gently in her hands to assess the damage. One of its pale grey, black-tipped wings hung limp, but otherwise it was quite robust. Stroking its head with her finger, she turned, intending to make her way back, speaking softly to calm the bird's fear, and wondering what to do with it.

In the distance she saw a man with his tan jacket hooked over his shoulder walking towards her. He was too far away for her to see his face clearly, but there was something familiar about his gait. He was very tall, with the same dark hair and taut grace, the same air of cool self-possession as Jordan. She looked into the sun's glare, blinking hard, telling herself that she was losing her mind, that it was her imagination playing tricks on her. But she sensed it was him. It was as if some tangible, powerful force told her so. She even recognised the elusive, tangy smell of his cologne, borne to her on the warm breeze.

On trembling limbs, still holding the injured bird in her hands, she stood stock still and waited, her heart pounding as she looked with loving eyes at his tall form, afraid to blink lest he disappeared, afraid to move, gazing at that sternly handsome face that haunted her dreams and tormented every hour of every day.

The closer he came the harder her heart hammered in nervous anticipation, with a mixture of hope and dread as she recalled their parting. What was he doing in Brighton? Why had he come? she thought wildly.

Had he finally regained his memory of the night she had spent in his bed and come to claim the necklace?

Or, merciful God, hope upon hope, had he come for her? Had he come to tell her how much she meant to him, that he couldn't live without her and he could not marry Alicia?

When he stopped and a pair of penetrating grey eyes looked straight into hers, she was too afraid to speak, to move, as she gazed at the unbearably handsome face that towered above her, his broad shoulders blocking out her view of anything but him. His white shirt, tucked into doe-coloured breeches, was open at the throat to reveal the strong muscles of his neck, and she fixed her gaze on a small pulse she saw beating just below the surface. An expression she couldn't recognise flickered on his face, and his eyes seemed bright beneath the shading of his hair. Then he smiled, the smile she knew so well.

'Hello, Jordan,' she heard herself say. 'How are you?' She knew it was a stupid, inadequate thing to say, but she had to say something, and with her heart beating so fast she could almost hear it, she couldn't think of anything else.

Chapter Fifteen

All the way down to Brighton Jordan had been re-
hearsing in his mind what he would say to Judith, and
now he was with her he couldn't remember a thing.
When she lifted her eyes to his and he saw the quiet
yielding in their clear depths, it nearly sent him to his
knees. He wanted to lose himself in her eyes, to pull
her into his arms and unburden his heart. Taking a
neutral course, he looked at the bird.

'What happened?' he asked, reaching out and gently
brushing its white plumage with the backs of his lean
fingers, because he didn't know what the hell to say
to her.

Judith met his gaze and swallowed nervously, smiling with shy uncertainty. 'I—I found it among the
rocks. I think it's injured its wing, poor thing.'

The sound of her voice was so soft and sweet,
Jordan almost dragged her to him. Instead he threw
his jacket onto a rock and took the bird from her.
Placing it on the smooth sand, they watched as it
limped away. When Jordan looked at Judith again his
face was inscrutable.

'You're surprised to see me?'

'Yes. I—I never expected to see you here in Brighton. H-How did you know where to find me?' she asked softly.

'I called on your aunt and she told me you had gone for a walk on the beach. It wasn't too difficult to locate you.'

'Why are you here?' she asked, unable to bear another moment of this awful suspense. With her new understanding of her own feelings, how she wished she understood his.

Jordan's brows drew together, and he continued to study her. 'What brought me here today has nothing whatsoever to do with the restorative values of this seaside resort.'

'No—I don't suppose it has,' she whispered. Acutely aware of her dishevelled appearance, she ran an ineffectual hand through her hair, which hung down her back in a shining, tangled cascade, thinking what a sight she must look. But at the admiration she saw in his eyes, and the inexplicable, lazy smile that swept over his face as he surveyed her—from her head to her small and slender bare feet, she had the staggering impression that he actually liked what he saw, that the girl walking on the beach was far more appealing to him than the prim schoolteacher. She had thought never to see him again, and now he was here she wanted to weep with joy.

'H-how are you?' she asked, echoing the first words she had spoken, giving him no indication of how she felt.

'All things considered, I am remarkably well,' he assured her dryly, fixing her with a level stare, 'for a man who has made love to a woman and been unable to recall her identity. It did nothing for my male ego, my self-esteem or my pride—and a man is most sensitive about his pride. Only the remembrance that the woman I made love to on the night of the ball was passionate, warm and responsive acted as a balm of sorts. She had an ardour that matched my own—a woman I could not equate to Alicia.'

The words hit Judith with a jolt, and hot, embarrassed colour flooded her cheeks. She looked up at him in helpless appeal. 'Oh!' she whispered, the silky smoothness of her voice beset with confusion. 'You—you know? How did you find out?'

'I worked it out for myself after Tom Parry—the man who took me home that night told me that no sooner did we arrive at the house than you emerged and took charge. I must thank you for getting me to my room without waking the entire household. Although how you managed it is quite beyond me. Alicia confirmed what Tom had told me.'

'I see. How she must hate me.'

'In that you are correct,' he answered with wry amusement. 'But at this moment I don't know who she hates most. You or me.'

'Do—do you know everything?' she asked hesitantly.

'Almost everything. What I don't know, I am sure you will fill me in on,' he said, a softness entering his eyes. Idly he brushed a tumbled curl from her cheek, becoming preoccupied with the way the wind caught her hair, lifting the tresses so that they streamed out like banners. He admired the way it sparkled in the sunlight like rich, dark brown honey. Here in this open, relaxed setting, with the sky as blue as sapphire, and the sea as calm as a mill pond, he could see she was a very beautiful young woman. Her face was flushed with the sun and exertion, and her eyes on closer inspection were not so much hazel as amber and cinnamon.

'You have lovely hair,' he murmured. 'You should always wear it so.'

Judith laughed and smoothed it back with a careless gesture. 'I don't think Miss Powell would approve if I were to appear in class with it in such abandon,' she replied, seeking safety in light humour, but she was vibrantly aware of the compelling magnetism emanating from Jordan's powerful body standing so close to her own.

Once again Jordan's gaze captured hers, probing with a blazing intensity. 'When I awoke the morning after the ball—still under the influence of the narcotic a certain tavern-keeper had applied to my drink—for which he has yet to be brought to account, I was in a somewhat nebulous state. Finding Alicia in my bed confused me even more. My memory of everything that had occurred was unclear, with disjointed, faceless shadows flitting about in my mind.'

'You don't have to explain, Jordan.'

'Yes I do. I owe you that, at least. When Alicia told me she had been with me all night—that we had made love, I doubted it but I could not disprove it. And you let me go on believing it—which was quite wrong of you, Judith,' he admonished, 'but we will go into that later. I was soundly caught in a trap. Every time I thought of marrying Alicia, I was tormented with images of you. You see, my desire for you was unquenchable. It nearly drove me insane. Ever since that night you have put me through a living hell.'

His voice sounded harsh, as if forged from his chest. Reaching out, he threaded his fingers through her hair and framed her face with his hands, gazing down at her lovely golden features, knowing perfectly well that he deserved her hatred and contempt for what he had done to her.

'My behaviour to you that night was unforgivable—but I sincerely hope you can find it in your heart to do so, and allow me to put things right. Circumstances, I'm afraid, played a heavy hand upon my actions. When I realised that you were the one who had shared my bed—having touched you, and not being able to remember—I became most anxious to touch you again.'

'You did much more than touch,' she whispered shyly.

'I know—and I intend doing so again,' he told her fiercely. 'I intend taking you to bed and making love to you as thoroughly and leisurely as I can. I accept that the loss of your virtue was largely my fault, and I find the responsibility a heavy burden to bear. If I could turn back the clock and put everything right, I would, believe me, but it's too late for that. For a whole week I have been dying inside because of what I did to you.'

Judith gave him a tearful smile, feeling herself melting at the tenderness she saw in his expression. An aching lump began to swell in her throat. 'It's been a difficult week for me too.'

Unable to look at her a moment longer and not hold her, Jordan pulled her against him with stunning force, his mouth opening over hers in a kiss that demanded she return it with equal passion. With unbelievable joy Judith slid her hands up his chest and around his neck. Beneath the thin fabric of his shirt, his chest was solid and warm. She arched herself against his rigid thighs, and Jordan shuddered with pleasure, his hands caressing her back, and then pulling her hips tighter to him. He groaned aloud with rampaging desire, and with the pleasure of having her in his arms and feeling the sweet softness of her mouth.

Tearing his lips from hers, he placed scorching kisses on her cheek, her temples. 'Say you forgive me,' he murmured. 'Say it, Judith.'

All the forgiveness that filled her heart was in her eyes for Jordan to see, a forgiveness so intense he was humbled by it. And when she opened her mouth to tell him so he silenced her words with his lips, his kiss becoming hungry, searching, primitive and potent, sending her spinning off into another world of exquisite bliss. Slowly she began to resurface as the pressure of his lips lessened, but she didn't surface from the state of mindless pleasure until he broke contact with her mouth and raised his head.

Breathing deeply, Jordan looked down at her glowing eyes and soft mouth and had an impulse to bend his head and kiss them again, but a loud burst of laughter from a jolly party of people coming onto the beach snapped them both back to the present. Irritated by the lack of privacy available to them, he shot the group an irate, disapproving scowl.

'Let's find somewhere quiet where we can talk.'

Taking Judith's hand he led her towards a dry piece of sand close by. Lulled by his kiss and the lazy slap of the water on the shore, finding a place in the shade she sank down, tucking her feet beneath her skirts. A welcome breeze rippled off the water, and she turned her head better to feel its coolness on her cheeks. Jordan sat with his back against a rock and drew one leg up at the knee, resting his arm across it. A heavy, dark fall of hair had tumbled over his brow. With a casual gesture he brushed it back, before taking her hand once more and placing it to his lips. He looked into the wavering depths of her large, clear eyes, as if seeking the answer to some burning question.

'I want you to be perfectly honest with me, Judith. It is important to me that you tell me the truth, because ever since I discovered it was you I made love to that night, I've been in hell. Do you have any idea how much I hate myself—how I feel every time I think of what I did to you?'

'Please, don't,' she whispered.

She wanted to tell him that it was the most wonderful thing that had ever happened to her, that she had felt completely, incredibly, unconditionally his, and that if it were never to happen again, she would be content to live on the memory for the rest of her life. Her pride and her passion were waging a terrible war inside her. Jordan had given her no indication that he was looking for a permanent partner, a helpmate, and as things stood she could only assume that he wanted what women could give him, as a means to slake his physical lust. She wouldn't humiliate herself by letting him know how much she craved his kisses, his touch.

'I've said that you are forgiven,' she went on, 'even though you did think I was an Eastern dancing-girl and paid me generously for my services,' she said with a whimsical smile.

Jordan grimaced. 'I'm not proud of that, either.'

'Why did you go to the Crescent Moon that night?' she asked curiously.

'I knew that was where Khan's servants could be found when not attending their master. I hoped to find out more about Khan's visit to London, and to confirm my suspicion that he—and Minton—were behind what happened to me at Blackwall. Unfortunately,' Jordan remarked dryly, 'they must have seen me first—hence what followed.' Still holding Judith's hand, after a moment's silence he looked at her once more, his expression one of deep concern. 'For my peace of mind, what I must know is did I force you into my bed? Could you have got away from me?'

She gulped, nodding slowly. 'Yes,' she confessed, her voice a whisper. 'If I'd tried.'

'Then why didn't you?' Jordan questioned, his gaze searching hers.

'I—I don't know.' She sighed deeply. 'I've made such a mess of everything, haven't I? It was a mistake—I can see that now.'

'A mistake that cannot be put aside. So,' he murmured, his eyes gleaming seductively from beneath lowered lids, 'I can only assume that you stayed purely for your own enjoyment.'

'It looks like that,' she replied, her smile sheepish. 'My behaviour was quite shameless.'

'Absolutely,' he agreed. 'And outrageous.'

'Now you're mocking me,' she reproached lightly.

He grinned. 'No I'm not. You're much too adorable to mock.'

'And if I were to tell you that I acted purely on impulse?'

His lips twisted with cynicism. 'I can't imagine you doing anything on impulse. You're far too sensible for that—and I always thought you too prim and proper to let any man touch you as I did out of wedlock.'

'So did I, so what I did goes to prove I'm not always sensible. I can be extremely foolish.'

'The only foolish thing you've done was to climb into my bed. Do you regret your foolishness?'

Judith shook her head, and with a raw ache in her voice she said, 'No.'

Jordan saw tears shimmering in her lovely eyes, and watched one trace its way down her cheek. 'Thank God for that,' he said hoarsely. 'That was my second greatest fear.'

'And what was the first?'

'That I inadvertently hurt you,' he said, with something like despair in his voice.

He was looking at her hard, and she could almost feel the pain inside him, sharp as crystal pieces of ice. 'It's all right. You didn't hurt me. What I did was wrong. I knew the rules, and I broke every one of them when I climbed into your bed,' she admitted quietly.

'For God's sake, Judith,' he said, his voice edged with remorse. 'Will you stop exonerating me. I know what I am capable of when my ardour's aroused.'

She gave him a wayward smile. 'Since you put it like that, you certainly can't be complimented on your subtlety. But—you were most persuasive,' she murmured, tilting her head sideways and laughing lightly.

Jordan grinned. 'You have the advantage over me, but I have no doubt of my abilities.'

'I believe you. I'm sure you've proven yourself to countless ladies in the past.'

'True, but it is the one who has made the deepest impression that has eluded me. My only regret is that almost everything about that night is still obscure, and I despise my weakness.' His face suddenly grew sombre as he considered his next words. 'There is something else we need to discuss. I think you already know what I am going to ask.'

His voice was calm, much too calm, carefully modulated, and that worried Judith. She felt a weak, tremulous feeling inside. 'I think you want me to explain how it came about that Alicia found her way into your bed.' When he nodded she drew a long breath. 'You must believe me when I tell you that when I left I had no idea Alicia would step into it and pretend she had been there all night.' She went on to tell him the whole story, simply, without trying to hide the anger she had felt towards Alicia for her conniving interference and treachery.

Jordan listened without interrupting. Only when she had finished did he speak. 'And the necklace?' When she glanced at him sharply he smiled thinly. 'That is one thing I do remember about that night.'

'You—you thought I was a woman of ill repute and—'

'Gave you the necklace in receipt of your favours,' he finished, a brittle quality having entered his voice. 'Why did you keep it? Why didn't you take it off before your left my room?'

'I—I didn't intend to keep it,' she answered in a small voice, hoping he didn't think that. 'And just in case you are wondering, I have it safe around my neck. You must understand that when I left you I was not in full possession of my thoughts. To be quite honest, I forgot all about it until I returned to my room. After that it was too late. When you arrived at Landsdowne and announced your betrothal to Alicia— when I discovered the lengths she had gone to to secure you, I—I did consider giving it to her—'

'Why? To sanction her deceit?' Jordan said. His voice was mocking, his stare accusing and never wavering from her face.

Judith nodded. 'Something like that,' she admitted wretchedly.

Jordan was disappointed with her reply. 'One thing I have always admired in you is your determination always to speak your mind, your honesty and your courage, but this time the truth digs deep, Judith.'

She flinched, drawing away from him a little. The tenderness of a moment before was no longer evident. Jordan sat regarding her, his face an impenetrable mask. She realised suddenly that there was so much she didn't know about him, that he'd been a soldier in some of the most remote and savage areas of India for years—the ability to hide his thoughts was as much a part of him as his handsome features and dove-grey eyes. The tremulous feeling increased.

'Why are you looking at me like that?'

'Suppose you tell me why you didn't give Alicia the necklace?' he countered.

'You—might not like the answer.'

'Try me,' he clipped, refusing to spare her until he knew the whole of it.

She drew a long, fortifying breath, raising her eyes to his impassive face, speaking awkwardly. 'I—I thought—' Dropping her eyes, she faltered, unable to proceed beneath his penetrating gaze.

'I suppose it was when you thought that you might be carrying my child,' he said quickly, taking pity on her confusion and coming to her rescue.

She nodded, swallowing hard. 'Yes. I—I didn't know if a child might result from what we did to-gether,' she whispered, realising as she spoke that she would be adding more pain and guilt to his memory of that night.

'And has it?' he asked impatiently, his eyes as hard as ice floes.

She flushed. 'I don't know. It—it's too soon to say.'

He nodded, continuing to look at her, his face expressionless. 'And what did you intend doing about it—should you find yourself *enceinte*? Would you have had the child adopted?'

Bristling at his crisp tone she looked at him sharply, deeply offended by his question. 'No. I would never do that,' she answered fiercely. 'Whatever my circumstances, I would never part with my own child. It's just that—I hoped it wouldn't happen.'

'Why? Does the thought of bearing my child bring you such misery?'

'Of course not,' she answered, repaying his sarcasm with characteristic honesty. 'I would be proud to bear your child, Jordan, and I would not fail it—but I would prefer not to do so out of wedlock. I have no wish for any child of mine to bear the stigma of illegitimacy.'

His eyes were hard and probing. 'And if there should be a child, did you intend informing the father?'

'I confess that my mind shied away from any confrontation with you, but I have examined very carefully what I would do, and was forced to conclude that I would tell you. I firmly believe that every man has a right to know his child, and every child its father. That was why I kept the necklace,' she explained, conscious of the diamond caressing her bare skin between her breasts. 'It would prove beyond doubt that I was the woman in your bed that night, and that the child was yours.'

'And did you not consider the dire consequences of telling me I had fathered a child when I was married to Alicia?'

'I would have found out before you married her. I would have told you, and after that the rest would be up to you. But one thing you must understand, Jordan, is that if I should find myself in such a delicate condition, I had thought of going away until after the birth. I wouldn't want anything from you. The last thing I wanted was for you to feel under any obligation to me.'

Jordan sighed, feeling the tension of the last few moments go out of him. Reaching out, he gently caught her shoulders and drew her close beside him so that she leaned against the rock. Holding her in his arms he turned her to face him. Desire was there in his silver gaze, and something more, something so profound it held Judith spellbound. 'You little fool. I am going to marry you,' he said finally. 'I will make you my wife—child or no child.' For a moment Jordan thought that she was not going to answer him, and when she did it was in a whisper.

'Your—your wife? I—I did not think... When—when I left Landsdowne I never expected to see you again. Please don't feel you have an obligation towards me.'

'I don't.'

Judith stared at him, knowing he was doing the honourable thing because he had taken her virtue and because there was every possibility that she might be carrying his child. Not for one moment did she delude herself into believing he loved her, but how she wished he would say it, even if he didn't mean it. She had no doubt that she was deeply and irresistibly in love with him, and she would nurse her secret until, God willing, in time he would come to feel the same about her.

When he spoke his voice was low and his eyes gleamed, so gentle, so full of tenderness. 'Any man would be proud to have you as his wife, Judith.'

'But—you're a gentleman,' she said. 'I'm a nobody—a schoolteacher. Men of your class don't marry women like me. Your friends—society—would reject you. You'd be ostracised. It wouldn't be right, Jordan. I'm not of your world—whereas Alicia is.'

'I think I should be the judge of that. And, anyway, do you seriously believe that would matter to me? If so you do not know me.'

Judith unclasped the necklace and pulled it out of her dress, handing it to him. 'This is yours. Keep it safe, Jordan. It's beautiful—and extremely valuable, too, I imagine. If my aunt could have her way she would sell it and live off the proceeds for the rest of her life.'

Jordan looked down at the exquisite gem for a moment before bringing his gaze back to hers. The wind ruffled his hair, and giving her a rueful smile he got to his feet. 'If she were to do so, she would be able to live like a queen, and no mistake.' Taking Judith's hand, he hoisted her to her feet, picking up his jacket. Taking a handkerchief from an inside pocket, he wrapped the necklace in it and put it back, casually hooking it over his shoulder. 'When we are married I will shower you in jewels, my love,' he said, placing his free arm about her waist as they slowly made their way back along the now empty beach. 'Unfortunately, this particular jewel is not mine to give.'

'Who does it belong to?'

'The Ranee of Ranjipur—the Rajah's widow. When he died of injuries he received in a riding accident, his wife was in Calcutta visiting her family. Knowing the state of Ranjipur would be annexed and all his treasures confiscated, before he died the Rajah placed the necklace in my care—to give to his wife. When he entrusted it to me I had no idea of the trouble it would bring. The jewel—which at one time would have been worn in a turban and belongs to the state regalia, has been prized by various owners in his family for hundreds of years, and he was reluctant to surrender it to the British.'

'He must have trusted you a great deal to place it in your care.'

'He did. Over the years we became close friends. It was an affection that survived until his death. After that a revolt ensued—led by Prince Chandu, who wanted to proclaim himself ruler and make the state of Ranjipur independent. Afraid for her own life and that of her only surviving daughter, his wife—along with her daughter and a large contingent of servants—

left for Bombay, where they boarded a ship for the Red Sea. From there they travelled overland to Alexandria, where I have learned the Ranee has decided to spend a little time. I expect her to arrive in England very soon, when I shall be able to relieve myself of the necklace.'

'And what happened to Ranjipur? I recall you telling me that it was annexed by the British.'

'It was. Ranjipur is of strategic importance to the British, and what Prince Chandu intended was not acceptable to them. They stormed the Rajah's palace. Many people on both sides died in the fighting. Prince Chandu escaped back to his own lands and there he remains.'

'So, apart from the necklace, all the Rajah's wealth became the property of the British?'

'Some of it—gold and jewels beyond anything you and I could imagine. Prince Chandu creamed off most of it before they could get to it.'

'Goodness! I can't believe I've been carrying such a precious object around my neck all this time. Is this the reason behind my abduction and the assaults on you, do you think?'

'Yes. I'm certain Prince Chandu has promised Jehan Kahn and Minton a bounty if they can retrieve it.'

'Why do you hate Lord Minton so much, Jordan?' she asked, glancing up at him. 'It was evident to me when the two of you came face to face on the night of the ball.'

Pulling away from her, Jordan became perfectly still, his stare hot and unblinking on the distant horizon. Judith saw something move in the depths of his eyes, and his body tensed. She was reminded of the tell-tale twitch of a stalking tiger's tail, precursor to the kill. He was a seething mass of feelings, and the first emotion to erupt was anger.

'Because the man is a sadist and a murderer. He enjoys hurting people weaker than himself. He is also totally corrupt and stands accused of colluding with the Thugs—professional stranglers, their ranks consisting of thieves and brigands.' He glanced at Judith. 'You will have heard of them.'

Judith nodded. Yes, she knew all about the incredible secret society that roamed India in gangs in the guise of pilgrims and merchants. It was a murder organisation which befriended travellers before strangling them with a cloth, in one corner of which was knotted a silver coin consecrated by the Kali, the goddess of destruction—which gave a religious backing to their activities, although they were not above making a profit out of the proceedings.

'Then you will know that local rulers sometimes protect this fanatical sect, and share their ill-gotten gains, overflowing their coffers with jewels and rupees beyond price. Minton was one of them, and he made my life as a soldier trying to track down these murderers—to make it safe for travellers to go about their business—almost impossible. His greed knew no bounds.' His voice became low and trembled slightly. 'I also hold him responsible for the death of the

Rajah's eldest daughter. To me, this was the blackest of all his crimes.'

'Why?'

'She was married to Chandu's son when she was just fifteen. At sixteen he died and she was to become suttee.'

A chill stole over Judith and she shuddered. Suttee, belonging to the higher castes of Hinduism, was the custom of burning widows alive on the funeral pyres of their husbands. It was a holy practice, one which Judith thought hideous and cruel. The widow had to die painfully, and should she escape the flames, she could expect no pity from her own people, who would push her back onto the pyre. It was a practice the English sought hard to abolish, but it still went on.

'At the earnest request of the Rajah, who considered suttee a hateful business despite it being an accepted part of his religion, my superiors sent me to Prince Chandu to prevent it.'

'And did you?' Judith asked in a small, hopeful voice.

He nodded, his expression grim. 'On the whole I respect the customs of India, and I understand why the English are slow to interfere with a custom sanctioned by religion, but the practice of condemning widows to a fiery hell cannot be right. If it has to be, then the act must be voluntary, and there are widows who love their husbands so much they choose to burn with them of their own free will. But nine times out of ten they go to the flames in terror.'

'I know. I have heard of the practice, but I've never witnessed it. It's suicide.'

'Which is not a crime to the Hindus—but murder is, and I consider it murder forcibly to burn widows. I knew the Rajah's daughter. Her name was Anjali. She was full of laughter, kind and gentle, and her father adored her. When her husband lay dying, she wrote to her father, begging him to come for her. Prince Chandu would not allow it, so I went in his place. When I arrived Anjali's husband was already dead. I appealed to Chandu to allow Anjali to return to her father, but he refused my request.

'I sought out Minton, but he had the ear of Prince Chandu and would do nothing. He had power in the district and he could have halted the suttee—had he wished. He chose not to do so. I already knew what little regard he had for honour and fair play when a generous bribe was being dangled beneath his nose like a carrot to a donkey. I have no doubt Chandu rewarded him handsomely for his co-operation. That was the moment the matter became personal.'

Jordan's voice, so flat a moment before, shook with a restrained fury. 'With no time to spare I had to act quickly, and on the night before the funeral, myself and two of my most experienced soldiers stole into Chandu's palace and rescued Anjali and took her back to her father.

'Nothing was heard from Chandu, and as the months went by everyone thought the matter was ended. But Chandu was like a sleeping tiger. He believed it was his duty to his dead son to see that his widow died. By her pain she would release her husband from the burdens of his earthly sins, earning him aeons of blessedness in heaven. When the Rajah left his palace to seek enlightenment on a pilgrimage to the holy places, Chandu sent men to capture her. They succeeded and took her back.'

Judith felt herself trembling, and gooseflesh lifted the hairs on the back of her neck.

'The distraught Ranee sent for me and I went after Anjali, but I was too late.' A fine sweat had broken out on his temples and his fists were clenched. His mouth closed tight for a moment, until he found the strength to go on.

'I will never forget it. I will never forget the swaying crowd, the chanting of the holy men—the lonely figure of a young girl, half crazed with terror as she was bound and forced onto the pyre. I still hear her screams. There was nothing I could do but watch as the fire consumed her, feeding avariciously on that small thing in its midst, the noise it made sounding so much like the roaring in my ears. I couldn't even get near her to put a bullet in her heart to hasten her death.

'I watched until her screams died with her, when her spirit had begun its journey on a road to heavenly beatitude, to lie beside that of her husband, beyond the reach of man's cruelty. Beside the pyre I saw Minton and Chandu seated on gilded chairs. Chandu was attired in flowing robes of crimson and gold and decked in rubies. They were gloating—laughing.'

Momentarily falling silent, Jordan recalled that the hard look he had given Minton had only been a small measure of the fury that had possessed him—fury at Minton for allowing the burning of Prince Chandu's beautiful, sixteen-year-old daughter-in-law to take place, and his own inability to prevent it.

'Half mad with fury, I wanted to kill Minton,' he continued at length, 'to throw him into the flames, and I couldn't for the life of me remember why I couldn't, beyond the fact that he was an Englishman like myself.'

Sick and outraged by what he had told her, Judith had been holding her breath and now let it out. She slowly began to understand his hatred of Lord Minton, and the look of strain on his face. Not knowing what to say, she squeezed his hand, feeling the tension going out of him with the end of the story. He smiled briefly, then put an arm round her and pulled her towards him.

'So you too have your demons—like me,' she murmured, meeting his gaze quietly. 'What happened to me is in my memory like the ache of an unhealed wound—as it is with you. I'm sorry, Jordan. I wish I could say something to make it easier. But I can't. Nothing can alter what has happened—or bring Anjali back. People say that time is a great healer. They are usually right but not always.'

Jordan looked down at her. The sheer intensity of his feelings seemed to resonate along the empty shore. Her eyes and the quiet, unblinking way she had of looking at a person reminded him of some ancient mystic—as though she could see a good deal farther than most people. Her face was calm and full of understanding. It was also looking at him with an expression that made him lower his head without conscious thought. The kiss he placed on her lips was brief and tender, yet as remarkable in its impact as though they had just plighted their troth.

He raised his head, but the warmth of it lingered on Judith's lips, so that she could still feel it. She breathed in the taste of it, seeking to hold on to it. The moment was interrupted by the raucous cry of a gull swooping overhead.

'Come back with me to London,' Jordan said. 'I want you with me—so I'll know that you're safe.'

'As much as I would like to, I can't go with you, Jordan. Not just now. I would like to spend a little time in Brighton with Aunt Cynthia. She is to be married soon and will be moving to Chichester.' She smiled, standing on her toes and planting a light kiss on Jordan's lips in an attempt to alleviate his concern. 'I'll be all right. Don't worry about me.'

'But I do. My darling girl,' he said softly. 'You gave me all of yourself, and held nothing back. You give me honesty when I ask for it—it isn't in you to lie and I thank God for it. I won't lose you now I've found you, Judith.'

She frowned, looking at him steadily. 'You speak as if you are afraid something will happen?'

'I don't know. I hope not.' His voice was just as fast as the possessive tightening of his arm round her waist once more. 'We are bound, you and I, and noth-

ing is going to part us. We will be married very soon.
I promise.'

'I would like that,' Judith whispered, her eyes shining with happiness.

Chapter Sixteen

When Jordan had left Brighton, later that day, with the sun sinking in a blaze of crimson on the horizon and still basking in the glow of his embrace, Judith returned to the beach to mull over everything that had happened.

On meeting Jordan, her aunt had been impressed, telling Judith as she watched his splendid carriage drive away that he was a fine-looking man. When he had said farewell to the woman he intended to wed, it was more than interest that had lingered in his eyes, and her aunt had curiously enquired as to his reason for coming to Brighton. Judith had calmly told her it was to collect the necklace, but her aunt had not been deceived.

Swallowing her disappointment over the loss of the precious necklace, Cynthia had cautiously asked if there was anything in their relationship. Judith had merely smiled secretly, not yet ready to share her confidence with anyone. The future that had looked so bleak and meaningless without the man she loved was suddenly filled with hope.

In the dying light of the setting sun she returned to the house, taking no notice of the carriage standing close by. All the windows were dark, and then she remembered that her aunt was visiting a friend a few streets away. The first thing she heard on opening the door was someone moving about in the drawing-room.

'Aunt Cynthia!' she called, thinking the maker of the noise must be her aunt, having come home early. 'I didn't expect you—'

The words died on her lips as she pushed the drawing-room door open. The fading light revealed a man searching through the drawers of a large dresser and carelessly discarding things onto the floor, his huge frame seeming to fill the whole room as he worked. She stopped dead at the sight of the intruder and choked back a scream, every instinct telling her even before he turned that it was Lord Minton.

The shock of recognition when he greeted her with a profoundly mocking bow was mingled with incredulity.

'You are alone?'

She nodded.

The sharp eyes flickered back and forth between her and the door, as if assessing her truthfulness. Instinctively Judith knew why he had come. He must suspect her of having the necklace—although how he had come by the knowledge was quite beyond her just then. Trying not to show her fear, she threw him a cold glance.

'What are you doing here?' she asked, struggling with the nervous tension that was sapping the strength from her quaking limbs. 'You have no right to be in this house. How did you get in?'

With a flick of his eyes he indicated the window her aunt had left unlatched. 'It wasn't difficult,' he said in his deep baritone voice. 'Pardon me for not bothering to knock,' he drawled, 'but there was no one at home to let me in.'

'What are you looking for? There is nothing here that could possibly belong to you. Please go away.'

He laughed, and under the drooping lids the pupils of his eyes seemed to burn. 'No, lady. You'll have to put up with me for a bit. I stay until I have what I came for.'

'There is nothing here that could possibly interest you,' she seethed. Her voice was shaking and her hands were clenched in the folds of her skirt, the fabric clutched between her fingers. 'I have nothing to give you.'

'Ah, Miss Wyatt, that is where you are quite wrong,' he countered, feeling his jaded senses coming to life as he watched the tiny pulse throbbing just above her collar-bone. In her anger she was so young and fragile, and wary. 'You have two things that interest me.'

The lurid smile that stretched his lips as he looked her over left Judith in no doubt about his meaning. Fear began to claw at her stomach, and a spark that forbade acquiescence appeared like heat at the back of her eyes.

The sight of it filled Lord Minton with anticipation. 'I told you at the ball that we had something to discuss,' he went on, 'and I see you are at liberty to be of assistance to me now.'

His threat combined with the physical bulk of the man—the sheer power of him—made Judith tremble. Out of the corner of her eye she glimpsed her aunt's long, silver paper knife on her desk where she wrote her letters. She grabbed for it and brought it to bear in front of her. 'Stay away from me,' she hissed, mustering firmness through her fear.

Lord Minton's face remained calm when he looked at her. Her opposition was the most piquant thing he had felt in months. His laughter was brutally mocking. 'Your hand trembles. I do not think you have the strength to hold the knife, let alone use it.' Slowly, confidently, he walked towards her. She backed away and he laughed again.

An onrush of panic was loosed within Judith's mind. She turned to flee, but Lord Minton's arm shot out, knocking the paper knife from her hand. Suddenly she was caught and held fast in an iron grip. Holding her with one hand, he produced a thin cord from his jacket pocket and quickly bound her wrists firmly together behind her.

Her cry of pain echoed hollowly in the room. 'How dare you!' she cried, appalled and angered by the ferocity of his assault. 'Let me go.'

His eyes glittering with a singular malice, he took her arm and yanked her towards him, twisting his fingers in her hair, forcing her head back, and kissed her with a deliberate brutality that made her squirm. His

hands pressed the fabric over her breasts and her horrified gasp only provoked more laughter.

He spoke harshly into her ear. 'You little bitch. Did
you think I would let you escape me—especially now
when I know that *he* wants you?' The *he* he referred
to being Jordan, which Judith understood. 'Even in
temper you're a pleasing sight.'

With an acrobatic litheness that amazed him, Judith
writhed away from him and spat in his leering face.
He struck her with the speed of a snake, catching her
across the mouth with the back of his hand. She tumbled to her knees at his feet, blood welling from her
bruised lips.

Her hair awry, tears streamed down her cheeks, but
she glared at him without blinking, her eyes snapping
up at him with a promise of vengeance, letting the
stinging pain serve to feed her anger. 'You'll pay for
that,' she seethed. 'I swear it.'

Lord Minton jerked her back to her feet by a fist in
her hair, the cocksure smile acquiring a malevolent
twist. 'I think not, lady.'

'What are you proposing to do with me?'

'Since you ask, unless you produce the necklace—
which I know Grant gave to you—I intend to enjoy
myself with that soft little body of yours until you're
black and blue, before wringing that pretty neck. In
fact,' he murmured, the evil in his eyes plain for her
to see, even though they were half shuttered, 'I have
a mind to do that in any case. It would be worth elim-
inating you in order to get at Grant—to punish him
for past slights, and destroy him for ever.' The young

woman's tear-stained face was a real mask of terror, and he savoured her panic.

Her lips throbbing from the blow, Judith was certain that Lord Minton's clear, ruthless mind, which had done nothing to halt the burning of a terrified young widow, would not hesitate to end her own life. She was in the clutches of a depraved and dangerous man, and she could see no way of escape. 'And if I tell you that I don't have the necklace?'

'I wouldn't believe you.'

She swallowed nervously. 'How is it that you are so well-informed?'

'In my position it is a matter of life or death to know as much as possible—about friends and foes—and it is often in my best interest to make the acquaintance of the friends of my foes.'

'You talk in riddles, Lord Minton,' Judith scoffed, her watchful eyes shining like stars in the dim light. 'I think what you are saying is that someone has betrayed Jordan to you.'

'Shall we say a certain lady was none too pleased about being passed over by Grant for you.'

'Alicia!' Judith gasped, remembering seeing the two of them together at the ball, and the camaraderie that had sprung up between them. 'So—she has acted from sheer spite.'

Lord Minton's smile was chilling. 'Exactly. A typical example of a woman scorned, you might say. Now, tell me where you have hidden the necklace. As you see, I have searched the house from top to bottom.' His eyes narrowed, fastening on her bosom. 'Maybe it's not so far away from me, after all.'

With a sudden jerk, he ripped the fabric of her gown and shift to her waist, revealing her exquisite flesh.

Reacting instinctively, Judith kicked him hard on the shin. 'How dare you,' she shrieked, her voice trembling with outrage rather than fear. 'You loathsome animal. I no longer have the necklace, I tell you. I gave it to Jordan when he came earlier. You're too late!'

Lord Minton stiffened, his eyes gleaming like twin daggers. The full force of his rage was ready to explode. 'Grant? He's been here?'

'Yes,' she flung at him, wishing her hands were free so she could cover her partially exposed breasts. 'He has taken the necklace back to London.'

Again Lord Minton yanked her hair, pulling her close. She uttered a yelp of pain as the roots dragged at her scalp, and he laughed fiendishly. 'So, this changes things. He has the necklace. I have you. It will be interesting to see just how valuable you are to him.'

'Jordan will never yield to the demands of a blackmailer,' she spat, giving him a scalding glare.

'He will, if he wants you back alive. A valuable hostage against the release of the diamond? Oh, yes. I am sure he will consider my demands very seriously when he receives my note. I made a serious mistake in thinking you were of no consequence to him when I took you the first time.'

'So it was you who abducted me.'

'And let you go. I can see now that I should have held onto you.'

'And Mr Khan? Was he a party to it?' She had no wish to bandy words with him, and yet she could not help but be curious.

'Khan?' His lips twisted scornfully. 'No. He thinks as ill of me as I do of him—just like Grant and me.' His face darkened with a malevolent frown, hatred leaping from his close set eyes. 'Now there's a man I'd take pleasure in killing—slowly. Every slight, every time he gave orders and expected me to obey, every time that bastard looked down his nose at me, I remember—and he'll pay for it. I would like to see all that arrogant power brought to its knees and humbled.

'Khan and I are only together out of necessity. He's a fool and also expendable. He wants to retrieve the necklace for no other reason than to secure his own position at the court of Prince Chandu—a man I am certain Grant has told you about. Khan has been sent to England not only to retrieve the annexed state of Ranjipur for Chandu, but also the diamond, and Chandu will not care to hear of two failures. Unless one of his missions is accomplished, Khan will die.'

'Perhaps he will remain in London.'

'Chandu's arm is far-reaching. It is one or the other—the state of Ranjipur, or the diamond.'

'Whereas you want the diamond for yourself.'

'Exactly.'

'Even though it will mean you leaving England for good.'

'If I have the diamond, when I have turned such a treasure into money, the gain to myself will be well worth the sacrifice. The British and the charges hanging over me can go to hell. Where I am going they will never find me.'

'Jordan was right about you. I believe you would sell your soul to the devil for the right amount of money. You said yourself that Prince Chandu's arm is far-reaching,' she reminded him coldly, her look one of profound disgust. 'If that is so then I would advise you to find a very deep hole in which to hide.'

Lord Minton shrugged his shoulders, unperturbed by this. 'I know the east. There are places I know of where not even Chandu will be able to find me.'

'And Mr Khan has no idea of your nefarious plot, and that you have come to Brighton?'

'None.'

'I see. What was he doing in Greenwich on the day I encountered him?'

Lord Minton shrugged. 'Curiosity, mainly. He wanted to see where Grant lived, hoping to search the house. He soon gave up on the idea.'

'And were you behind the assault on Jordan that day at Blackwall?'

'I was,' he admitted coolly, seeing no reason to deny it. 'Unfortunately I hired a pair of bungling, incompetent fools to do the work, and one of them ended up dead.'

'I know. I was there. And the night he was drugged.'

'That was Khan and myself. We suspected he might be carrying the necklace on his person, and we would have succeeded in searching him had not a group of his friends turned up and taken him home.'

'What are you going to do with me?'

His laugh was cruel. She was looking round the room like a cornered animal, obviously thinking of escape and calculating her chances. She was intelligent, and he sensed she would not give up easily. 'Why—I shall take you on board the boat I've hired that's waiting to take me to France. Unfortunately things have not gone as planned and I do not yet have the jewel I have long coveted. But with you to barter with, I don't believe I shall have long to wait. Now come along. We are wasting time.'

Taking her arm, he dragged her towards the door. Judith struggled and screamed deliberately, hoping to attract someone's attention.

'Screaming's useless,' Lord Minton hissed into her ear. 'There's no one to hear you, and the man on the box of my coach is my own servant. You will learn to keep your mouth shut, for there will be no other to help or protect you, save me.'

He pulled a gag across her mouth against further outcry and flung his iron-thewed arm around her. Lifting her off her feet, he carried her outside into the darkened street and shoved her into the waiting coach, where she fell upon the seat. Ordering the driver to take him to the boat, he climbed in after her and pulled down the shades.

Judith continued to struggle, to lash out with her feet, kicking him wherever she could, until a broad fist struck out, hitting her hard on the side of the jaw. Abruptly his accompanying words reverberated hollowly down that long final plummet and she slipped into total blackness.

On his return journey to Greenwich, Jordan indulged himself in the pleasurable occupation of dwelling on his future wife. Just thinking of her caused his chest to constrict with emotion, and there was an unfamiliar lump in his throat.

Closing his eyes, he leaned his head back, harbouring not the slightest doubt of what he felt for Judith. He loved her with a passion that was deeply rooted within his soul. She filled him with a feeling that was a mixture of awe, joy, and reverence, and he could not believe she had been the one who had sent him to unparalleled heights of desire and unequalled depths of satisfaction on that one night they had shared. The mere thought that already a child of his might be growing within her womb filled him with a feeling so intense, so profoundly proud, that he almost burst with it—although he did realise that for proprieties' sake, it would be best for their first child not to be born too soon into their marriage.

With regret, he realised that he had not made the depth of his feelings clear to her, and that he had failed to explain that he'd never known there were feelings like this, that he could neither see nor touch her without wanting to satisfy his craving for her. He also realised that he had not told her the most important thing of all—that he loved her.

He was a quarter of his way to London when the occupants of a carriage coming towards him caught his attention. The turbaned Indian was sitting ramrod straight and looking impassively ahead, his two servants facing him. Immediately all Jordan's senses were alert. It was Jehan Khan, and he was heading for Brighton. Why? And where was Minton? He had an acute premonition of danger—that Minton might already be in Brighton, seeking out Judith.

Ordering his driver to turn the carriage around, he tensed, his mind recklessly leaping ahead and climbing mountains before he'd reached the foothills. A vision of Judith completely at the mercy of Minton set his mind on fire. She could no more stand against him than a child.

It was dark when he arrived back at the house he had left just a short while ago.

'Oh, Lord Grant,' Cynthia said, letting him in. 'Thank goodness you're here. I really do not know what to do next.'

Her apparent distress and the state of the ransacked house sent a chill through Jordan. 'Miss Wyatt, please calm down and tell me what has happened.'

'Oh, dear! How I wish I knew.'

'Where is Judith?'

Cynthia slowly shook her head in absolute bewilderment. 'I really do not know. I've just arrived home after visiting a friend, and I find—this—and no sign of my niece. Who can have done this? What can it mean? Judith has completely disappeared.'

Pain lanced through Jordan. It was so sharp that he could scarce keep himself from shaking the woman in front of him. 'Disappeared? Are you certain? Have you looked for her?'

'No—I—I haven't had time.'

'When did you last see her?' Jordan demanded, clenching his hands in frustration.

'The last I saw of her was at about six o'clock. When I left the house she was getting ready to go for a walk on the promenade—which she does every evening when she comes to Brighton.'

'Could she have called on anyone—friends, perhaps?'

Cynthia shook her head. 'No. She never visits anyone unless I am with her.'

'What about the servants?'

'I—I only have the one, and she doesn't live in.'

'And when you left the house, did you see anyone loitering outside—a carriage, perhaps? Anything suspicious?'

'No, I don't recall seeing anything of a suspicious nature,' she answered, feeling uncomfortable beneath Lord Grant's probing stare, as if he thought it was her fault that Judith had gone missing. Suddenly he turned on his heel and strode towards the door. 'Where are you going?' she asked in alarm, having no wish to be left by herself in case the intruder returned.

'To look for her.'

'Oh, dear! Lord Grant, do you think she has been kidnapped—or worse?'

Jordan spun round, his manner abrupt. Then he saw the woman standing in the middle of the room wringing her hands, her eyes clouded with anxiety. Going back to her he laid a calming hand on her arm and forced his expression into less severe lines. 'You are jumping to conclusions. We do not yet know she has been harmed.'

'But—the person who did this,' she said, indicating the shambles all around her. 'Perhaps Judith interrupted him and he's taken her with him—or murdered her. Perhaps she is lying injured or dead somewhere. Oh, dear!' She placed her hands to her cheeks at the sheer horror of such a dreadful thing happening to her niece.

'I beg you do not distress yourself, Miss Wyatt. I am almost certain that I know the identity of the person who did this, and if I am right then I can assure you that it has nothing whatsoever to do with you. He came here to look for something he believed was in your niece's possession, and when he didn't find what he wanted he will have taken Judith. I fully expect him to communicate with me in some way.'

'Do you mean he will demand a ransom?'

Jordan stared at her wordlessly, his eyes a pale, misted grey.

'Dear God,' she cried, her voice vibrating about the room, in danger of being overcome by her emotions as her anxiety grew. 'Where can she be? Where can he have taken her?' Her eyes appealed to the man in

front of her. His face looked grim. Gone was the softness she had seen earlier, and the charm she had found
so appealing. In its place was a steely determination
of a battle-hardened soldier.

'I do not know. But I will find her,' he said, with
determination. 'I promise you that.' And he had to do
it before Jehan Khan got to Minton.

Jordan was striding down the path to speak to his
driver when a youth carrying a lantern appeared in
front of him. His eyes narrowed with suspicion. 'Who
are you, and what is your business with Miss Wyatt?'

'Name's Freddie Scales, sir,' the youth supplied,
holding something out to him that looked like a letter.
'Gentleman gave me this half an hour ago and told
me to deliver it to Miss Wyatt.'

Jordan took it. 'Who was this gentleman?'

'Dunno, sir,' Freddie replied, fidgeting awkwardly
on his feet beneath the penetrating stare.

'What is it?' Cynthia asked, coming out of the
house.

'A letter addressed to you—although I suspect there
are instructions inside asking you to have the letter
forwarded to me in London.'

'Then please open it quickly,' Cynthia whispered,
her voice frantic. 'I couldn't.'

Jordan ripped it open. He was right. The missive
was meant to be forwarded to him at Greenwich. After
scanning what was written he shoved it into his
pocket, his expression grim. 'I was right. She is being
taken to Dieppe.'

'France?' Cynthia gasped, horrified. 'Is she in danger?'

'Probably.' Jordan knew Judith would be feeling terrified, and the thought of her in Minton's power knifed through his heart and was enough to make him forget the necklace secure in his inside breast pocket.

Cynthia glanced at him as a thought occurred her. 'Lord Grant, why did you come back to Brighton?'

'It's a long story, Miss Wyatt. Under the circumstances I think an explanation will have to wait. I must go after Judith.' His expression was one of gravity when he looked at her. 'I will instruct my driver to remain at your house until I return, but for your own safety it might be advisable for you to seek the hospitality of one of your friends—for tonight, at least. There is someone else in Brighton who may call on you, and it would be best for you not to be here.'

She nodded. 'Yes,' she whispered. 'I will take your advice.'

Jordan looked at the youth. 'Freddie, where can I get a boat?'

Freddie looked vague. 'Nowhere I can think of. Not at this time o' night.'

'Think, lad,' Jordan said insistently. 'What does your father do?'

'Nothin'. He's dead—lost at sea in a squall, he was. I live wi' Rory—me brother.'

'And what does your brother do?' Jordan asked, trying hard not to show his frustration and impatience with the lad.

Freddie shuffled his feet uncomfortably. 'He's a fisherman.'

Jordan let out a long sigh of relief. At last he thought he was getting somewhere. 'And is your brother at home?'

'No, sir. He's wettin' his whistle at the Ship, and he'll not take kindly to being interrupted in his drinkin' after finishin' his day's work,' he informed the gentleman, intent on saving his own skin. Rory might treat the womenfolk in his house with something little short of reverence, but when it came to his young brother, he was not averse to giving him a cuff on the ear if he disturbed his hour at the Ship after a hard day's fishing.

'He will,' Jordan said with firm conviction, 'when faced with an offer he can't refuse. Come on, lad, take me to him.'

Cynthia went back inside the house, shaken and deeply shocked by Judith's disappearance, and she fervently hoped that whoever had taken her would let her go unharmed. However, she decided against leaving the house. She wanted to be on hand should Lord Grant find her and bring her back.

In her own way she had become fond of her niece, and had begun to look forward to her visits to Brighton. This was the main reason why she had informed her of her early return from the Continent, in the hope that she would find the time to come down— although she would never confess to it.

To openly display affection was something Cynthia found awkward, and it had been much easier to play on the gastric ailment that was troubling her at the time. It had not been serious and it had had the desired effect—although now she was beginning to regret ever having written to Judith. If she hadn't she would be safe and well in Greenwich with her friend Charlotte.

Chapter Seventeen

There was no shortage of taverns in Brighton, and Freddie took Jordan to one close to the front that catered for fishermen. Pushing open the low door they went inside, being met by a reek of alcohol, human sweat, and a babble of voices. Freddie took Jordan towards a table where a big man with skin like leather and piercing blue eyes beneath bushy black brows was sitting. He had a mug of ale in front of him, and was contentedly smoking a clay pipe. Immediately Jordan took the chair opposite.

'You are Rory Scales?'

'Aye,' Rory replied, quietly taking stock of the stranger. Humble fisherman he might be, but he was not unobservant. Neither was he a poor judge of men, and there was no mistaking the imposing, vigorous bearing of the man facing him, who carried himself with all the confidence of a seasoned soldier.

'Your brother tells me you have a boat.'

The man glanced at him dubiously and nodded. 'What of it?'

'I need one immediately to take me to sea. Can you help me?'

Rory shook his head, puffing thoughtfully at his pipe. 'You're the second man to approach me in the last three hours—and I'll tell you what I told him. Not tonight.'

'And why didn't you take him? Wasn't he generous enough?'

'Not generous enough for the risks involved. I wanted the money all right—but France?' He shook his head slowly. 'Didn't like the look of him, either.'

Jordan grinned thinly. 'I applaud your judgement. Still, someone must have been tempted by his offer?'

'Aye—a ne'er-do-well by the name of Jed Taylor— a drunk who beats his wife and anyone else who gets in his way when he's that way out. Mention of gold is always enough to make him prick his ears up. He'll do anythin' when he hears the jangle of coins.'

Jordan leaned forward, lowering his voice. 'Listen, Rory, it is imperative that I go after that boat. I must catch up with it before it reaches Dieppe. I am not without means, and I will more than double what the man offered. Will you take me? He has a woman with him—and I will tell you that she is not his sweetheart. She will not have gone willingly. I am obliged to go after her. It could be a matter of life or death.'

For a moment interest mingled with anger flickered in Rory's eyes. Cherishing the memory of his dead mother, being blessed with two little girls who were the apples of his eye, and a love for his wife, Letty, that verged on worship, he had no time for men who showed no respect for their womenfolk.

Fine and dandy the man was who had approached him earlier, but there had been something ugly beneath his skin, and the prospect of finding himself alone with him at sea made him shudder. He was certain the man had no scruples and would have sold his own mother for the right price, and killed her for a bit more. Leaning heavily across the table he thrust his face close to Jordan's.

'You're in luck. I'm a great respecter of women and don't like to hear of them being ill-treated, so I'll take you. But it depends.'

'On what?'

'Whether or not you pay half now.'

Jordan nodded, glad he'd had the presence of mind to bring some coins with him. Taking a purse from his pocket he discreetly passed it across to the fisherman. 'There's twenty guineas in there.'

Rory took it and pocketed it. 'Just so that's understood. And the rest?'

'Unfortunately I don't have any more money with me. I am Lord Grant, and I give you my word that I will have an equal amount sent to you as soon as I return to London—and more if we succeed.'

'And why should I trust your word, Lord Grant?' Rory allowed considerable scepticism to show in his voice.

Jordan arched his brows and fixed him with a level gaze across the table top. 'No one has ever had cause to doubt my word, Mr Scales.'

Rory sat for a moment, contemplating the other man, and then he nodded. 'Aye, I'll trust you. Just one more thing. Whatever you and that other chap are involved in is something that's no concern of mine. I reckon they've nearly an hour start on us, but the state Jed and his mate were in when they left here, they'll not be making good time so we should catch up with them in mid-Channel.' He turned to Freddie, who had been watching the proceedings with wide-eyed interest. 'Go home, lad. Tell Letty where I am and that she's not to worry.'

When Freddie had scampered out of the inn, Jordan turned to Rory. 'Did anyone see them leave?' he asked, wondering if anyone might have tried to stop Minton bundling a struggling woman into a boat—his mind refused to contemplate the thought that Minton might have rendered her incapable of fight.

'Shouldn't think so.'

'Is there anyone else we can recruit? Another man at the oars will make all the difference.'

'I can do better than that. Wait here.'

Rory returned accompanied by three more fishermen, tall and broad-shouldered, all eager to supplement their meagre incomes any way they could, and without question. With no need for conversation they hastened towards the beach, where boats were drawn up on the shingle above the high-water mark. Fortunately the tide had just turned and it didn't take them long to drag the boat into the water. Climbing in, they pushed it clear of the shore with their oars. It was a clear night. The moon's gleam painted the water in a silver sheen, and the stars were like a million eyes looking down on them.

'Shall we light the lantern?' Rory asked.

'No,' Jordan answered. 'The moon will provide us with enough light. Our friends in the other boat will have no idea they are being pursued, and I have no wish to alert them until it's too late for them to escape. Double your pace, lads, and I'll make it worth your while.'

With the creak and splash of the oars they put out to sea, rowing rhythmically and with precision, moving their whole bodies with every stroke. With nothing to see but the blackness of the water against the sky, Jordan scoured ahead for a light. Fortunately the sea was calm, with only the slightest swell.

There was a time when crossing the Channel at night would have been a risky business—when smuggling had been in its heyday, with contraband being brought across from the Continent on every tide. Now there was little chance of meeting the revenue cutters. The crime had declined since the end of the Napoleonic wars—not because the preventative system worked, but because the customs duties imposed no longer made it profitable.

It was close to midnight when Jordan saw the dull glow of a light bobbing in the far distance, alerting all his senses. 'Row, men—harder,' he said, speaking through gritted teeth. 'If that's our quarry we're gaining on them.' He took out his pistol and primed it.

'God in heaven! Is there to be shooting?' someone

gasped in a horrified voice.

'I hope not, but I know what I'm dealing with.'

When Judith regained consciousness there was a searing pain inside her head. Mercifully her wrists were no longer bound. Bruised and shaken by her rough handling, she found herself lying on the bottom of a boat, the stench of fish and bilge water turning her stomach. Hearing the gentle slap of water against the hull and the splash of oars, she knew she was at sea and drifting off into the unknown. Her heart sank with despair.

Someone was sitting close by speaking in low tones to the oarsmen. Lord Minton was no more than a silhouette, black against the lantern's glow. The close proximity of her kidnapper made her shiver, and she felt a sudden sense of panic sweep over her, and a premonition of the dangers that lay ahead of her in France.

As if sensing her scrutiny, Lord Minton turned his head. He observed the whiteness of her face, and how lifeless she was, and as always when he was in the presence of someone smaller and weaker than himself, her distress acted pleasurably upon him. It brought a vicious tang to his excitement when he thought of the pain and fury that would consume Grant when he discovered his intended bride had been abducted yet again.

'Sit there and be quiet,' he growled, her presence losing its flavour as he got to wondering if the lad he'd hired to deliver the note to the girl's aunt had done so.

His coach driver—who was also his personal servant and had been with him throughout his time in India—could have taken the letter direct to Grant at Greenwich, but wanting to stall for time until he was safely in France, and knowing it would take a little longer if he sent the letter via the girl's aunt, he'd decided to use the lad and instructed his servant to lie low for a few weeks, for it was vital that he avoided coming into contact with Jehan Khan.

Judith heard Lord Minton's words through a haze of exhaustion. With throbbing head and smarting eyes she saw the two oarsmen facing her, although with their backs against the moon it was impossible for her to make out their features. Who were they? she wondered. Fishermen, most likely, she decided, who had taken Lord Minton's money in return for the Channel crossing with no questions asked—which was why they totally ignored the existence of a helpless female aboard their boat.

She shrank closer to the side of the boat, away from the nearness of her abductor, resigning herself to the movement of the swaying boat. Looking up, she gazed with passionate intensity at the stars shining brightly in the sky. How she longed to escape from this hell Lord Minton was inflicting on her. It was a time of great peril and she felt like a frightened child without protection, drained of courage and all capacity for thought, helpless and without the smallest hope.

Her fatigue was such that she fell into a light doze, which gave her a moment's respite from her terror, in which she dreamed she was being held close in

Jordan's arms, and that he was whispering tender words of endearment from his lips. But the dream faded when noises penetrated the night air, the sound dragging her back to the world.

Suddenly something seemed to be happening. A voice shouted for them to heave to, causing Lord Minton to swear comprehensively. He stood up and ordered the two men to row harder, but already a boat was drawing alongside. The men stopped rowing and the boat began to rock to and fro as someone clambered aboard.

Judith's eyes became riveted on the figure, her thundering heart drowning out every other sound. She was able to distinguish his features in the light, and for a moment she thought she must be dreaming, but that keen, fine-boned face and firm lips, the unruly black hair being ruffled by the salt wind, were indelibly printed on her mind. Her heart gave a joyful leap and cried out his name long before her lips framed the word. 'Jordan!'

Suddenly a pistol exploded, shattering the night. Jordan fell to his knees beside Judith and let the ball pass harmlessly close to his ear, and he felt the breath of its passing upon his cheek. He cursed softly and fired his own pistol. There was a grunt as the ball hit its target, but Lord Minton was not sufficiently injured to give up without a fight. He was on his enemy like a flash, but despite his muscular bulk, in his weakened state and with a fire burning in his shoulder, he was no match for the other's might.

There was little room for manoeuvre in the small boat. It rocked madly as Jordan struck Minton in the ribs, the other fist coming down in a numbing blow on the point of his shoulder. Winded, Lord Minton's broad, vigorous body lay slumped down in the boat. There was a look of intense surprise on his face, and a spreading rosette of blood on the front of his coat from his injured right shoulder.

'Move, and you're a dead man,' Jordan said through clenched teeth.

Jed Taylor and his companion, resting on their oars, shuffled back on their seats, staring at the newcomer with wide-eyed alarm. His black hair, curling in a thick mass above his fierce silver eyes, was brushed back with an impatient hand. His uncompromising jaw was set as hard as granite, and his shoulders were hunched powerfully beneath his jacket.

Rory had climbed aboard and Jordan handed him a pistol. 'Watch him,' he growled, indicating the injured man, 'and if he moves shoot him.' Jordan then turned and glanced at the small, dejected figure huddled in the bottom of the boat. It was the one he loved and sought. 'Judith!' he whispered, going down on one knee beside her. With aching gentleness he pulled her into his arms.

'Thank God you are safe!' Threading his fingers through her sweet-scented hair, he framed her face between his hands and gazed at her. 'If anything had happened to you I would never have forgiven myself for leaving you alone in Brighton. I love you,' he whispered hoarsely. 'Dear God, Judith! How I love you. I love you so much I would gladly give up my life for you. Your face might have eluded me that night, but you stole my heart and gave me yours. I know you did. I could see it in your eyes when you looked at me that day at Landsdowne when we parted.'

The naked anguish in his voice brought tears to Judith's eyes as she looked adoringly at him, and the shattering sincerity and tenderness of his words sent a jolting tremor up her spine. Happiness began to spread through her until it was so intense she ached from it. She tried to speak, to express her joy, her love, but everything that had happened to her in the last two hours at Lord Minton's hands had used up all her resistance. She allowed him to draw her back into his arms, and they clung to each other in silence, too relieved and deeply moved for speech, seeming to forget the fishermen conversing noisily among themselves existed.

After a moment, Jordan gently held her away from him, tenderly smoothing back the hair from her face. 'It's all right, my love. It's all over,' he said.

'How frightened I have been,' she whispered, drawing a long, shaky breath. 'Thank goodness you came after me—but I never expected you quite so soon.'

Briefly Jordan explained how he came to be there. Anger blazed in his eyes when he saw the evidence of Minton's brutal viciousness—her swollen lips and torn dress, and the feeble attempt she had made to draw it together for modesty's sake. How could one slender girl endure such cruelty? 'If that blackguard has hurt you I might just change my mind and kill him now,' he seethed.

'I may be shaky-kneed with fright, but I'm not hurt, Jordan,' she said quickly, a wobbly smile curving her lips. She noticed how strained he looked, as if he, too, had gone through a great ordeal in the past few hours. 'A few scratches and bruises—you can see for yourself—but basically I'm sound.'

Jordan put a gentle hand beneath her chin and tilted up her face. He traced the bruise on her chin with his finger, and when she winced he drew in his breath, and cursed softly. 'I could have spared you this. I should have known when I left you that I was putting your life at risk. When I found you gone—I thought—I feared—' His arms were round her once more. 'The villain set a pretty trap for me and I'm lucky to get you back. We both know what Minton was doing in Brighton. He must have been disappointed when he found you didn't have the necklace. But how did he know you had it in the first place?'

'Alicia told him,' Judith informed him simply.

The truth hit him then, and all the things that had puzzled him clicked neatly into place. The unspeakable depths of Alicia's treachery made him tremble with rage. 'When I told her I would not marry her and sent her back to her father, I never realised what vengeance she harboured, or the lengths she would go to to appease that vengeance. But perhaps even Alicia would have thought twice about approaching Minton, had she known the power of evil that inhabits the man.' Becoming aware of the others around them, he got to his feet. 'Come, we will speak of this later. Let me help you into the other boat.'

A terrible, consuming hatred flared in Lord Minton's eyes when he looked up at his powerful assailant etched against the pale light. Defeat had come as a crushing blow. 'Why don't you finish me?' he hissed, breathing shortly. The answer was a hard, bright silver stare that seared him to the backbone.

'I'm sorely tempted, Minton—and had I any sense I would. For too long you have escaped your fate— and you have been a burden on my flesh from the moment I first set eyes on you. You took the woman I am to marry with no other cause but to make me surrender that which you seek to possess.' Removing the necklace from his breast pocket, after removing the handkerchief still wrapped round it, he let the diamond pendant dangle loosely though his fingers, his smile one of savagery when Lord Minton's eyes feasted on it greedily.

Jordan watched his adversary shift his gaze, from the jewel he'd sought so fiercely to obtain, to him, the round buttons of his eyes watchful, like those of a cornered rat. 'Take a good look at it, Minton, for it will be your last. This is what it has all been about— this diamond that belongs to the Ranee of Ranjipur, which I intend delivering to her in person.'

Nothing moved in the boat or beyond but the shimmer of moonlight on water. The face above the wounded man was a blur, but he could feel the spasm of hatred and disgust, the revulsion, that rose from the man's core, radiating through his flesh. Unable to blink, to break the hard silver gaze that held him frozen, Lord Minton felt his body shrink.

Replacing the necklace in his pocket, Jordan went on, very, very softly, to list Minton's crimes, each word enunciated. The first two were against the Rajah of Ranjipur, his third directed against himself. 'It was your henchmen who assaulted me at the docks that day, and when that failed you had me drugged in an attempt to secure the diamond for yourself.

'Your final crime is your abduction and assault of Miss Wyatt—twice. That, Minton, is quite a list. Your luck turned when you were summoned back to England to face charges of corruption. But still with your eye on the main chance, you saw there was something worth the taking, something that could set you up for life if only you could lay your thieving hands on it. But the game's up. You've run your course—had your day—and if I don't kill you, Chandu will.

'Unfortunately you will live—for now. I cannot, in all honour, kill you in cold blood. You will see a surgeon in Brighton to tend your wound, and at a date that is convenient to me we will settle what is between us on a personal basis.'

Jordan's voice lacked nothing in conviction, quiet as it was. There was a moment's silence, broken only by the lap of the water against the hull, when no one in either boat seemed to breathe. 'Follow us,' he told Jed Taylor. 'And don't even think about trying to escape. Minton will be charged with Miss Wyatt's abduction—and you two of aiding him in his nefarious plot. You became accessories when you took his money and agreed to take him to France.'

'But we had nothing to do with it,' Jed spluttered objectionably.

'I'm afraid you will find it hard to make any judge believe that.'

Having put the house to rights, Cynthia was pacing the carpet in a state of extreme anxiety when Jordan arrived with an exhausted Judith. She gave a start when they entered.

'Heaven be praised!' she ejaculated. 'It is you, Judith, and me half out of my mind with worry. Why, anything might have happened to you.'

'I am back safe and unharmed, Aunt Cynthia,' Judith said, managing a tremulous smile.

Cynthia shook her head, unconvinced by such dishevelment. 'But—your poor face is bruised—and your dress... Oh, my dear!' she gasped in distress, taking her hand in both her own. 'You—you weren't—'

'I wasn't ravished. I suffered nothing worse than a little rough handling,' she assured her aunt quietly, deeply touched by the older woman's genuine concern and obvious relief that she had returned. She was warmed by it, and hoped that after four years of resentment, she was beginning to see some redeeming features in her one remaining relative at last. 'I'm so sorry about the mess, but I see you've managed to put everything back.'

'The truth is, having to remain here and wait, I was glad to have something to do. The dragging inactivity was worse than being out there looking for you,' she said, ushering her niece to a comfortable chair by the fire before turning her attention to Lord Grant. 'You will both be glad of a little brandy, I think, after your ordeal. And then I would like an explanation.'

'Thank you, but no brandy for me,' Jordan said. 'I will leave you to put Judith to bed where she belongs. Explanations will have to wait, I'm afraid. I must get back to the beach.'

'But—must you go now?' Judith asked in a small voice, when her aunt had disappeared into the kitchen.

'I have to. There is much yet to be settled. What has happened is serious and must be reported to the proper authorities.'

'Does it have to be?'

Jordan's eyes narrowed. 'Are you saying you don't want Minton to be charged with your abduction?'

Judith heard the astonishment in his tone and sighed resignedly. 'You must do what you think is right. What I want is to forget. I am safe now, and so are you—and that is all I care about.'

With aching gentleness Jordan took her in his arms, his gaze probing with flaming warmth into hers. Bending his head, he caressed her lips lightly with his own. 'You echo my thoughts entirely, my love. Nothing matters to me but you. I love you, Judith, and my desire for you is hard driven. But I have not forgotten that Jehan Khan is at liberty in Brighton. It cannot be ignored, so I will leave my coachman here for your protection until I return.'

She looked at him in alarm. 'You will be careful? Promise me.'

His eyes held hers as he tenderly brushed a tangled curl from her cheek. 'I will. I promise.'

'Well!' Cynthia exclaimed in astonishment when he'd gone. 'So that's the way of things!'

Judith smiled. 'Yes, Aunt. It is.'

'And has he asked you to marry him?' she asked, seating herself opposite.

Judith nodded. 'I am sure he will speak to you about it in due course, Aunt.'

Cynthia perched excitedly on the edge of the chair opposite, trying to imagine what it would mean to her personally, having a niece married into such a prestigious family as the Grants of Greenwich. 'I never expected a gentleman of Lord Grant's means to offer for you.' She looked directly at her niece, her expression one of gravity. 'You would be very foolish to refuse him, Judith.'

'I have no intention of doing any such thing.'

'I am glad to hear it. I confess I was concerned that you were upset about me having to sell the house, but this makes me feel a whole lot better. Are you sure it's what you want?'

Judith nodded, settling back into the chair. Secure in the knowledge that Jordan loved her, she felt certain that there was no other man in the whole world for her. 'It's everything. I love him so much. Sometimes, what I feel frightens me. When I came to England, I could never imagine another world for myself and thanked God I was successful in the one allotted to me. But Jordan changed all that.'

Suddenly she recalled what her mother had once told her, that there had been a gentleman in her aunt's life whom everyone had thought she would marry. But he had left her for someone else. Apparently, it had been a rather tragic business at the time, leaving her aunt broken-hearted and bitterly disappointed. But she had bottled up her feelings and got on with her life.

Judith glanced across at her, wondering how much she had suffered because of it. 'H—have you ever loved very deeply, Aunt Cynthia?' she dared to ask quietly. Her aunt's eyes misted, and for a moment her life seemed to be suspended by memory of a tragic love. Drawing a deep breath, she half-turned her face away, and Judith was struck by its mournful look.

'Yes,' she replied at length. 'Once. Its loss is too painful and its presence too demanding. I swore when he left me for another that I had done with love—and I kept my word to myself. That way life is more straightforward. It suits me. Mr Wakeman is quiet and uncomplicated and will suit me well enough,' she said with quiet resignation.

'I'm glad of that, Aunt,' Judith murmured, looking at her as if seeing her for the first time, realising there was an underlying sensitivity and fragility about her, which until now she had not been aware of. At last she was able to understand her aunt a little, and to think of her with a kind of tenderness. The small revelation of what was in her heart had won her affection, too. However, if their relationship was going to improve, they would have to ease into it.

'Will you return to London with Lord Grant, Judith?'

'Would you mind if I remain here in Brighton with you for a while, Aunt? I want to make the most of it—before you marry Mr Wakeman and move to Chichester.'

'I would like that,' she smiled.

'Then I shall—and when Jordan and I are married, you and Mr Wakeman must visit us in London. I must also write to Miss Powell at the academy and inform her of all that has transpired.'

'At least your marriage will take care of that problem. You will no longer have the need to take up employment to support yourself.'

'I may not need to, Aunt, but I am determined to remain involved with the academy in some capacity.'

Her aunt glanced at her sceptically. 'You may find that your husband will object most strongly to that.'

'He won't,' Judith replied with a smile of confidence when she recalled the conversation at the dinner table on her first evening at Landsdowne, when she had made her opinions plain to everyone and seen the spark of admiration in Jordan's eyes. He had told her afterwards that he was by no means prejudiced against females with brains, adding that she had taught him something new, and he was beginning to think that there was no substitute for a clear-sighted, intelligent woman. She hoped he would still feel that way when she was his wife.

Chapter Eighteen

The beach was a long, pale ribbon of light against the black sea, and dawn was breaking on the horizon when Jordan strode to the water's edge and helped Jed Taylor and his companion pull the boat carrying Jeremy Minton up onto the shingle. After securing a promise from Jordan that the remainder of what he owed would be forthcoming, Rory and the others had already gone to their homes. Jordan stood aside as Jed helped Minton from the small craft. His face was a hardened mask of icy wrath as his eyes blazed at his enemy, and the air between them was filled with hate and hostility.

Without a word they turned to leave the beach, when Jehan Khan, dressed in white robes and an extravagant turban, appeared before them like an apparition. His carriage was drawn up on the promenade, his two servants standing like statues a few paces behind him. Jehan Khan's unexpected arrival and princely bearing, set against the backdrop of the Prince Regent's Royal Pavilion, with its eastern domes and minarets, brought the two gaping fishermen to a halt.

Khan's hooded eyes were fixed and unblinking. His stare did not waver from Lord Minton's stumbling form. They came face to face. The Indian's black eyes narrowed and glittered dangerously.

'Welcome back,' he said smoothly, his voice of a thin, high-pitched timbre. 'Your sudden departure was not without reason. I had almost begun to fear I would have to go to France in search of you.'

'So,' Lord Minton hissed, 'you set your blood-hounds onto me, Khan.'

'I didn't need to. In your haste to reach Brighton you carelessly left the letter sent to you by Miss Paxton in the top drawer of your desk. It didn't take me long to find it.' The dislike and distrust Khan felt for Minton had turned into a consuming hatred at this latest treachery, and it showed in the deadly glitter in his coal-black eyes.

'You will regret this, Lord Minton. You have not only gone against me, but Prince Chandu, also. I always knew you would bite his hand when your luck turned. I've seen it coming for a long time. You have played a double game with the wrong man, and you will find it hasn't paid you. Of course, I knew you wanted the diamond, but the desperate measures you have gone to to obtain it I cannot allow to pass. You are wounded, I see. Your work, I suspect, Grant-sahib.'

Khan's eyes lingered briefly on Jordan, reminding him of a cobra's eyes beneath its hood—staring and malevolent. They shifted back to Lord Minton.

'I promise you I will not wound you, Lord Minton. I shall do myself the honour of killing you.' His voice was flat and deadly, and Minton stared at him with frustrated anger and pain.

Jordan was too far away to prevent Khan from driving a knife to the hilt into Minton's chest. It was done swiftly and cleanly, which was the case in all Khan's dealings. Minton fell on his hands and knees, but succeeded in staggering to his feet and lurching towards Khan, hands outstretched, with a sleepwalker's face.

He knew the folly of trying to double cross Prince Chandu, and retribution had come quickly in the form of Jehan Khan. Khan slowly backed out of his reach as Minton tripped, and with a final convulsion that fixed a grin in a hideous rictus upon his face, he coughed up an amazing quantity of bright red frothing blood, and fell dead at his feet.

With his blank face, his white robes and the blood on the hand still holding the thin-bladed knife, Khan truly resembled some demon cast up out of the pit. Jordan knew the kind of creature Chandu's envoy was. He knew what depths of evil and sadistic cruelty lay behind that face. Minton's death would not lie heavy on his conscience. He lifted his eyes to Jordan.

'It is done, Grant-sahib. I grew weary of his presence, his treachery and his lies, and so—as one would do to a scorpion about to strike—I killed him. It must have occurred to you that he was in the pay of Prince Chandu.'

'There is little that escapes me, Khan.'

'My master made him rich, but his palm itched for more. He wanted the diamond of Ranjipur for himself.'

'I know that, too. But this is not the frontier region of India, where you indulge in tribal warfare. This is England, and you have just murdered a man. You will be called to account for your crime.'

'I think not, and please—do not try to apprehend me,' Khan said on a warning note, indicating his servants hovering close, clutching weapons of their own which they kept concealed in the folds of their robes. 'I realise it is now dangerous for me to stay here, so I shall simply disappear. Now the government has made it plain that they will not grant Prince Chandu the state of Ranjipur—and since you are to give the Ranee the necklace my master sought to possess, there is nothing to keep me here. It is time for me to return to India.'

He bowed his head ceremoniously, his face taking on a neutral expression. The huge black pearl in his turban caught the light of the rising sun as he turned and walked slowly back to his carriage, and as he did so the white silk of his robe billowed out behind him, so that for a moment it seemed to Jordan that he was looking at a departing ghost. A sudden chill descended on the three men left on the beach, and no one spoke until the carriage had disappeared along the empty promenade.

When Jordan arrived at Miss Wyatt's house in mid-morning, he found Judith alone. Without moving, she looked across the room at him, her face pale, her eyes questioning.

'Is it over?'

'Yes, it's over.' His voice was solemn. Wearily he moved towards her. 'It's good news—or bad, depending on how you take it. Minton is dead, Judith. He can do no more harm.'

She was stricken. 'You—you killed him?'

'No. Jehan Khan did. I lost no time in reporting your abduction and Minton's murder to the local magistrate. I disclosed the identity of the murderer, but I know there is little hope of Jehan Khan being apprehended and arrested. He's as cunning as a fox, and will disappear without trace.'

A moan of relief, of torment, tore from Judith's chest. She came wordlessly into his arms, kissing him with a silent desperation that matched his own, pressing herself to him, crushing her soft mouth to his. The passing of carriages out in the street brought them back to reality and they stood, arms still entwined, gazing at each other.

'I can't believe it's over, Jordan. I can't believe you're here, holding me at last,' she whispered. 'Just a few hours ago everything seemed so—so—'

'Futile?' he provided in the deep, compelling voice that never failed to wreak havoc on her body, her soul, and her heart.

She nodded. 'And hopeless. Dear Lord, when I regained consciousness and found myself in that boat with Lord Minton, I was already missing you so much.'

Jordan answered her with his mouth, his warm lips moving fiercely on hers, as he kissed her with a raw, urgent hunger that made her feel helpless. Her hands crept up his muscular male chest, fastening around his neck, allowing her lips to yield to his kiss, parting beneath the sensual pressure. The sensation of his hardening body crushed against hers was all so achingly, poignantly familiar to her, because she had experienced it before and lived it in her dreams a million times.

Dragging his mouth from hers, Jordan gazed down at her flushed face, at the half-moons of her dark lashes, her unselfish ardour having a devastating effect on his starved body.

'Open your eyes, little one,' he whispered.

She obeyed and found herself meeting his half-shuttered eyes, seeing in them the changes that passion had made in him. A muscle moved spasmodically in his throat, his face was hard and dark, his lips sensual, his voice low.

'We will be married just as soon as it can be arranged.'

His eyes gazed into hers, plumbing their innermost depths, and Judith was overwhelmed at the passionate desire she read in them. She rested her hand against his shaven cheek. 'By your side I will happily stand, Jordan, if you want me there. But my marriage to you must not stop my work. I would still like to be involved in some kind of employment at the academy. I cannot do as convention demands—a lady of leisure, with nothing to do but run a house. It is important to me that I am involved in something productive. You do understand, don't you?' She lifted her eyes to his pleadingly, watching with a mixture of anxiety and hope for his reaction.

A wry smile touched his mouth, and he gave in without a struggle. 'You're always so practical, my love, and of course I wouldn't stand in your way if you want to involve yourself in matters at the academy,' he said decisively, 'but my mind is on productivity of a different kind—a process that might be in motion already, don't forget.'

The intensity of his gaze ploughed through her composure. 'I haven't forgotten,' she could not resist teasing. Then she became serious. 'But if I'm not—'

He raised his brows in amused challenge. 'You very soon will be.'

'Jordan—there is something I have to tell you.'

'What?' he queried.

'I—what I mean to say is—there is no baby.'

'You are certain of this?'

She nodded. 'As certain as a woman can be about such things.'

His face remained expressionless. 'Are you disappointed?'

'Relieved,' she confessed.

'But you do want my baby?'

'Desperately. I was simply worried about the timing.' she whispered, pressing a kiss against his throat.

Grinning wickedly, Jordan cupped her face between his hands, brushing his thumbs over her smooth cheeks. 'Keep doing that and you could find yourself

with child sooner than is decent,' he murmured. 'As
soon as you are my wife, I intend to spend every night
in the pleasurable occupation of siring my heir. If I
don't succeed, it won't be for want of trying. I'm terribly selfish, my love, and I want us to be married
without delay.'

Judith's cheeks turned scarlet, but an answering
sparkle lit her eyes. 'So do I. But won't everyone think
that is highly irregular?'

'I don't give a damn about what everyone else
thinks. Besides, everything about our relationship has
been highly irregular, in every way.'

'I fear the news that we are to marry will cause a
terrible scandal.'

'A few eyebrows are bound to be raised, of course.'

'I am prepared for gossip—even to be cut, but I am
far too happy to care.'

'That's the kind of spirit I expect from you. And
we will be happy, my love. I promise. As soon as the
wedding is over I must leave for India on Company
business. We will go together and make it our hon-
eymoon. I intend showing you the beauty of the foothills as well as the serenity and quiet beauty of the
distant Himalayas. We will stay in Delhi, where we
can watch the magic of the moonflowers opening together—and press some more in a book to remember
our time there. Does that appeal to you?'

Judith stared at him, unable to comprehend what he
had said. 'India?' she whispered, swallowing hard and
looking at him warily. 'Jordan—you do not jest with
me?'

'I would not jest about something which I know means a great deal to you. Come, what do you say? I know you would like to return.'

Unable to put her thoughts into words or to stem her feelings, she threw her arms about his neck and wept tears of absolute joy. India was hundreds of miles away, but already she could feel her life stretching away to unimaginable horizons. She could smell the bazaars, the sweet flowering orange blossoms, jasmine and frangipani—the smell of home.

'Am I to understand from this outpouring of emotion that you are happy with the arrangement?' Jordan asked softly.

When she raised her tear bright eyes to his she smiled broadly. 'I'm very happy. I don't know what to say—except thank you, Jordan—with all my heart. I am just so happy I could die.'

He grinned, placing a kiss on her brow. 'Don't you dare. I can't get married without you,' he teased. 'Now, can't I persuade you to return to London with me?'

'I will stay in Brighton for a little while, if you don't mind. I know Aunt Cynthia would like me to.'

His brows arched quizzically. 'You and your aunt seem to be getting on remarkably well, all of a sudden. Do I detect a softening in your attitudes towards each other?'

'Yes. Which is why I would like to remain a little longer. Perhaps two weeks. You don't mind, do you, Jordan?'

'Mind? Of course I mind,' he said, his arms going round her once more, his breath sending vibrant warmth spilling through her veins. 'I can't bear being apart from you. But you corrupt me with your delightful distractions, my love. I've been idle for two days, and I'll have to work twice as hard when I return to London to make up for it.'

When it was time for Judith to leave Brighton, Jordan sent the carriage for her, refusing even to consider allowing her to use the Brighton to London stagecoach as she had done previously. As he was unable to come himself, Charlotte arrived with Emily, and after partaking of Aunt Cynthia's hospitality—she was absolutely delighted to entertain two such distinguished ladies—the four of them went for a stroll along the promenade.

After bidding her aunt farewell—with a fondness always absent on their previous partings, Judith set off for London with her two companions, the entire conversation from Brighton to Greenwich being about the arrangements to be made for her wedding to Jordan.

Like everyone else, Charlotte had been horrified when, on his return to Landsdowne, Jordan had told them of the unfortunate events that had shadowed him since his return to England, and how Judith had become innocently drawn into the dastardly Lord Minton's web of treachery, and the brutal treatment she had received at his hands when he had abducted her again. However, she was ecstatic at the way things had turned out, and that her dear friend was to be her sister-in-law—but then, she said with a haughty toss of her blonde curls, she had always known she would be.

On reaching Landsdowne they were met by Lady Grant, who was highly delighted to receive her future daughter-in-law safe and well, and she sincerely hoped the whole unfortunate episode concerning Lord Minton was well and truly behind them. Judith was a remarkable young woman, who would make her son a far more fitting wife than Alicia ever could, and since he had returned from Brighton, she had never seen him so relaxed and happy.

'Where is Jordan? Can I see him?' Judith asked, unable to contain her impatience.

'Of course you can, just as soon as he returns.'

Judith had a sudden sense of disappointment. For days now she had been living with the one thought of seeing him and being with him for ever—sharing their lives together—and now she found she must wait a little longer. So great was her disappointment that it came as something of a shock to hear Lady Grant laugh.

'Don't worry, my dear. He is not far away. He arrived from town early, and so impatient was he to see you, he has gone to work his frustration out on his poor horse and is riding in the park.'

Judith relaxed, her face breaking out into a smile. 'Oh, is that all? Then out of pity for his poor horse, I feel I must go and find him.'

The sky being overcast, there were few people in the park. She hadn't been walking very long when the sound of galloping hoofbeats made itself heard, and she paused, seeing a horse and rider coming towards her. The noise grew louder, nearer, and in a moment they were upon her. In danger of being ridden down, she stepped back. So still was she standing in the shade of the trees that it was likely Jordan had not seen her.

Held spellbound by the wildness of horse and rider, and the sheer beauty of the gallop and the man in the saddle, she gasped—a tide of love rolling over her and almost drowning her, a torrent that, had she had any doubts about marrying this man, would have swept them away.

When she stepped out of the trees the great horse reared back, its slender legs pawing the air, then dropped them to the ground and stood quiet, while its master sprang to the ground with athletic ease. He strode towards her, his eyes smiling, and swept her up into his arms.

'I've missed you,' Judith said quietly, looking up at him, loving him, the mere sight of him and the way his dark hair fell carelessly over his brow twisting her insides into hot, tight knots of yearning.

'And I you,' he murmured, looking at her with adoration in his eyes. 'I love you wholeheartedly and without reserve. You are my future, Judith. Without you my life is incomplete. I have arranged for us to be married a month from now. Miss Powell has suggested that you stay with her until the wedding. Do you have any objections to that?'

'Only one.' Her smile was impish.

He frowned. 'Oh?'

'Why do we have to wait so long? Couldn't you have arranged it sooner?'

'Minx,' he said, catching her up into his arms once more and spinning her round, their laughter drawing the attention of a group of people strolling close by.

Slipping his arm about her waist and taking the reins, together they made their way slowly out of the park.

'Have you heard anything of Alicia, Jordan?' Judith asked on a more serious note. 'Do you know if she's still in Kent?'

He nodded. 'And expected to remain so. Indefinitely.'

'Oh? You surprise me. I thought she disliked the country intensely.'

'So she does. It was unfortunate for Alicia that Emily informed their father of her unacceptable behaviour while she was our guest here at Landsdowne, and the devious methods she used to entrap me into wedlock. It was like pouring oil over red-hot coals,' he chuckled softly.

'What do you mean?'

'That moral, hugely respected man erupted like a volcano. During Alicia's absence he learned of her affair with his steward, Philip Mason, from the wife of an acquaintance—who probably told him for some spiteful reason of her own. According to Edmund, this, combined with her disgraceful antics here in London, motivated that usually mild-mannered man into action. He was outraged, his temper unrestrained.'

'Why, what on earth did he do?'

Jordan grinned down at her. 'Determined to curb his daughter's wild ways once and for all—to punish her, to teach her a lesson she will never forget—he insists she will wed his steward before the month is out.'

Judith stared at him incredulously. 'Alicia will never agree to that. She is far too proud, too arrogant, ever to submit to marrying a man of such low social standing.'

'Oh, she ranted and railed against it, but even Alicia cannot stand against her father when his mind is made up. It is hardly the expedient marriage he had planned for his daughter, you understand, but her affair with Philip Mason has become common gossip and Alicia's reputation is in ruins. Her father is determined that she will pay for the shame she has brought upon the family, that nothing will impede the marriage—and his steward is highly delighted with the arrangement.'

'Then, despite their affair, he cannot be aware of the true nature of the woman he is marrying.'

'I doubt anyone will ever know the true workings of Alicia's mind, but however you look at it, Philip Mason stands to gain from the marriage in a material sense. All her life Alicia has been a sore trial to her father. He called her wanton—accusing her of inheriting bad blood from an uncle on her mother's side—and bad blood will always out in the end. I doubt Alicia will ever get over the humiliation and shame of being forced to marry one of her father's employees. She'll never be able to hold her head up in society again, so I doubt she will venture far from home—at least, not in the foreseeable future.'

Judith felt a stirring of exultation and overwhelming relief that she wouldn't have to face Alicia again if she didn't want to, leaving her thankful. She waited for the pang of sadness she might feel when a woman is forced into a marriage against her will, but none was forthcoming.

'Speaking of Alicia brings to mind one other who has tried to harm you,' she said. 'Jehan Khan! Have you heard what has become of him?'

'No. Although I suspect he will be on his way to India by now. The Ranee of Ranjipur has arrived in London with her daughter. I will take you to meet her.'

'I would like that. Is she to remain in London indefinitely?'

'No. She intends to return to India and seek asylum in her brother's domain, where she should be safe from Chandu's evil machinations.'

'Will it be granted?'

'Yes. Her brother owes loyalty to the Ranee's husband, and will make her welcome.'

'You have given her the necklace?'

He nodded. 'To be perfectly honest, it was a relief to be rid of it—although she did offer to loan it to you to wear with your wedding gown.'

'She did? Oh—I don't know what to say,' Judith said, looking away, not wishing to give offence by refusing such a generous offer; but in truth, she never wanted to see that particular treasure ever again.

Jordan smiled, reading her thoughts exactly. 'Don't worry, my love. I took the liberty of refusing on your behalf.' He grinned when she raised her eyes to his. 'I have jewels of my own to adorn the neck of my bride on her wedding day—but no jewel on earth is as exquisite as you. To me, my love, you are a rare gem indeed—a jewel beyond price.'

For Judith her wedding day had a distinct aura of unreality. Never had she believed she could be so happy. In a church aglow with candlelight and perfumed with lavish blooms, among a sea of smiling faces and a vicar waiting with the marriage book open in his hands, on Edmund's arm and with Charlotte in attendance, it was with a sense of quiet joy that she walked down the aisle to take her place beside Jordan.

Turning, Jordan felt as if his chest would burst at the sight that greeted him. Holding a spray of white lilies, Judith was a vision of ethereal loveliness in cream and white. A special kind of radiance was gathered into her face beneath the dawn mist of her veil. She was glowing, but it was her smile that tugged his heart the most. So filled with peace and contentment, it was the most beautiful smile he had ever seen, and in her eyes he saw all the love in the world, the promise of unborn children, and a lifetime of happiness and love together.

After speaking their vows they were pronounced husband and wife. A grand banquet and reception followed, which to the happy couple seemed like an eternity of smiling and being polite, until they found the opportunity to slip away.

In no time at all Judith fell under the spell of her husband's heavy-lidded gaze and inviting smile. Fuelled by weeks of abstinence, desire began to beat fiercely in Jordan's veins and he pulled her close, his mouth opening over hers with sudden urgency. They kissed deeply, almost savagely, pausing only long enough to cast off their clothes, before falling onto the bed, their bodies melting feverishly, entwining at last. Waves of pure, physical pleasure washed over them. Lost in the physical bliss of their union, of giving to the other and finding everything and much more in return, they each knew that theirs was a special kind of love.

Later, sated and spent, entwined in the afterglow of passion, the quiet of the bedroom was wafted by sighs. After a while of being wrapped in each other's arms, Jordan raised himself so that he could look down at Judith's sleeping face, unable to believe that she belonged to him at last. He was much enamoured of this adorable young wife of his, and there was much more to her than he had ever realised. Bending his head, he placed a lingering kiss on her parted lips, breathing in the delicious fragrance of her. She opened her eyes and he smiled.

'Welcome home, my love,' he said softly, for he knew without doubt that this was not the first time he had made love to his wife, and that the mysterious woman who had shared his bed on the night of the ball had returned to him. What they had was meant to be. It was like the fish in the sea, the ever-changing seasons, and the moon and the stars in the sky. It was eternal, and should the earth cease to exist, they would still go on.

Judith was the woman he would love to the end of his life, and beyond.

* * * * *

HISTORICAL ROMANCE™

LARGE PRINT

THE NOTORIOUS MARRIAGE

Nicola Cornick

Debutante Eleanor Trevithick's elopement with Kit, Lord Mostyn, was enough to have the gossips in an uproar. But then it was heard that her new husband had disappeared a day after the wedding…and their marriage became the most notorious in town!

Kit returned five long months later, not at liberty to explain the secret assignment that had forced his departure. Yet he was still determined to win back his bride's affections! Could he succeed? Perhaps if he continued the marriage exactly where it had started—in the bedroom.

RAVEN'S HONOUR

Claire Thornton

When Major Cole Raven rescues Honor from a rushing river in war-torn Spain he knows he could find love with this brave, beautiful – unattainable – young woman. An oath to a dying soldier to protect Honor throws them together and, with the dangers of war all around them, an irresistible passion flares.

The handsome Major stirs Honor's spirit as never before, but responsibilities await as they return to England—family duties which will force Cole to deny what he most desires. Unless he can find a way of keeping his honour as well as the woman he loves…

MILLS & BOON®

HISTORICAL ROMANCE™

LARGE PRINT

THE DUTIFUL RAKE
Elizabeth Rolls

Marcus, Earl of Rutherford, is used to flirting with scandal, but when he places Miss Marguerite Fellowes's spotless reputation in jeopardy, he's challenged to do the honourable thing.

Marcus makes it clear theirs will be a marriage based on duty, not love. But then he watches as proud Meg blossoms in London society. Tantalised by her evident passion for life, suddenly the dutiful husband finds himself with far from innocent desires….

LORD CALTHORPE'S PROMISE
Sylvia Andrew

Lord Adam Calthorpe had been rash to promise to look out for a fellow soldier's sister when he was killed at the battle of Waterloo. Katharine Payne was a golden-eyed virago who flouted Adam's authority at every turn!

Maybe taking her to stay with his mother for the Season would absolve him of his responsibilities—not that such a headstrong chit, however enchanting, would ever find herself a husband. Only when an unscrupulous man started pursuing her did Adam come to realise that fulfilling his promise might involve marrying the girl himself…

MILLS & BOON®

HISTORICAL ROMANCE™

LARGE PRINT

RINALDI'S REVENGE
Paula Marshall

As ruler of a small but wealthy Italian duchy, Elena de' Carisendi fears her land will be taken from her by force. Her only chance for survival is to hire an army to protect her, and mercenary Marco Rinaldi is the best soldier money can buy.

Marco will fight off all invaders, and he'd pose even more of a deterrent if they were to wed. Strong and commanding, he awakes the sensual woman in her, but it appears he harbours a dark secret, with their marriage part of his plan for revenge…

Renaissance Italy
…*condottiere*, **conspiracy, passionate conquest…**

LADY LAVINIA'S MATCH
Mary Nicols

When their parents married, James, Earl of Corringham, and Lady Lavinia Stanmore became as close as brother and sister. Now, years later, James has outgrown his rakish ways and is burning with a love for her that he longs to reveal.

However, he faces a rival in the shape of the mysterious Lord Wincote. Torn between James and the handsome stranger, Lavinia's feelings are thrown into turmoil. But is this man really what he seems? The more Lord Wincote persists, the more Lavinia wonders if she shouldn't be looking for love a little closer to home…

Regency

MILLS & BOON®

HISTORICAL ROMANCE™

LARGE PRINT

MARRYING THE MAJOR
Joanna Maitland

Back from the Peninsular Wars, Major Hugo Stratton is scarred and embittered, much altered from the laughing young man Emma Fitzwilliam has fantasised about over the years.

Now the toast of London Society, beautiful Emma inflames Hugo's blood like no other woman. She is tantalised by glimpses of the man she knew in the recluse he has become. But it's patently obvious that Hugo considers himself to be far from the eligible catch she deserves. So how will they fare when a situation arises which forces a marriage between them…?

THE ROGUE'S SEDUCTION
Georgina Devon

Ten years ago Lillith, Lady de Lisle, was forced to stand up the man she loved at the altar in favour of a richer husband. Now a widow, she suddenly finds herself the target of her thwarted lover's revenge.

Jason Beaumair, Earl of Perth, plans to abduct and seduce this beautiful woman in return for her cruel rejection of him. He'll certainly never fall for her again! But nothing can prepare him for what their night of passion will bring…

MILLS & BOON®

HIST1202 L